Engineering Love

FRIENDS OF THE UNEXPECTED ROYALS

BOOK TWO

TOMI TABB

Cover Design by Gigi Blume

Published by

Pas de Chat Publications

First Edition, 2025

E-Book ISBN: 978-1-969184-21-5

Paperback ISBN: 978-1-969184-02-4

Hardback ISBN: 978-1-969184-13-0

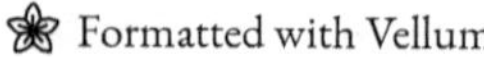 Formatted with Vellum

To Baby Tabb

Contents

Alice and Art's World   vii

Chapter 1   1
Chapter 2   15
Chapter 3   23
Chapter 4   35
Chapter 5   49
Chapter 6   55
Chapter 7   65
Chapter 8   79
Chapter 9   89
Chapter 10   101
Chapter 11   111
Chapter 12   123
Chapter 13   135
Chapter 14   147
Chapter 15   157
Chapter 16   169
Chapter 17   175
Chapter 18   183
Chapter 19   195
Chapter 20   207
Chapter 21   217
Chapter 22   227
Chapter 23   237
Chapter 24   247
Chapter 25   255
Chapter 26   265
Chapter 27   277
Chapter 28   287
Epilogue   297

Dear Reader 309
Acknowledgments 311
About the Author 313
Also by Tomi Tabb 315

Alice and Art's World

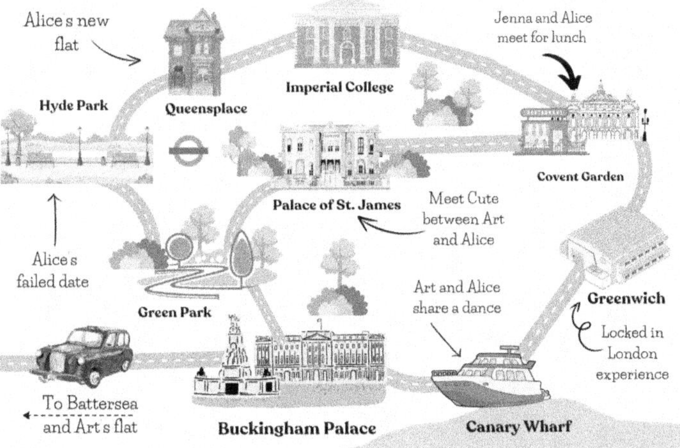

One

"Papa!" I burst through the doors to my father's study. "Your secretary told me you were up here. I was so excited that I couldn't wait a moment longer. You're the first person I wanted to see. I've missed you so much."

My father clears his throat and blinks slowly, shooting me a bemused expression. My cheeks sear with heat and the words die on my lips. Seated opposite my father is a man with salt-and-pepper hair and a neat beard, dressed in a three-piece pin-striped suit. His brows are furrowed in a deep V. Of course this would be the one time I chose *not* to knock.

I incline my head. "Forgive me, Father. Prime Minister. I, er . . . didn't realize you two had a meeting scheduled for today. Please accept my sincerest apologies for interrupting you." I take a few steps backward, inching toward the doors. "I'll return later."

"Welcome home, Alice. Why don't you wait for me in my sitting room? I'll join you shortly. Prime Minister Carrington and I were just wrapping up our discussion," my father says.

"Yes, sir. Apologies again, Prime Minister."

The PM nods curtly. He's all business and not one who cares much for idle chitchat. Secretly, Papa doesn't care much for him, but he'll never ever let his personal opinions be known. As the king of the United Kingdom, he's an expert at masking his thoughts and emotions. The ultimate poker player.

I exit and turn right, entering the adjacent room, softly closing the door behind me. Franny, our family's springer spaniel, immediately pops up from her favorite sleeping spot by the fire and trots over to greet me. I kneel down. She sniffs my hand and rolls over onto her back, exposing her tummy to me. "How's my favorite girl? I've missed you too!"

My fingers find all her favorite spots, and her tail wags wildly from side to side. "You know, your daughter Lillian is doing well. She's gotten just as big as you. I'm overdue to bring her to see you. Would you like that?" My hand travels under her chin. "Would you?" Franny barks and licks my hand.

Standing up, I brush a few stray pieces of Franny's hair off my trousers. This is one of my favorite rooms in the palace. Growing up, I spent so many hours in here with Papa. I'd sit on the rug and read next to Franny while he went through the day's correspondence at his desk.

The decor hasn't changed much. The far wall still contains his expansive collection of books on military history. The antique globe and collection of ships in bottles are still displayed on the mantel above the fireplace. Crossing the room, I pull open the top drawer on the right-hand side. There're a few empty wrappers and a Cadbury Flake bar inside, his favorite candy.

"What would people say if they knew my father's tastes were so simple?" I giggle.

A knock sounds on the connecting door. A moment later, Papa emerges. "If you're looking for some chocolate,

I'm sorry to say there isn't much left. Your brother raided my supply last week and forgot to mention it to me. I haven't had the chance to ask my secretary pick up some replacements."

"May I have the Cadbury Flake bar?"

"Sure. But only if you come and give your favorite father a hug."

"You're my only father." I laugh.

He wraps his arms around me and kisses the top of my head. The fine fabric of his suit brushes against my bare arms. I soak in the fresh scent of sandalwood and leather. "I've missed you. It's good to have you home again."

"I've missed you too." Seeing my family over video chat is brilliant, but it's no replacement for physically having them near me. For the last eight months, I've been traveling all over Europe, taking a gap year between finishing sixth form and beginning university.

"When did you arrive home?" He releases me, and hands me the chocolate bar from the drawer as we both sit down on the sofa.

"A few hours ago."

"You're early. We didn't expect you home until tomorrow." He chuckles.

"It's been an amazing once-in-a-lifetime experience seeing so many places, but the last few weeks, I've started to feel homesick. I couldn't wait to be back on English soil and see you."

Papa flashes me a Cheshire cat smile. I see a flash of my older brother Eddie in him. "Have you at least seen your mum yet?"

"I'd planned to, but her secretary said she won't be back from the children's hospital expansion opening in Cornwall until late afternoon."

"Why don't you plan to stay for dinner tonight. We'll turn

it into a welcome home celebration. Edmund was already due to join us."

"I'd like that."

Papa crosses one leg over the other. "Well, don't keep an old man waiting . . . how was it?"

"Inspiring." My eyes flutter and adrenaline floods my system as I relive the last few months. I've traveled through Europe before as a princess, but never as a private citizen or for such an extended period of time. "Reading about architecture is one thing, but seeing it up close is . . ." I blow a chef's kiss.

"And what were the top three highlights of your trip?"

"Only three?"

He nods.

"Um . . . hiking to the top of Brunelleschi's dome at sunset in Florence, exploring the medieval structures of Toledo, and . . . I guess spending time studying the Roman aqueducts outside Rome."

"I thought the Roman aqueducts would be number one on your list. You've been fascinated by them since you were a child," he teases.

"You put me on the spot," I poke back.

We share a laugh. "How was your meeting with the PM?"

Papa pinches his lips together. "About as fun as watching wet paint dry."

I snort. "What did he want?"

"The PM is calling elections in six weeks. He's urging me to postpone all previously planned engagements until then, including the state visit from the emperor and empress of Japan. He wants the public's attention to be on the elections, not us."

"I don't understand." I frown. "Does that mean Trooping the Colour and the Order of the Garter ceremony will be called off too?"

"No, those will still go on. There're too many important

guests and visiting dignitaries involved. It's everything else that'll have to be put on hold."

What Papa doesn't mention are the tourist dollars that'll flood London's economy for the week. The PM can't have business owners angered with him. My jaw clenches. "In other words, all the causes that matter."

Historically, we don't involve ourselves in politics. It's always been the family's standard practice to go along with what the PM wants. I don't understand why we should have to give up our visits to places like the children's hospital so the PM can conduct dinner fundraisers. But then again, it's Prime Minister Carrington, and he only cares about one person. Himself. He'll do anything to stay in office even though his party is probably doomed.

"Let's not let Prime Minister Carrington ruin our day. Why don't you show me some trip photos. Then we'll talk a little about what else you have planned for the rest of the summer before you start uni."

I sit up taller. A few alarms start ringing in my head. There's something I haven't mentioned to my parents yet about where I plan to live come fall.

"Sure." My voice wavers. "Where do you want to start?"

"Wherever you'd like."

Later, after we've enjoyed some tea and mini Victorian sponge cakes—Papa's favorite indulgence when Mum isn't around—he brings up the one topic I'd hope we could avoid.

"I know you have your heart set on moving into your own flat, but what about the cottages at Kensington Palace? They're much nicer than anything you'll find around Imperial College. Not to mention you can move in whenever you'd like."

"That's generous of you, Papa, but moving into a Kensington cottage wouldn't be much different than my current flat. I've always lived in a property owned by the crown. It's time for me to have a place that's mine."

At present, I live inside one of the apartments at St. James's Palace in the heart of Central London. It's a beautiful, historical home that anyone would be lucky to call their own, but it's always been intended to be a temporary base while I traveled during my gap year. I'll be starting at Imperial College here in London in September, three months from now. It's my plan to move into my own place by then.

Papa taps his fingers against the arm of the sofa. "So, we're back to square one."

"Afraid so."

He sighs deeply.

"I don't suppose you and Mum have reconsidered property locations?" I ask hopefully. My parents are being sticklers about the neighborhoods they'll consider allowing me to move into.

"No. The furthest your mum and I will allow you to move is still Earl's Court. We want you to be within a five-kilometer radius of school."

His tone is firm—it's going to be a challenge convincing him to change his mind. My chest grows tight. I'm running out of time. What he doesn't know is that before I left, I bought a flat. But it's not exactly in one of the neighborhoods he'll approve of. I'm going to need help and a plan of attack before I approach him about it.

A knock sounds at the door.

"Enter," Papa says.

The door opens, revealing his private secretary. "Sir, I'm sorry to interrupt you, but there's a call from the PM on line two."

My father's jaw clenches. "Tell him, I'll be with him shortly."

"Yes, sir."

Papa removes his reading glasses and stands, starting toward his office. "Ali, I'm sorry to have to cut this short, but I'll see you at dinner tonight?"

"Of course." I nod.

We hug, and I leave the room, my mind a jumble of thoughts.

"WELL, PRINCESS? HOW DID IT GO?" BRUCE, THE head of my security detail, asks as he drives us back to St. James's Palace. He's been my personal protection officer for the last eight years. We have an easy relationship between us. He's in his mid-fifties and has dark-brown hair and kind brown eyes.

I rub my temples. "No changes on the flat situation. Mum and dad still want me to find a place that's within their approved bubble. We're back to where we were before I left."

"I'm sorry," he says in a sympathetic tone. "Did you try and lay out the argument just as we'd practiced?"

"There was no point. I could tell he wasn't going to budge without Mum around." I stare out the window at the tourists gathered near the front gates of Buckingham Palace, snapping selfies and watching the famed foot guards stand in their sentry boxes. It's funny, they'd do anything to see the inside of the palace, while I'd love nothing more than to escape it. Heaviness fills me.

"You know, ma'am, I wouldn't give up hope yet. I'm sure everything will work out just fine when the timing is right."

"I hope so."

"It's only June. You still have plenty of time." He glances back at me in the rearview mirror. "Have you thought about enlisting your brother or Ms. Collins? She seems to have a gift for pulling off what others deem impossible."

"Hmm, I haven't." A jolt of energy shoots through my body at the thought of Eddie's fiancée. "You're right. Amanda might be the perfect person to get somewhere with my parents."

Amanda is a spunky American who met my brother about five years ago. She loves all things Disney, and before moving permanently to the UK, she worked as a flight attendant. These days, she helps my brother run his charitable organization.

On paper, it doesn't seem like she and my brother would have anything in common. They were like water and oil. But now, I can't imagine them *not* being together. Amanda and Eddie are living, breathing proof that opposites attract. Even though we aren't *technically* sisters yet, I still consider her to be one.

Pulling out my mobile, I tap on the green bubble icon and start typing a new text message.

ALICE

Hey, A.

I only have to wait a few seconds for her to respond.

AMANDA

Ali! You're back! I need to see you ASAP!

My body shakes with laughter. That's Amanda for you. She'd drop everything she's doing to see me.

ALICE

Agreed! It's been too long. Are you free tonight? Eddie is doing dinner with Papa and I'm joining them.

AMANDA

I wasn't planning to, but if you're going to be there, count me in.

ALICE

Brilliant, because I could use your help.

AMANDA

Awesome sauce. What do you need?

ALICE

Help convincing Papa not to be a stick in
the mud.

AMANDA

Oh? I'm gonna need more info to go on
than that.

ALICE

The short version of the story is, I bought a
flat. And I haven't told my parents yet.

AMANDA

What? I'm calling you right now!

A moment later, my mobile lights up. I swipe to answer it. Amanda's image fills the screen, with her unruly curly red hair, green eyes, and a smattering of freckles.

"Shouldn't you be at work?" I joke.

"Family comes first." The screen wobbles as she sets her tablet down. "And I'm due for a break. I've been working on planning this fundraising dinner for Charlie's all day. Now spill! Tell me everything."

"The car ride home isn't that long."

"Okay, then just the Spark Notes version."

"Last October, I found a property listing that I fell in love with. It may not be the prettiest place, but the stained-glass windows, the crown molding, and all the character features more than make up for how it looks. To my shock, it was in budget and in the cutest north London neighborhood. So I made an offer, and it was accepted!"

Amanda's eyes widen. "You made an offer? Just like that?"

"I know it might not have been the smartest thing to do, but you know how fast London property moves. As soon as a place is listed, it's practically sold. I didn't want someone else to get it." My cheeks burn hot. "If I didn't like the place, I knew I could always back out of the deal. Except, um . . . time seems to have gotten away from me."

Her eyes narrow. "What do you mean?"

"I wasn't the best at checking my email and messages while I was gone."

Amanda groans. "Time's up, isn't it?"

I nod slowly, swallowing hard. "The deal closed Thursday, and I'm due to pick up the keys later this week."

"Well, I guess there's no going back now. What do you need from me?"

"Do you think you could help me put together a presentation with some dummy listings and the place I bought? I thought we could pretend we've found a few flats that I'm seriously considering. Mum won't be there tonight, and it'll help buy me some time to come up with a better plan on how I'm going to break the news to them."

Amanda gives me a thumbs-up. "Not a half-bad idea. Do you want a PowerPoint?"

"Only if it's not too much trouble."

She waves me off. "Never. Making them is relaxing for me. I'll send over a mock-up to you when I'm done. Give me a couple hours."

"Thank you so much, A."

"You're welcome." She winks. "And Ali, welcome home."

Tucking my mobile back into my purse, I let out a sigh of relief. "Amanda is in."

"That's brilliant. If anyone can help convince the king, it's her. She's a hard woman to say no to." The car pulls into the palace complex. Bruce cuts the engine. "Shall I put the car away, or do you have any other errands planned before dinner?"

"No. I'll be in until we leave at seven. I have a massive amount of unpacking to do."

Bruce chuckles. "Have you made any headway on the eight suitcases of books you brought back?"

"Not yet. But I did ask my brother's secretary to order a bookshelf, some floating shelves, and a terrarium for me. I'm hoping they'll turn up today."

"Rearranging your room again?"

I nod. Bruce knows whenever I need a project to stay busy, I often take to doing up my room. I like to think it allows my creative juices to flow. My brother, however, would disagree and says it's an excuse for me to buy more furniture I don't need. But that's not true. Everything I buy is out of necessity, like the new bookshelf. Otherwise, I would literally have no more space for my massive book and film collection.

"I'll keep my eyes open for any deliveries. If anything turns up, I'll text you."

"Thanks, Bruce."

He steps out of the car and opens the door for me. As I walk up the three steps to the entryway, he snaps his fingers together, "Oh, ma'am. There is one thing I forgot to mention."

I glance over my shoulder.

"Do remember the meeting I took after I dropped you off at the palace?"

"Yes?"

"Well, the two new members who've been assigned to your detail will be here after lunch to introduce themselves to you."

Two new team members? What does he mean? I take a few shaky breaths. I don't remember hearing anything about my needing more security. It was one thing while I was abroad to have some extra bodies around, but now that I'm home, every-thing should just go back to normal.

Just as I open my mouth to quiz him about the sudden changes, his mobile rings. He ignores it, giving me his full and undivided attention, but I know that when he's on duty, the only calls he receives are important ones. "You should prob-ably answer that," I say, my voice quivering.

"Yes, I should, but did you have any questions first?"

Yes, I have a million questions. But I'll have to limit myself to asking the most important ones. "Why are there new offi-cers coming onboard?" I croak.

"I'm being reassigned."

My hand flies to my chest and I press down on my breast-bone. "Reassigned?" I sputter. "What? I don't understand."

"Princess, it's been one of the greatest honors of my career to serve you these last few years, but my superiors have collec-tively agreed that your entering university spells the end of my time as your lead protection officer." He shoots me a sad smile. "I've been allowed to stay with you much longer than an officer is normally allowed. You need a bodyguard who is younger and fitter than me."

"But you *are* young and fit," I insist.

He may have a few gray hairs sprinkled into the brown, and a couple more fine lines than the day we met, but Bruce is in good shape. He runs five miles every morning and has always finished with top marks on the annual fitness test given to members of the security detail.

"I'm chuffed you think so." He chuckles "But on this account, I agree with my bosses. My mind is as sharp as ever, but my reflexes and body have slowed. I can't protect you the same way I could when you were a teenager. I'd never forgive myself if something happened to you because I couldn't react fast enough."

His mobile begins ringing again. "We can discuss it later," he says.

I nod and take my leave, taking slow shuffling steps from the front to my flat. Sadness wells up inside of me. There's nobody who can replace Bruce. He's my friend and one of the few people I can be myself around.

I pause in front of a portrait of one of my ancestors, wearing the State Crown, holding the king's orb and scepter and wearing a long, flowing red robe. I'm reminded that I'm a member of the royal family. For hundreds of years, the decisions my relatives made were law. "You wouldn't let Bruce go so easily, would you?" I ask it.

"Well, you know what, neither will I." I clench my fists together and lift my chin. "He's not leaving me without a fight."

Two

Around two, I order a tea service, and invite Bruce to join me in my sitting room before the new team members are due to arrive. I'm trying to be open-minded, but a part of me wants to automatically dislike the new bodyguards.

They aren't the man I have eight years of history with. Bruce *knows* me. He's been right by my side supporting me through all the crap of the last two years. He is one of the few people outside my family who has my complete trust and won't betray me. How do I know I can trust these new chaps?

"Ma'am, the spread looks wonderful." His eyes are dancing as he spies what's been set out on the trolley. "You've remembered all my favorites."

"I've tried." I stare at my hands, fighting to keep a few tears from escaping. "Can I ask you something? It's kind of personal in nature. Don't feel pressured to answer it if you don't want to."

"Now you've piqued my curiosity. What's on your mind?" he asks, sitting down next to me and pouring himself a cuppa.

"Will you tell me a little more about your children?" I lift my chin, studying him from under my lashes. Bruce has never talked much about his family. I know he has two sons, but until now, I've never given them much thought. I was so young and in my own world when Bruce started with me. Now that I'm older, my perspective on everything has changed.

His eyes widen. He hesitates before slowly answering, "My two boys are both around Edmund's age. One of them has followed in my footsteps and joined the police force. The other is working toward his Masters in Business."

"You must be so proud." I do the mental calculations. Eddie is twenty-five, which means that his sons would also be in their early to mid-twenties. My shoulders hunch. My body suddenly feels heavy. I swallow hard, feeling guiltier than ever. "I'm sorry if I've kept you from them."

"Kept me from them?" Bruce's eyes widen and he blinks a few times in confusion.

"How many birthdays, graduations, anniversaries, family vacations, and other special occasions have you missed out on because of me?" My voice comes out weak.

"A few, but none of those were ever your fault. My family understands that my being a protection officer is an honor and a privilege. And that that equates to long hours, travel, and other extra duties." He places a hand on top of mine and squeezes it, sending a renewed surge of energy through my exhausted body. The jet lag is finally beginning to catch up with me. "Believe me when I say, I wouldn't be doing this without my wife's support. We've always made all our decisions together, as a team. If I've missed out on an important occasion, it was with her blessing."

"She sounds like a lovely woman."

"She is. A real diamond. I was lucky the day she accepted me." Bruce's eyes sparkle in a way that shows he's thinking about her.

"I'd love to meet her someday."

"You already have." Bruce grins. "My Abigail works for your aunt."

I inhale sharply. There's only one person I know by that name. "Abigail . . . as in Abigail Martins? My aunt's private secretary?"

"The one and only."

I shouldn't be shocked, but I am. I can picture the bright green eyes and light-brown hair of Bruce's wife clearly. She may be in her mid-fifties, but she has one of those ageless faces that makes her appear much younger than she actually is. Whenever I've interacted with her, she's been kind, and has always offered me a toffee. Hearing that both Bruce and his wife work for my family make it much easier to understand how they'd be able to put up with his demanding job.

"Now it's my turn to ask you, ma'am. Why the sudden interest?"

"Earlier, you caught me by surprise with your big news. It's taken me a few hours to process it all. All these memories of our time together have been floating through my mind. You've been such a huge part of my life, and I'd like to think we were friends." I squeeze Bruce's hand and look away. "But it's hit me that I haven't been a very decent one to you. I've never asked if you'd like more time with your family." A new wave of guilt hits me.

"Princess, you *are* my friend. And I have taken time away when I've needed it. Until now, my work and private lives needed to stay separate to remain professional. It's why even though you *have* asked me questions about my family, I've deflected them."

"Bruce, what do you mean by 'until now'? What's changed?"

"There's no easy way to say this, but in two short weeks, you'll no longer be under my charge."

"So soon?" I gasp. "I thought we'd have a few more months together." Ugh. The news keeps getting worse.

"Unfortunately, it's better to rip the plaster off now. That way you and your new agents will have enough time settle into a comfortable routine before the school term begins."

I want to shout and complain to him about how unfair it is, but throwing a tantrum won't do any good. I'm supposed to be an adult. I'm twenty, not a child. I need to handle this with maturity. Even if I'm feeling sick to my stomach over the situation, it's beyond my control. There is no arguing with the security office. I'll just have to do what a good princess is trained to do—keep calm and carry on. "Will you stay in touch with me?" I ask softly.

"Of course. You can count on it."

My neck and ears warm, and I release his hand. In many ways, Bruce is like my second father.

The corners of his eyes crinkle as he takes a sip of his tea. A faint twinge of pink appears on his own cheeks. I've never seen him so flustered.

I pour myself my own cuppa with shaky hands and change the subject. "What comes next for you? Will you still be based out of the palace?"

"That would be my first choice." He sets his teacup down. "The details still haven't been fully worked out, but I'd very much like to become a part of the committee that selects and trains future protection officers."

That sounds perfect for him. I make a mental note to write a statement of support and have Papa put in a good word for Bruce. It's the least I can do considering all his years of service to me. "Have you had a hand in choosing the officers we're expecting today?"

"No, but your father has." He adds a cranberry-orange scone to his plate. "And from what I've heard, he's picked the best available candidates for you. They've both graduated at the top of their training course."

"So you haven't met either of them?"

"No, but odds are, they'll both be as charming as me." He winks, puffing out his chest.

My body shakes with laughter. "Let's hope so."

A few moments later, a knock sounds at the door. I stand, fully intending to answer it, but Bruce is quicker and beats me to the punch. The door swings open to reveal a suit-clad man and woman.

Pushing aside my weariness, I plaster a smile on my face and wave. Despite my not wanting them here, I'd still like to make a good first impression. "Cheers, and welcome. I'm Alice, it's nice to meet you both. Please, come in."

They enter the room, and Bruce closes the door behind them. Both appear to be in their early- to mid-twenties and carry themselves with a sense of overconfidence, an important quality to have as a protection officer.

The woman curtsies, and the man bows. I wonder how long it's going to take for me to train them to ignore proper protocols around me when we're in private. I've tried hard with Bruce, and have succeeded for the most part, but I've never been able to break him from the habit of calling me ma'am, Princess, or Your Highness.

"Ma'am," the woman says, "I'm Angela." She flashes me a cheeky grin.

Angela is even in height as me at about five four. A pair of tortoiseshell glasses is perched on the bridge of her nose. It works well with her strong jawline. Her curly dark-brown hair has been secured into a tight, low bun. The creases of her suit are pressed to perfection.

We shake hands. It's firm, just like Papa's. "Ex-military?" I wager a guess.

"Yes, ma'am. RAF." She lights up and tucks her arms

behind her back, just as a military officer might when they're standing at ease.

"Thank you for your service. I'm lucky to have you with me." Before I can stop myself, I ask the cliche question, "Were you a pilot?"

"Yes, ma'am. I'm fully qualified to fly the C-17 Globemaster and the Atlas C-1." She studies my clueless face and quickly clarifies, "They're both transport planes."

"Wow," I murmur. My respect for her has just gone up tenfold. I know from Papa that the pool of female aviators is small. Angela has probably had to work hard her entire career to prove herself in a field that's historically been dominated by men. In this, we're alike. I want to become a structural engineer, another field where there aren't many women. "I hope the transition from the air to the ground has gone smoothly."

"Yes, ma'am, it has. I can handle anything that's thrown my direction."

My gaze travels to the man. "Ma'am. I'm Arthur," he says.

He has light-brown hair and hazel eyes. While he's not overly tall, about five eight, his shoulders are broad. His three-piece suit is immaculately cut and contours perfectly to his body, leaving little doubt in my mind about the powerful physique that's hiding underneath it all. I stare for a moment longer than necessary, then quickly return his handshake. It's short and to the point. There's no smile or flicker of any emotion. He's already an expert at donning a mask.

"A pleasure." My voice comes out slightly higher than normal. I clear my throat and gesture to the couch, willing myself to focus. "Are you ex-military too?"

"No, ma'am." He doesn't elaborate.

"All right, then, please, have a seat. I'd love to spend a few minutes getting to know each of you a little better."

"The feeling is mutual." Angela nods.

Arthur remains quiet, but wordlessly follows her lead and

sits across from me. His eyes appraise me as if he's assessing my worth. It's as if something icy cold is passing through my spine. Despite what the public may think, I don't appreciate being stared at. It's the reason I avoid being photographed and appearing in public as much as humanly possible.

"Bruce Martins is the current head of my detail. Er . . ." I search the room for him. He's stepped out of earshot and is on the mobile in the far corner near my dog Lillian. "I'm sure he'll join us shortly, then I'll be able to properly introduce you to him."

"We've met," Arthur says, crossing his arms and clenching his jaw.

That's curious. Bruce said he hadn't met the new team members. I study Arthur a little closer and have to wonder, does he not like Bruce? Everyone loves him. How could they not? He's the epitome of what a gentleman should be. He always keeps his calm and has never said a cross or ill word about anyone. At least that I'm aware of.

My eyebrows twitch. The interest I had in this man a few moments ago has suddenly evaporated, replaced with a bitter taste in my mouth. *Arthur, you are not creating a very good impression with me.*

"You might have, I haven't." Angela pats his arm and crosses her legs. "I'd love to meet him when we're able."

"Brilliant. In the meantime, please help yourself to tea."

"Don't mind if we do." Angela arches her eyebrow at Arthur and nods to the tea. He sighs, then finally relents, pouring himself a cup and ignoring the food offerings. Angela, on the other hand, helps herself to a few finger sandwiches and a mini fruit scone.

Three

The only reason I'm able to stop myself from ripping the hair off my head in frustration at Arthur's one-word answers is because I've been trained since birth to be a proper hostess. No matter what tactic I employ, the man is like a robot who's only capable of saying "yes, ma'am" or "no, ma'am." Any time I ask an open-ended question, Angela jumps in and answers on his behalf. It's exhausting, and I don't think my tired brain can stand it much longer.

Our conversation so far has gone something like this:

"Have you been with the Met Police long?"

"No, ma'am."

"It's been about three years for him and two years for me," Angela adds.

"At least I won't be your first assignment," I joke.

"No, ma'am." Arthur's face remains blank.

Silence ensues before Angela again comes to the rescue, filling the awkward silence. "We've both worked our way up through the ranks. For the last couple of months, we've been assigned to the Foreign Dignitary Protection Division."

"That's fantastic. Angela, I know you were previously with the RAF, but what about you Arthur?"

"He's been with the force since he finished uni." Arthur nods curtly to confirm what Angela said.

"Which uni did you attend?"

"He studied at the University of Manchester."

By this point, I've begun to wonder if he's doing it on purpose to annoy me. His body language is closed off and he keeps checking his watch. That tells me he doesn't want to be here.

If that's the case, fine. Leave. He wouldn't be missed. I'll happily keep Bruce until the security office can find a replacement. In fact, I think I'll talk to Papa about it later. Two can play at this game. I'll just ignore him until this meeting is over.

"Apologies, Princess. There was an issue with the head office that needed to be ironed out." Bruce tucks his mobile away and sits next to me. "How are you all getting on?"

"Swimmingly," I joke. My tone borders on sarcasm.

Bruce glances at me. His eyebrows knit together in a frown for a split second before he's back to his smiling self. He leans over the coffee table and offers his hand to Angela. "Hiya, I'm Bruce Martins." When he sets eyes on Arthur, however, he suddenly stiffens. The corners of his eyes widen. His mouth opens and closes. Arthur frowns even deeper and doesn't extend his hand. Bruce doesn't move—all he can do is stare.

The room stays silent for several seconds. I tilt my head to the side, eyes darting between the two, but whatever is being exchanged between them is something that's unreadable. All I can do is continue to be a decent hostess.

"Right, then." I set my teacup down with a little more force than usual. It clatters against the saucer. Everyone's attention turns to me. "How about if we turn the tables. I'm sure by now you have some questions for me you might like to ask."

"Yes, ma'am. I do." Angela nods. "We've been informed by the security office that for the summer, our daily schedules will mirror yours. Just for my reference, I'd like to get a feel for what types of activities you do on a given day."

That's a simple enough question. I exhale and relax against the back of the couch. "So there's really two types of days that I might have. Days with preplanned public engagements and days without. For the remainder of June and July, I'm slated to appear at the Princess Alice Cup, Trooping the Colour, Royal Ascot, and one or two garden parties at Buckingham Palace."

I pause, giving her a moment to take a few notes on her mobile. "The PM has asked my father to place a hold on all other public appearances for the next few weeks until after the elections. On a normal day for me, if I'm leaving the palace complex, it's usually to go riding, play tennis, or spend time with my family."

"Don't forget, Princess, you *do* have a part-time job," Bruce gently reminds me.

"Oh yes. I work in the palace stables on the weekends from about six a.m. to two p.m."

"I think you two will find Princess Alice to be an easy charge to work with," he says. "She's got a good head on her shoulders and has never made any trouble for me."

My body warms at the compliment. I can feel the tips of my ears and neck heating up. I quickly reach for tea and take a long sip, hiding my face.

"Brilliant." Angela glances up from her mobile. "I know it's a little early to ask since you haven't registered for classes yet, but what about once you start uni."

I swallow slowly, frowning. "I'll be in classes and studying during the week. If I have any spare time, I'll probably try and fit in some riding since the stables are close to Imperial's campus."

"That's not exactly what I meant." Angela rubs the back

of her neck. "I was curious . . . that is, um . . . do you see your-self embracing the full uni experience?"

"It works best with Her Highness if you ask her questions directly." Bruce half coughs, half laughs. "Ma'am, Angela is trying to politely find out if you intend to frequent nightclubs."

Angela is taken aback by his frankness. She nearly drops her mobile. Arthur's left eyebrow rises a millimeter.

"No." I wrinkle my nose. "It's *not* my thing. If I wanted to drink expensive alcohol and act stupid, I'd rather do it at home in my pajamas."

One, my older brother did enough clubbing for the both of us when he was my age. Two, going out involves having a social life, which I lack. I make it a point of staying away from being bait for the press. The media has ruined my life enough for a lifetime, especially after last year.

"It sounds like we have that in common." Angela smiles. "My ideal night is curling up on the sofa with a hot chocolate and a good book or a film."

"Do you enjoy rom-coms?" I scoot forward in my seat. "Books and films are a guilty pleasure of mine."

"I do." Her eyes glimmer with excitement.

I know who's going to be my plus-one when we get new rom-coms at the Buckingham Palace cinema. "Bruce finds them too predictable. He's a thriller and sci-fi bloke. But the familiar storylines are what I love about them. From the meet-cute to the happily ever after, you know exactly what you're going to get."

"Here, here."

I know I said I'd ignore Arthur, but there's a nagging feeling inside my chest urging me to make an effort to include him. "What about you, Arthur? What types of films do you enjoy?" I don't expect an answer.

"Comedy." His tone is flat as he glances at his watch again.

"That's great."

Good deed done; I spend the next few minutes monopolizing Angela in conversation by swapping favorite films and what we love about them. At the top of her list are *My Big Fat Greek Wedding*, *13 Going on 30*, and *Notting Hill*. While my current top three are *Love Actually*, *Crazy Rich Asians*, and *Enchanted*.

"Ladies, I hate to interrupt, but unfortunately, we'll have to wrap this up. I just received a text from the security office. You two are needed back downstairs to finish processing your badges." Bruce looks at Angela and Arthur.

"More paperwork." Angela sighs.

"It's never-ending," Arthur mutters.

"It was nice meeting you two." I shake their hands one final time.

"Thank you for tea, ma'am," Angela says.

Arthur gives me a curt nod.

"I'll walk you two out." Bruce opens the door, locks eyes with Arthur, and mouths the word *hallway* to him.

Something flickers behind Arthur's eyes. He offers Bruce the slightest of nods.

They all exit, and I'm left alone. I wish Angela could've stayed longer. She's brilliant. I enjoyed spending some time getting to know her, but I understand that she's here to work, not to idly chitchat with me. I let out a sigh of relief. At least I have a good feeling about her. Arthur, however, needs to go.

FAMILY DINNERS AT BUCKINGHAM PALACE AREN'T AT all like film and television make them out to be. During the day, we may dress formally, but come evening, when the business of state has been concluded, we dress casually, usually in jeans and T-shirts. Except for Papa. He prefers plaid button-up shirts, which he owns in every pattern and color imaginable.

Mum and Papa started the tradition of family dinner night when we were children to try and give us a taste of a normal life. Once a week, the palace chefs would have a night off and they'd let Eddie and me order takeaway. It was always something we looked forward to. We'd be on our best behavior so Papa wouldn't have any reason to cancel our special dinner.

As adults, our schedules keep us apart more than when we're together, but Papa still makes an effort to make sure we have at least one family dinner a month. Tonight, it was Eddie's turn to order. We have about twenty containers of Chinese food spread out over the dining room table. That may seem like a lot, but he and Papa can easily eat half of them. It's one of the reasons I always help myself to the bao buns first. They're the first item to disappear if you're not fast enough.

"Amanda, I'm glad you were able to join us tonight," Papa says as he dumps half a container of chow mein onto his plate, followed by some orange chicken, white rice, steamed veggies, and crispy honey walnut shrimp.

"Me too. I couldn't pass up on the chance to see Alice." She grins. "There are soooooooooo many things I want to ask you about your trip. It seems like you were gone forever."

Amanda has bright green eyes, and a personality as vibrant as her curly red hair. She's been engaged to my brother for four years and has become a close friend.

"Not forever, only a couple months."

"In Amanda's world, that's forever." Eddie snorts. Like Papa, he packs his plate as full as he can manage, like he's a human rubbish compactor.

Physically, Eddie has been dubbed the male version of me. We have the same sandy-blond hair, blue eyes, button nose, and cheeky smiles. However, that's where the similarities end. Unlike me, he received the height gene that runs on Papa's side of the family. Eddie stands just over six feet tall to my petite five-four frame. He's also much more outgoing than me.

"You'd better save some for your mum. I bet she'll be starving when she gets back," Amanda elbows him.

"Don't worry about Agnus. She rang me earlier letting me know that the opening reception ran longer than planned. She only left Cornwall about an hour ago and won't be back until late. She'll pick up some dinner on her way home." Papa seats himself at the head of the table. "Although, it *would* be nice if there were a few leftovers for her to enjoy tomorrow." He locks eyes with my brother.

Eddie takes the hint and stops loading his plate, joining Papa at the table next to Amanda. "So, sister dearest . . ." he begins. "What was the most embarrassing thing that happened to you?"

"You haven't seen Alice in eight months and *that's* the first thing you decide to ask her?" Amanda groans.

"Yes." He shrugs. "She'd probably ask me the same thing."

He's right, I probably would if our positions were reversed. I take a moment to think about all the places I've visited.

"Okay, here's a good story for you. On the day I arrived in Venice, our train was a few hours late. I was able to rearrange most of my plans, but one thing I knew we had to try and squeeze in was a visit to the Guggenheim Museum. It was going to be closed two of the three days we were there. So we dashed to the hotel, did the world's quickest check-in, and darted off to the museum."

"What's funny about that?" Eddie asks.

Amanda shoots him a *Be patient* look.

I ignore him and continue. "After we'd had dinner and returned to the hotel, I went up to my room and found a trail of rose petals, scented candles, towels folded in the shape of swans, chocolate strawberries, and a bottle of champagne. It was set up as if somebody thought I was there to celebrate a honeymoon."

Amanda and Eddie begin to laugh.

"Why the devil would they think that?" Papa's brows knit together.

"Bruce and I put our heads together, and the best explanation we could come up with was that the front desk must've seen one of the protection officers helping me carry my bags up to my room, and jumped to the conclusion we were newlyweds."

Papa joins in the laughter.

"The joke was on them. We never bothered to correct their mistake, and they didn't charge us for the treats. The strawberries were delicious."

"That's brilliant." Eddie wipes a small tear from the corner of his eyelid. "What other stories do you have?"

"Um . . . while I was in Spain, I did laundry, and didn't secure it on a clothesline correctly. I ended up dropping all my clothes onto the street below. That was pretty bad."

I shake my head, remembering how fast I had to sprint down the steps from my hotel room to the street and scramble to pick up my bras and knickers. The security team thought something bad had happened and chased after me. I was mortified to have to explain about the shower of clothing, but at the very least they didn't see my undergarments.

Amanda jumps into the conversation and recounts a few memorable moments from her time working as a flight attendant. My favorite is probably the story of the time she tried to speak to the pilot, and instead of using the intercom to tell him to turn up the heat in the cabin, she accidentally used the PA system. We spend so much time laughing that the muscles in my face and stomach become sore.

After the washing up has been taken care of and takeaway containers safely tucked into the refrigerator, the four of us migrate into the sitting room. We have mugs of hot tea and are munching on a delicious lemon loaf cake Amanda baked for dessert. Spirits are high. My eyes are burning, and I'm about ready to fall asleep, but that's when Amanda decides to make her presentation to Papa.

"Reggie, if you don't mind, there is a little something Alice and I would like to discuss with you." She nods to me.

I down the rest of my tea and hope the sugar from the dessert will give me a second wind.

"Of course, I'm all ears," he says.

With scary precision, Amanda whips out her iPad and turns on the screen mirroring. Her presentation appears on the telly.

"Property in London, as you may know, is among the most expensive and competitive markets in the world. As soon as a listing springs up online, it's as good as sold." She changes slides. "Alice told me that she's aiming to purchase a flat in one of the neighborhoods within a five-kilometer radius of Imperial College."

Eddie and Papa stare at the screen as a series of maps, charts, and graphs appear. Amanda walks them through the average cost of a property in each neighborhood and what my money can buy.

"Now, if we extend our search radius even two kilometers, to this zone, you'll notice that the prices drop off more than ten percent. *And* with the added benefit of improved safety and access to green space. Now, there are three properties that Alice and I thought might be worth you having a look over . . ."

I cross my fingers behind my back and hope for the best. She's doing a killer job. If she weren't going to be the future queen, she'd make a brilliant CEO. I'm so glad she's on my side.

"Alice, some of these are knackered." Eddie's eyes narrow.

"Why are you only interested in places that need so much doing up?"

"Three main reasons. Number one, I'll be able to customize the place exactly as I want it. Number two, I want a character property. And number three, doing work is the best way to get value for your money."

The thing about this flat is that when I say I wanted a place that is solely my own, I meant it. I'm footing the purchase of it from the trust fund my grandad left me, not my parents. It's true, there were places available in better condition than the place I bought, but they were well outside my million-and-a-half-pound budget.

"I don't know, Alice. Your brother is right." My father removes his reading glasses. "What if your mum and I offered to assist you with the purchase? You'd be able to find a better building."

"I appreciate that, but the answer's no. This is my baby."

"Very well." He sighs. "I'll take into consideration the flats Amanda has shown us tonight, but your mum will have the final say."

Internally, I'm jumping for joy. Papa hasn't ruled out the flat I bought. That's a huge win in my book. It makes everything one step easier in breaking the news to him in a few days when I officially pick up the keys. "Thank you, Papa." I hug him tightly. Amanda offers me a subtle high five behind his back.

As the evening winds down, Mum arrives home. She's clearly as exhausted as me and has a hard time hiding her yawns. Eddie, Amanda, and I spend a couple minutes chatting with her, but we collectively agree it's time to head home.

"Do you need a ride, Ali?" My brother grabs his coat and helps Amanda into hers.

"Sure, that would be great; I just have one thing I need to ask Papa about."

"Okay, we'll be waiting in the car. Come down whenever you're ready."

Approaching my father, who's in the kitchen wiping down the counter, I clear my throat. "Papa?"

"Oh, Alice, I thought you'd left."

"Not yet. I . . . I just had one more thing I wanted to mention to you before I forgot." I try and sound as nonchalant as possible.

"Yes?" He places the dish towel next to the sink and leans against the counter.

"I met my new security officers this afternoon. Angela is fantastic—I like her a lot—but the other one, Arthur . . . we didn't get on very well. I, um . . . just wanted to see if it might be possible to reassign him."

"I see." Papa blinks slowly. "And what exactly, pray tell, did you not care for about Arthur? Did he misbehave?"

"No, not exactly. He just, um . . . wasn't very talkative." I'm frustrated with how weak and feeble that excuse sounds. I had this entire speech rehearsed in my head and now my mind's gone blank.

"Alice, that's *not* a valid reason to reassign him." Papa crosses his arms. "I know that anyone who comes after Bruce has large shoes to fill, but trust me, Arthur is the right person for your detail. I remember reading his file. He earned top marks across the board on all his tests and had several outstanding recommendations from his superiors. Give him some time."

Papa's tone is firm. There's no room for negotiation with him. Arthur is not going anywhere. I decide to make one last-ditch attempt, knowing it's a lost cause. I widen my eyes and school my face as best I can into the "Daddy's little girl" look. "Even if I asked with a cherry on top?"

"Alice . . ." My father places a hand on my shoulder. "How about this: Give the man until the end of summer. If you're still not getting on with him by the time school begins, we'll reassess the situation. Does that sound fair?"

"Yes, sir."

"Good. We'll circle back to this in a few months' time." He kisses the top of my head and walks me to the door. I bid him good night and walk down to the car.

I'll take tonight as a partial win-win. I may not have been able to get rid of Arthur yet, but at least I'm better off than when I started the night. There's an end date in sight.

Four

The next evening, I receive a call from Amanda. Placing the phone on speaker, I answer, "Hello?"

Instead of hearing Amanda's voice, the song "The Boys Are Back in Town" and a mean guitar solo blare out. I have to hold my mobile a few inches from my ear.

"Alice! I've been waiting all day to call you! I wasn't able to ask you for the nitty-gritty details of your trip last night with your dad and brother around, but Eddie is *finally* out of the house. So fill me in!"

I'm confused. I'd thought I'd done a decent job covering most of the details at dinner. "What else do you want to know? More about the museums? The architecture? The shopping?"

"No, silly. There's no way you can go away for eight months without rubbing elbows with some cute guys. How many dates did you go on?"

"Zero."

"Ah, come on, Ali, this is me you're talking to. I promise I won't say anything to Eddie."

"It's true!" I protest. "Remember who you're dealing with

—Ms. Antisocial. I didn't go out. I stayed in most nights. It was too risky. The goal was to escape the world and find myself, not invite the media back in."

"Oh, Ali." Amanda sighs. "I'd hoped you would've allowed yourself to have a little fun. It wouldn't have hurt you to go to a bar or a pub and see if you could score a date with guy. Not every person you meet is out to get you."

"I had fun. It just didn't involve anyone outside my protection team." I know her heart is in the right place. It's just when you've had your entire world turned upside down once before, it's difficult to step outside the protective bubble you've built. "Besides, let's say I *did* manage to speak to a guy at a pub. Odds are, if my security team didn't scare him, I'd do it the moment I opened my mouth. You know how I am when I'm nervous. I start rambling about the first architectural feature that the pops into my mind. It's one of the reasons I'll never find a boyfriend."

"That's rubbish. There is someone for everybody out there! Besides, aren't you the one who's told me you get on better with guys than girls?"

"Yes, I did," I admit. She has me there.

"So, what's the problem?"

"Lads are only interested in how a girl looks. They don't care two bits about personality."

"There's where you're wrong. I guarantee you that there are guys out there who will like you for your brilliant brain and your personality. Look at your brother and me. We're total opposites. But we love each other for who we are."

A smile tugs at my lips. Amanda and my brother are indeed living, breathing proof of that.

"It sounds to me like you just need some practice to boost your confidence. If I have it my way, you'll have a boyfriend in no time," she muses. "What are you doing tonight?"

Technically speaking, I'm free. I was going to dive into one of the books I picked up on my trip, but I can't tell her that. "Laundry," I fib, knowing she'll see right through it.

"Pfft. Not anymore, you're not. The laundry can wait. Tonight, you're going out with Clara and me."

Clara is my cousin David's wife. She's a prima ballerina with the Westminster Ballet and one of the most genuinely kind people you could meet. She'd give you the pointe shoes and leotard off her body if you asked her for them.

"But Amanda, if the three of us go out, we'll stand out like a group of people who have decided to wear inflatable flamingo suits to a black-tie dinner. Every eye and camera will be on us." I can't imagine anything worse. My stomach fills with dread thinking about it. "Plus, I can guarantee that Eddie, David, or both will find a way to join us. Talk about an instant way to repel any guys."

"Ali, quit being a party pooper. Live a little. Can't is not a word that exists in my vocabulary. Trust me, it'll save us both a lot of time and energy if you just give in to me now."

"I don't know." I rub the back of my neck. Everything in my body is telling me not to engage with Amanda's plan. I'm mentally fighting with a two-ton rhinoceros, trying to be open-minded.

"If you come out tonight, I can guarantee the boys won't join us, and we'll go somewhere we can mix in with the crowd."

"Where were you thinking of going?" I pinch my nose, chiding myself for asking.

"Three places—the private members' club, the Keys at the Tower of London, or a mystery location. Each one of those is semi-private. Even our protection officers wouldn't have any trouble blending in."

My body feels like I'm playing a game of tug of war. On one hand, I have absolutely zero desire to go out. But on the other hand, as my therapist has repeatedly told me, the best cure to a problem is to face it head-on. Meaning that going out will help me get over my fear of being targeted by the paparazzi.

Compared to where I was before I left on my gap-year travels, I've made big strides. Being able to travel through Europe with near-total anonymity has shown me I *can* go out in public and have an enjoyable time. Plus, if I'm with Amanda and Clara, I know I'll be among family and well protected. I can trust them.

I rub my temples as I turn to another problem—the last date I went on. It had to have been at least two-and-a-half years ago. And the time before that? I squeeze my eyes shut and have a think. I'm fairly certain it was on the night after my fifteenth birthday. I distinctly remember having dinner with one of the blokes from the all-boys school down the road.

I swallow hard. Two dates. That's the extent of my romantic life. Two bloody dates. I can't start uni without having gone on a proper date. I'll be more of a social outcast than I already am. A surge of adrenaline courses through my body. Before I'm fully aware of what I'm agreeing to, I exclaim, "I'll do it!"

"You're learning well, my young padawan. Now, pick your poison. Where are we going tonight?"

"The mystery location."

I hear Amanda clapping. "Awesome sauce. I'll text you with the details. Wear something that has a skirt you can twirl in."

"Huh?"

"For the mystery location," she clarifies. "You'll need a skirt that gives you some movement. Trust me, it'll all make sense soon enough."

What does Amanda have in store for me? She and Eddie have a history of planning elaborate dates and get-togethers. What's waiting at the mystery location?

"Okay, um . . . I'll see you soon. I guess."

I hang up the call. Despite the anxiety and tightness in my chest, I'm going to see this outing through. Walking over to my closet, I plant my hands on my hips. There is a large selection of suits, formal gowns, coats, riding clothes, and my more casual everyday clothes, but a flowing skirt? I don't know if I own one. I'm a jeans and blouse kind of girl. It looks like I may have to improvise.

Twenty minutes later, my mobile lights up. I've been added to a group text message.

AMANDA

Who's excited for a girls' night out?

CLARA

Me!

ALICE

Me too.

AMANDA

Grinning emoji

CLARA

It's been ages since I've had a night off.
Where are we headed?

AMANDA

That's for me to know and you to find out.
I've sent the address to your security team.
David's driver is giving us a ride. We'll pick
you up in a half hour.

CLARA

A! That's not enough time to get ready!

ALICE

I'm ready.

AMANDA

So am I. C, it looks like it's just you who
needs time to get ready.

CLARA

Blushing emoji What's the dress code?

ALICE

To quote Amanda, wear a dress with a skirt
that has movement.

AMANDA

What she said. You'd better put those
famous quick-change skills to use. You
have twenty-nine more minutes.

ALICE

You sound like my dad.

AMANDA

Who do you think I learned it from?

ALICE

Winking emoji

AMANDA

See you soon!

MY MOUTH DROPS OPEN. STANDING OUTSIDE MY
doorway with his arms crossed, scowling, is the last person I
expected to find. "Arthur?" I sputter. "What are you doing
here?"

"My job," he huffs.

I resist the urge to face-palm. I wasn't exactly looking for a
literal answer. "I was expecting Bruce, that's all."

"He's unavailable." Arthur's tone is curt.

"Oh, okay." I close the entry door, and we start down the hall to the lift.

His strides are quick. I'm forced to walk faster than normal to keep up with him. He's dressed in the same black suit, white dress shirt, and blue-and-red-striped tie as yesterday.

"The Duchess of Leeds and Amanda Collins will be joining us. I'm not sure which car their driver will be in, but you may have to ride in one of the trailing cars with their security teams."

"I'm aware."

We step into the lift. The whirl of the machinery fills the awkward silence.

"I hadn't realized you and Angela were starting straightaway."

"It's our first day," he says flatly as he checks his mobile.

"Uh-huh. So, you'll be rotating with Angela and shadowing Bruce?"

"Yes."

"Except for tonight?

"Yes."

Why does he have to make conversations so difficult? It's so frustrating. Is he not used to speaking with other people? Maybe he thinks I'm just a silly princess. This is going to be a very, *very* long night. At least I'll have Clara and Amanda to distract me.

The lift door opens. He shoves the phone into his trouser pocket and power walks ahead of me. I shake my head and follow him to the front drive, where a black Range Rover has just pulled up.

Before the driver can open the back door, it flies open, and Amanda spills out. "Alice! You look smoking hot!" She wolf whistles.

Her energy and excitement help me forget Arthur. I give her my full attention. "It's the best I could do." I slowly spin in a circle. I've picked out a light-blue long-sleeved V-neck dress that ends just above my knees. I've paired it with my favorite knee-high black boots and a black belt. My hair is styled in a half-up, half-down look, my default. It's semi-casual, so I hope this will work for wherever our destination is for tonight.

"I love it." Pulling out her mobile, she snaps a photo of me. Then Amanda's gaze travels to Arthur. His stoic mask is firmly in place. She plasters a Cheshire cat grin on her face and waves. "Hi, I haven't seen you before. I'm Amanda, Collins, or AC. Nice to meet ya."

"Ma'am." He nods.

"And I'm Clara." My cousin's wife, a petite woman with dark-brown hair, waves from inside the car. "Excuse me for not getting out." She points to a walking boot on her foot. "My plantar fasciitis has flared again."

"Your Grace."

I let out a breath. He's bordering on rude, making no effort to give his name. Bruce would never do that. Arthur can act how he likes with me, but not with my family. "This is Arthur. He's my Bruce tonight."

"Cool beans. We're happy to have you with us. Our security guys are in the other car. They'll be excited to have you join them," Amanda says.

Arthur doesn't reply. Frowning, he wordlessly makes his way to the lead vehicle.

"I'm sorry for him."

"Don't worry about it. He just needs to be broken in." Amanda links her arm through mine. "More importantly, now that you're here, Ali, let's get this party started." We slide into the car and shut the door.

"Clara, your poor foot," I say sympathetically. Of all the

rotten luck. As a ballerina, her feet are her livelihood. "How long are you going to be out for this time?"

"Don't worry, it's more precautionary than anything else. I can dance. I just need to cut back on my rehearsal time. The older I get, the more my body seems to break down."

"I hope it doesn't hurt too much." I wonder if she's hiding any other injuries. Clara is as tough as they come. The week she met my cousin five years ago, she danced in a gala performance with a broken bone in her foot. Any other person would've pulled out, but not her. And secretly, I'm glad she didn't, because that gutsy move is what eventually earned her a contract with the Westminster Ballet and brought her to London. I can't imagine her not being married to my cousin and in my life.

"It's nothing I can't handle. This isn't any worse than a strained or pulled muscle. If it'll make you feel any better, David's been watching me like a mother hen. He'll make sure I actually rest."

We share a laugh. My cousin can definitely be a worrywart.

"Speaking of being protected, how are you getting along with your new protection team?" Clara asks. "Amanda mentioned on the way over that Bruce is retiring. It's such a shame. I like him a lot."

"Me too." My heart still feels heavy when I think about it, but I've begun getting used to the idea of not having him around. "The two newbies are a mixed bag. Arthur, you've met. He's professional to the point of being cold. I don't really have much to say about him. Angela, on the other hand, is lovely. Just from our initial conversation, it seems like we have a lot in common. She was so easy to talk to. I like her already."

"It sounds to me like Arthur is just doing his job. Give him some time to settle in. I'm sure he needs to adjust to the new situation too. It took a while for the lads on your cousin's team to warm up to me," Clara muses.

"That's what Amanda said."

"Great minds think alike." She elbows Clara. "And shy or not, the new Bruce is handsome."

"If you say so." I can't think of another decent thing to say about him. I pull a line out of Mr. Darcy's book. "I guess he has nice eyes." Not that I know what color they are. I haven't looked that closely.

"Amanda, you shouldn't encourage her. He's the *one* guy who's off-limits. You know the rules," Clara says. "Protection officers aren't allowed to date anyone they work for."

"Then it's a good thing I have zero interest in him. He's *not* my type." I wince at the thought of going on a date with someone like him.

Amanda twists her body to face me. "And what is your type?"

I shouldn't have opened my mouth. I don't know. I mutter the first thought that pops into my head, "Um . . . somebody who likes horses?"

Taking out her phone she opens the note app. "Hold on." Her nose wrinkles as she creates a list in the app. "Okay, what else?"

"Are we really doing this?"

"Come on, Ali, what else are you into? Beards? Tattoos? Piercings? Muscles? Eye color?"

"Er . . ." My palms grow sweaty and suddenly the car is too hot. I don't know what type of guy I'm into. It's never been a thing that's high on my priority list.

Clara places a cool, calming hand on my elbow. "Whatever you say stays between us girls. We promise none of it will leak out, especially to the boys. You can trust us." She glances at Amanda, then back to me. "Did you know that before I met David, I used to hang out at the bookshop near the Los Angeles Ballet Theatre during my breaks? I'd hoped to meet a guy there. But I never did. They were always taken.

To me, there was nothing more attractive than a man who reads."

Luckily for Clara, she met the perfect partner. David, like Papa, adores reading military history books. If you were to give them the name of a major battle, the two of them could go on for hours on end discussing how one decision made by a general or colonel impacted the outcome of said event.

"What about you, A? We know you've always had a thing for Eddie, but before you were an engaged woman, what types of profiles attracted you on dating apps?" Clara asks.

"Mainly guys who were open to going to Disneyland with me." She presses her lips together. "You'd think it wouldn't be asking much, but it was. Nine times out of ten, I'd exhaust them running from ride to ride and they'd strand me two hours into the date. It's their loss. They missed one of the world's best fireworks shows."

The embarrassment from a few moments ago flees the car. Clara and I giggle. These two are family. I can trust them. They'd never hurt me—unlike my former classmates. I take a deep breath. "What else are you attracted to? Tattoos?" I ask, needing a few more moments to compose myself.

"Yup, tattoos are cool by me. They just didn't rank as highly on my list of top attributes. Eddie has three, you know."

"Huh, I never knew that."

"They're in places that don't show much." She winks.

I cover my ears. "La la la. I don't need to hear that. I'll be scarred for life."

"They're on his shoulder blade, lower back, and his biceps." She rolls her eyes. "Places the *press* won't photograph. Anyway, quit stalling. What qualities or physical traits in a guy are important to you?"

That's the million-pound question. My eyes flutter and my voice grows quiet. "Besides horses, and being someone I can trust . . . er, I guess if I were looking, I'd like to find a guy who is motivated to go after his goals."

"Those are great, Ali! Keep them coming."

Putting their heads together, Amanda and Clara help me create a shortlist. My confidence is beginning to grow. It turns out that I *do* have things to look for in a man.

> Must Haves:
> -Enjoys horses, traveling, reading
> -Trustworthy
> -Confident and self-motivated
> -Emotionally mature
> -Open to DIY projects and working with his hands
> -Pet friendly
> Deal Breakers:
> -Looks down on women in STEM fields
> -Complainer
> -A man with a large ego who sees himself as the center of the universe
> -Has a long beard
> -Has facial tattoos

"This is perfect. Now you have a standard to help you determine if you'll click with one of the guys tonight." Amanda turns the screen off on her phone.

"You seem so hopeful I'll be able to talk to more than one bloke." I bite the inside of my lip. "What do you have planned?"

"You'll see." She laughs, her eyes sparkling with mirth.

The car comes to a stop. Glancing out the window, I realize we've arrived at a dock. I see the murky water of the Thames lapping against the stern of a sixty-foot-long yacht. The soft glow of a string of fairy lights casts a shimmering halo around a black-and-white polka-dot banner with a red heart at the entrance that reads "Club Babalou" in swirly letters.

The door opens, and Amanda, Clara, and I slide out. I stand and stare in awe for several moments. Goosebumps materialize on the back of my neck. There's a lingering scent of salt in the air and the sound of sea birds. Couples are walking up a red carpet, dressed to impress in tuxes and vintage-inspired gowns. A photographer stops them at the entrance and asks them to pose for photos using a vintage camera. The theme song to *I Love Lucy* plays in the background.

"What is this place?" I whisper.

"Tonight, it's Club Babalou, an *I Love Lucy*-themed dinner cruise." Amanda opens her purse and slips on a pair of white kid gloves. "Other nights, it's the yacht owned by the members' club, Charlie's."

"Leave it to you, A, to find something like this at the last minute," Clara jokes.

"Well, if we're being honest, I did most of the planning for tonight." Amanda's cheeks flush, but with the dim lighting, it looks more like she's applied blush. "This is their semi-annual fundraiser. Eddie had to cancel on me last minute to attend an event in Canterbury. I was going to stay home, but when you called and chose the mystery location, it seemed like we were meant to be here after all."

I subconsciously glance down at my dress, tugging at the skirt. "I wish I'd picked out something more formal, like an evening gown."

"Nope, that's exactly why I didn't tell you what the plan was. I wanted you to be the *real* you tonight. Not the princess. Trust me when I say the people here won't care about what you're wearing. They'll care about you being able to move on the dance floor." Amanda links her arms through mine and Clara's, and we walk up the ramp to the boat. "All right, ladies, let's go."

A photographer stops us. "Ladies, would you care for a photo?"

My gut reaction is to freeze, but Amanda pulls us in tighter to her. "You betcha!" she says.

The flashbulb goes off, and the photographer hands us a plastic card with a QR code. "You can download them after the event tonight. Have a swell time, ladies."

I exhale. This is a private event. There isn't a need to worry about any press being here. Or people at the dinner staring at me. My family has a long-standing relationship with Charlie's. Most of the members have seen us before and or are family friends. I *can* get through tonight.

Five

Each deck of the yacht is decorated as if we've stepped into a vintage Hollywood film. The lower deck is made up to resemble a 1950s kitchen, filled with brightly-colored appliances and a cherry-red table.

The upper deck has been converted into a living room. There's a sofa, coffee table, piano, and an oversized vintage boxy television. It takes me a moment to realize that the telly is hollow, and people can climb inside and pose for photos with different props, like large colorful novelty glasses, feather boas, and signs with different thought-bubble emojis.

Finally, the dining area on the main deck has been transformed into a nightclub. Each table has a black-and-white polka-dot tablecloth, red place settings, and a candelabra. There's a twelve-piece Latin band dressed in white suits playing a mixture of contemporary music and tunes that were popular in the 1950s and '60s.

"This is brilliant." I can't stop myself from grinning ear to ear. If there were ever a true *I Love Lucy* experience, this is it.

"Happy to hear you approve." Amanda winks.

We enjoy dinner and some musical entertainment with a

Ricky Ricardo impersonator before the dance floor officially opens up.

"Is it just me, or does everyone seem like they know what they're doing?" I whisper to Clara.

She lifts her head and studies the couples for several moments. "You're right. They're all dancing the same mambo. It wouldn't surprise me if Amanda organized dance lessons for ticketholders beforehand."

Suddenly, I feel the light touch of a hand on my shoulder. I twist in my seat. A lad in a white tuxedo with blond hair and brown eyes holds out his hand. "Miss, would you care to dance?"

"Um . . ."

"Go on and enjoy yourself," Clara urges. "If I can't dance, you might as well."

There goes my excuse for hanging out at the table. Now I don't have a reason to say no to him. "Are you sure? I *really* don't mind keeping you company," I emphasize.

"I have Amanda and my phone. I'm fine. Now go." She gently pushes my arm.

Amanda wanted to make tonight special. I owe it to her and Clara to participate in at least one dance. I can't be a wall-flower forever. Digging deep into my reserves of courage, I force a smile onto my face. "I'd love to," I answer, putting my hand into the man's.

"Brilliant." He sweeps me out of my chair and out onto the middle of the dance floor. "I'm Geoff."

"I'm Ali—son." I stop myself from giving my full name to him to buy a little time before I'm recognized. I'm curious to see how he'll treat me if he thinks I'm just another girl.

The band picks up their instruments and begins playing. Although Mum ensured that Eddie and I knew the basics of ballroom dancing, it's been a good long while since I've had to put any of that knowledge to use. I'm heavy on my feet.

Thank goodness my boots don't have heels. I'd be stumbling around like a baby fawn just learning how to walk. Forcing myself to relax, I let Geoff take the lead.

Our conversation stalls for a few moments. I hear the band and the buzz of conversation around us. Pulling from one of my go-to icebreaker questions, I ask, "So, Geoff, are you a Londoner?"

"I am now, but I grew up in Shropshire."

My eyes widen. "That's a dramatic change." Shropshire is one of the most rural counties in England. Situated on the Welsh border, it's packed full of endless wide-open fields and rolling hills.

"Yeah, it was. I couldn't wait to move far away from it. My parents might be keen on farming and running a B and B, but not me. Unlike London, there's nothing to do in Shropshire."

He places a hand on my waist and pulls me in a little closer to his body. He's tall, about six feet. I'm forced to look up at him.

"I wouldn't say that. There's quite a few national parks. And some lovely hiking trails."

"True, but they get old quickly. Once you've seen one field, all the others look the same."

"Uh-huh."

Geoff dominates our conversation, choosing to give me his life's story. I can't get much of a word in edgewise. When the music finally ends, I thank him, and before he can ask me for an encore dance, flee to the safety of my table. Except I never make it that far. Another guy named Nick blocks my pathway and claims me for a swing dance.

"How's your evening going so far? Are you enjoying the *I Love Lucy* theme? It's rather clever if you ask me," I say.

"You're enjoying this rubbish? It's so tacky. So American." He wrinkles his nose. "The band isn't playing anything decent. It's all old-timey stuff. And the food—for what a ticket costs, it should be a top-of-the-line menu, not items you could pick up at a takeaway counter. Then there's the . . ."

I suppress a groan and seriously consider making up an excuse to flee back to the safety of the dinner table. Out of all the guys I could've attracted, it happens to be a person who has the top characteristic on my deal-breaker list—a complainer. The next few minutes are going to be painfully long.

"What did you say your name was?" He furrows his brow.

"I didn't. It's Alison." I know using a fake name may be futile, but the less he knows about me, the better. I'm actually pretty shocked I haven't been recognized by either of my dance partners yet.

"Well, I like that you're quiet. The last girl I danced with talked too much."

The longer I spend in this bloke's presence, the angrier I become. Everything that comes out of his mouth is negative.

"If you hate everything about the themed dinner, why did you bother coming?"

"My mum made me escort her. She didn't want to come alone. If I didn't come, she threatened to withhold my quarterly allowance."

Is he joking? Where is his backbone? Find a job if you disagree with your mum. If he's having trouble now, how will he manage later in life? It irritates me that he's so immature. Nick has to be in his late twenties. I bet he's never worked a day in his life. Eddie and I may be part of a privileged family too, but our parents made sure we always made good use of our time.

We were expected to volunteer with different charities during our school holidays and even hold part-time jobs. The summer I turned sixteen, I remember Papa telling me that I'd be working as a salesclerk in the palace gift shop. It was important to him that we each had some real-life experience.

"Do you have a job?" I ask.

"Pfft. No. It's beneath me." He puffs out his chest. "*I come from one of the wealthiest families in the country.*"

That's the final straw. I can't stand his smugness and ego any longer. I drop my hands from him and step away. "Nick, you're a good dancer, but you need to work on your attitude and your conversation skills." I clench my fists. "Did you know that one of my good friends planned this event? And I think she's done an amazing job. You may not be enjoying it, but look around you." I gesture to the smiling couples surrounding us. "Everyone else is. If you don't have anything positive to say, I'd advise you to stay quiet. You never know who you'll manage to offend."

Turning on my heel, I leave him staring cluelessly around me and march over to the refreshment table for a nice cool drink. I blow a lock of hair out of my face and mutter, "After Mr. Entitled Motormouth, I never thought I'd appreciate the quiet."

"Ma'am."

I jump and splay my hand on my chest. My pulse beats wildly in my ears. "Arthur! Where did you come from?"

"I've been here," he says. He hands me a cup of juice.

"Thanks." As I take a long sip, the strawberry and cherry flavor hits my tongue. It's the perfect ratio of sweetness. I can't drink it quickly enough.

"Refill?"

"Um, sure. I guess I was thirstier than I thought."

Taking hold of my cup, he picks up a ladle and scoops a spoonful of juice from the punch bowl into it. I have to admit that even though I'm determined to have him replaced, he looks handsome in his black suit with a crisp white dress shirt.

"Was there a problem?" He nods toward Nick, who's claimed his next unwilling victim.

"Yes, but nothing you can fix. He's like a peacock who

only cares about preening his own feathers. He's the center of his own universe and unaware of anything else that's going on around him."

"I see."

"If I need rescuing in the future, don't worry, I'll let you know." I smack my lips together. "Should I make some sort of special signal to you if I need rescuing?"

He helps himself to a drink and frowns. "No. I'll be watching you."

"Are you sure? I can make it subtle. It can be something like me tugging on my ear?" I demonstrate, and somehow manage to tangle some of my hair in my hoop earrings. "Ugh." I place my cup down and reach for the offending piece of jewelry, tilting my head to the side. My cheeks warm in embarrassment.

"Do you need help, ma'am?"

"No, I've got it." I feel around for the backing of the earring and remove it. "But maybe you're right. We don't need a secret sign," I admit.

Arthur doesn't answer me, taking a long drink from his own punch.

"Excuse me?" Another lad, this time with red hair and a smattering of freckles, approaches us. I turn around. "Are you two together?" He glances at Arthur.

"No." Arthur takes a few steps away from me so he's standing alone to the side of the table.

"Brilliant." The redhead cracks a cheeky smile. "Care to have a go on the dance floor with me, Princess?"

"Um . . . sure."

He grabs my hand and leads me away from the table. With a fleeting glance, I notice that Arthur's gaze is indeed on me. He continues to track me like a submarine's sonar system. I have no doubts that nothing will escape his notice.

Six

"Ladies and gentlemen, it's been our pleasure to perform for you at Club Babalou. We hope we made tonight a memorable one for all of you. Regrettably, our evening has come to an end, but not before we play one final song."

The band picks up their instruments and begins playing "Cuban Pete," one of the signature songs from *I Love Lucy*. From my perch by the dessert table, I drum my fingers against the surface, humming along to the catchy melody.

"Are you done dancing?" Amanda asks, sneaking up to my left.

"It looks that way. I don't have a partner," I admit, continuing to watch the happy couples on the dance floor, swaying closely to one another. A small surge of jealousy flows through my veins, but my sitting out the last dance is my own fault. I've turned down the last few people who've asked me. "Maybe it's for the best. I've danced with about twenty different blokes, and talking to them has mentally exhausted me. I like dancing, but I'm all talked out. I am not used to having so many people around me."

"That's the excuse, but my question is do you want to dance?"

I rub the back of my neck. "I wouldn't mind it. I like this song."

"Cool beans, because I see someone I know is quiet who you can dance with." Tugging on my hand, she yanks me toward the adjoining table, where Arthur is standing with his arms crossed, leaning against the wall. He sees us approaching and immediately stiffens, standing like a soldier at attention. "Hey, Arthur," Amanda says.

"Ma'am."

"Ali is looking for a partner, and seeing as you're free, she'd love to have you take her out onto the dance floor." She places my hand in his. "Problem solved. Now to go find Clara. She's been sitting too long. One dance won't kill her." Amanda practically skips away from us.

"Um, sorry about that." I quickly tug my hand away. "I had no idea she was going to ask you. You don't have to dance with me. It's not in your job description."

"Technically speaking, it isn't. Unless it's something you ask me to do." He extends his hand back to me. My gaze travels up the length of his arm to his face. "Are you requesting a dance?"

My throat goes dry. I *do* want to dance. And not with any of the partners I've had tonight. I want it to be with someone who all I have to do is dance with. Not speak to. Arthur ticks all those boxes. "Yes." My voice is an octave higher than normal. "I am."

He nods and takes my hand in his. It's warm, and the tips of his fingers are calloused. He hesitates before placing his left hand on the small of my back and pulling me in closer to him. I let him lead.

We move side to side in a simple box-step pattern in the small area between the surrounding tables. His body is tense.

I'm nearly dragged along, like he's using me as a broom to try and sweep up a trail of dust. He has a surprising amount of strength in those arms. His attention keeps returning to his feet.

"You won't step on them, if that's what you're worried about."

He lifts his chin and grunts.

His grip loosens, but he continues to hold his shoulders high and step with all his weight on his heels. There are deep-set concentration lines on his forehead. It's not lost on me that he's way outside of his comfort zone.

He's probably counting down until we can leave. Nevertheless, his act of kindness isn't lost on me. I'll take it as an apology for the way our relationship has started. An olive branch of sorts.

"You're doing brilliantly. One of the best partners I've had all night."

Arthur's lips twitch. The folds of his eyes crinkle. For the briefest moment, I'm rewarded with a flash of his dimples. My heart stops and my breath catches. Whoa. Is that what he looks like when he doesn't have his mask in place? If Helen of Troy had a face that could launch a thousand ships, then Arthur has a face that could inspire a thousand sculptors. It's a face that would be at home in a statue gallery of Greek gods.

As the music slows, the steady beats are replaced by a reserved, tranquil tune. He pulls me an inch closer to him. It's a good feeling, but makes me nervous. I'm not used to being this close to a man. My body feels like it's a glass of champagne and the bubbles are rising to the top.

We rock side to side. My hands travel farther up his back, feeling the hard muscles beneath the fabric of his coat, before looping themselves around his neck. I catch the faint whiff of his cologne. It's a clean scent that reminds me of mint, vanilla, and some type of other herb I can't put my finger on.

"Art." He murmurs so low, I barely catch it.

"Huh?"

"I'd prefer going by the name Art. I've never liked being an Arthur."

"Of course. Why didn't you say so earlier?"

He presses his lips together, remaining silent.

I leave it at that, deciding not to press him any further. We're not on firm enough ground for me to delve into the man behind the facade yet. He's only managed to confuse me more than I already am with his break in character. We continue to dance until the last note of the music. The applause of the crowd breaks the spell, and Art drops my hands and steps away from me.

"Thank you," I whisper.

"Ma'am."

Walking back to the table, I gather my belongings and wait for Clara and Amanda to rejoin me. They're lingering on the dance floor, greeting the band and taking a few photos. My attention travels to the two protection officers shadowing them.

They stand at a respectful distance, chatting amongst themselves, yet stay alert at the same time, like lions guarding their pride, ready to pounce the moment the wind shifts. Art isn't with them. I don't need to turn to know he's probably standing behind me, trying to blend in with the wall. That's where I'd be.

Growing up, there was always a security team around me, but I never paid them much mind. It's like living in a room with brightly-colored wallpaper—you grow immune to their presence and forget they're there.

Bruce, however, changed all that. He was the first officer I had who was willing to be a friend in addition to being my bodyguard. I began to see the security team as people and not just names and faces. In time, I can only hope that's how my relationship with my new team will be.

~

ON THE WAY HOME, I BRING AMANDA AND CLARA UP to speed on how my night went.

"It was interesting, but it's not something I see myself doing again anytime soon." I try and keep my wording as diplomatic as possible. I enjoyed the parts of the evening where I could catch up with the girls, but talking to my partners involved too much interaction with other people for my liking.

"I know it wasn't your cup of tea, but still, I'm proud of you for putting yourself out there," Amanda gushes.

"Thanks," I murmur. I'm proud of myself too. Over the past few months, I've made big strides from being the girl who couldn't wait to escape the UK to becoming a woman who has some confidence and is able to attend events like this. But I know I still have a long way to go. Rebuilding who I am is not a sprint. It's a marathon.

"By my count, I consider tonight a win. You danced with . . ." Amanda reviews the tally in her note app. "A dozen different partners, and three of them twice. Give me the lowdown. Is there anyone who made an impression with you who might be date worthy?"

"You kept count?" My jaw drops. I'm partially annoyed, but also partially happy she was keeping an eye on me.

"I *told* you not to tell her. You sound like a crazed stalker." Clara sniggers.

"I had a bet going with Eddie. He thought you'd only manage to find five partners."

"And how many did you guess?" Clara asks.

"Ten." A smug smile appears on her lips. "Princey is going to owe me home-cooked breakfast in bed for a week!"

"My brother can't cook unless you count burned toast or microwaving Pot Noodles."

"Oh, he can manage a few dishes." Amanda winks. "He started getting lessons from me when we first began dating. He can make pancakes, beans on toast, sausages, and eggs for breakfast. But his specialty is grilling. He makes a mean steak."

"Impressive." I appraise her with a newfound respect. Who knew Eddie had it in him. Until he met Amanda, there was no way he would've ever set foot in the kitchen, unless it was to ask his chef to prepare something for him. She's changed him for the better.

Amanda is hands down one of the most talented self-taught bakers I've ever met. She'd be a shoo-in to win the celebrity edition of *The British Baking Championship* if she ever decided to enter. It's one of the few telly shows we watch religiously whenever a new series drops.

"Anyway, enough about Princey. Tell me about *you*. Did you meet anyone interesting or who stood out?" she asks.

Strangely, my mind jumps to my last dance with Art. He's the one person I danced with where it didn't feel forced. I can still feel his strong arms holding me up, and the easy side-to-side rocking motion. My fingers run over my forearms where he held me as a few goosebumps appear.

I frown. He doesn't count. Art was only doing his job. *Focus.* Who was the least irritating guy tonight? A few faces flash through my mind. "Out of everyone, the only bloke I'd seriously consider a contender is Eric, the accountant who resembled David Beckham."

We danced together twice. He was one of the only partners who took the time to listen to the responses to the questions he asked me. When I said I wasn't overly big on sports, he moved on from the topic. He also knew about horses. Having a common language made for an easy and natural conversation.

"Dark hair, tattoo sleeves, and a lean, mean body?" Amanda asks.

"I don't know about the tattoos, but yes, he was fit." I focus on pulling my boots off my feet and rub my aching arches.

"That's Eric Walsh." She snaps her fingers together. "He'd be a good match for you. I've talked to him a few times. He's reserved, but opens up once you get a chance to know him."

"And you know all this how?" Clara cocks her head to the side.

"Because he's friends with Eddie. They served in the Life Guards together for four years."

I process the information. That explains the bit about him knowing about horses. If he was a member of the Life Guards, Eric would've worked with horses for at least two years in the Household Cavalry before moving over to the infantry side of the regiment.

"Do you know how old he is?" I ask.

"I think he's twenty-three? He was one of the younger members of Eddie's squadron."

I nod. Unofficially, I've set the max age of men I'm willing to date at twenty-five. I know age is just a number, and if the right person comes along, exceptions can be made. However, I find that for me personally, I tend to have more in common with the twenty-five and under group.

I stare out the window and take a few steadying breaths. I'm ready to take another step forward. "If you think that highly of Eric, I'm willing to do lunch with him."

Amanda squees and claps her hands together.

"Tone it down a notch, A. Use your indoor voice," Clara prompts.

"Sorry. I'm just so excited Ali said yes to a date!"

Clara shakes her head, a smile tugging at the corners of her lips.

"What is your schedule like next week? I can arrange all the details for the outing, if you'd like. I want everything to go *perfectly*. If it all plays out, who knows. Maybe he'll become your boyfriend!"

"Let's not get ahead of ourselves." I suddenly feeling light-headed at the thought of a boyfriend. "I'll text you tomorrow after I meet with Mum. I need to see what public events she expects me to appear at. But if you want to plan the date, please, feel free to take the lead."

"You won't regret it!" Amanda nods. "Tell you what, I'll get things started by finding out what Eric's schedule looks like, then touch base with you."

"Sounds like a plan."

We hear a gentle snore. Clara's head rests against the window of the car.

Amanda leans close and whispers into my ear, "Just between you and me, I have a feeling C is going to have some *big* news to share with us soon. She's been extraordinarily tired of late and nauseous when it comes to certain smells."

It takes a few moments for her words to register. Then a lightbulb clicks on inside my head. I bite back a gasp as my heartbeat picks up for a moment. "Are you sure?"

"No, I'm not. For now, it's just a hunch. C and I have been friends since we were teens. I know her as well as I know myself. I'm planning to ask her about it later this week."

I cross my fingers. Clara and David have been married a little over four years. I know how much the pair of them have wanted to become parents. I can only hope Amanda's hunch is right.

Throughout the remainder of the ride, I can't help but ponder all the changes taking place around me. My thoughts turn to Amanda and Eddie. They've been engaged for about five years. They've talked about getting married since Eddie completed his military service last year and made the transition to being a full-time working royal. They've been driving Mum and Papa mad over their lack of plans for their wedding.

"Amanda?"

"Hmm?"

I brush a stray piece of lint off my dress. "I'm just curious; have you and Eddie had any conversations about your wedding?"

"On and off. It's the big elephant in the room." She closes her eyes and rests her head against the back of the seat. "We're getting pressured from both my family and yours to hurry up and make our plans. We've both agreed on next year, but when is TBD. It'll probably be in the summer." Her shoulders hunch. "The truth is, neither of us wants a big ceremony. If it were up to us, we'd have a private event at Disneyland Paris with just our immediate families present, but unfortunately, that's not going to fly."

I grimace. She's right. Eddie is the heir to Papa's throne and the next head of state. People have been talking about the next big royal wedding since the day their engagement was announced. The public expects a big ceremony, just like Clara and David had. Eddie and Amanda are going to have a minimum of five to six hundred guests.

"I suppose there isn't much point in putting off a serious talk too much longer. The more time that passes, the worse the pressure becomes. We might as well get the ball rolling. Goodness knows we're more than ready to officially become husband and wife."

A blanket of warmth spreads over my body at her words, like relaxing in a nice hot spa. I want Amanda to officially become my sister. I just hope they'll get some say in their plans. Mum has been waiting her turn for years to help plan a wedding, but her level of enthusiasm rivals my aunt Charlotte's. She may turn into a mum-zilla.

<h1 style="text-align:center">Seven</h1>

I settle back into the rhythm of life in London over the next week. Although we're scaled back on royal engagements, Mum has still managed to fill my diary. I've learned over the years it's not worth using my energy to fight her over it. It's better to accept what she says, put in a few appearances, and move on. Even if they bring me a great deal of anxiety, theoretically, the more I participate, the easier they'll become.

I text Amanda back on Wednesday morning.

ALICE

Cheers, Amanda, sorry it's taken me so long to get back to you. It looks like next Tuesday or Wednesday can work for lunch.

AMANDA

Perfecto. I'll let Eric know. I think Tuesday is gonna work best for him. Hold, please.

I wait for her response.

AMANDA

> Yup. Tuesday is his best day.

My eyes widen. She's gotten an answer already?

ALICE

> That was fast!

AMANDA

> It helps that he's standing right next to me.

I shake my head. They must both be at Charlie's.

ALICE

> *Laughing emoji*

AMANDA

> He wants to know if lunch is still good.

ALICE

> Yeah, it is. I know you mentioned you'd take care of the details, but I just thought I'd put it out there that if said plans involved horses, it might help me be less nervous going into the date.

AMANDA

> If that's what you want, I'll make it happen. Plan on meeting him at 11:30 and riding sometime in the midafternoon.

ALICE

> Jotting it into my agenda now.

Plans with Eric settled, I turn my attention to more pressing matters—plotting out my future home. I call Bruce.

"Good morning, Princess," he greets me after two rings.

"Hiya, Bruce."

"How can I assist you this morning?"

"I'd like to take a drive out to Queen's Park."

"Queen's Park? In north London? Hmm, that's a peculiar place."

"I have some property business in the area to take care of." I walk across my sitting room and select my black peacoat from the coat closet.

"Oh, congratulations, Princess. I told you your parents would come around to the idea of you living a few kilometers outside Kensington."

"Um, thanks, but I'm still working on changing their minds."

"I see. Will you be doing a property viewing to show them in the future?"

"No." I wince. "I, er . . . bought a flat last November and we're finalizing the deal today."

"Princess, please don't tell me you went behind their backs?" Bruce's tone oozes disappointment.

"Technically speaking, I've shown them the listing. I just haven't mentioned that I was in the process of purchasing it." My voice comes out weak.

"Ma'am, you need to tell them. And the sooner the better." He takes a long breath. "You are an incredibly bright young woman, but there are some things where it's best to have an expert's help. Buying property is one of them. At the very least, I hope you did a proper viewing and read through the surveyor's report in detail."

I sink down onto my bed. I've spent hours and hours of time searching for a property, and researching how the process is done. But between the family dinner, going out with Amanda, meeting with Mum, and returning to my part-time job working in the stables, I've been strapped for time.

My heart thuds against my ribs. The one piece of advice every single SearchTube video, and home-reno program on the telly reiterates is to read the surveyor's report before you finalize a property sale. I told myself I'd do it when I got home from Europe, but time has slipped away from me, and now, I'm going to have to pay the price. I dry swallow.

"I haven't done either of those things," I whisper.

"Well, I suppose it's too late to do anything about it." I hear Bruce mutter a few words in the background. "You'll just have to hope for the best and learn from this experience."

I squeeze my eyes shut. I can picture the looks of disappointment on my parents' faces when they hear about what I've done. I hope against all odds I haven't made a colossal mistake. I haven't seen the property in person. Maybe the flat will be exactly as it was described on the website, and it won't have any major issues except cosmetic ones. It'll make begging for forgiveness a million times easier.

"I'll let Arthur know to expect a text from you when you're ready to go out."

"You're not coming?" I feel like my heart's brushed up against the sharp needles of a cactus.

"Not today. Angela and I still have some logistics training to cover. Arthur, on the other hand, has just finished."

"Okay," I say, my voice cracking. "I'll be ready in twenty minutes."

I disconnect the call and stare at the phone blankly for a few moments. An entire morning alone with Arthur. No, Art, I correct myself. He asked me not to call him Arthur. We may not be on the best of terms, but it's a request I'll honor.

Why am I making such a big deal about this? I can handle the grump for a few hours. He'll drive me to the building, I'll walk around with him trailing me, then we'll come home. It's not a big deal. It's just business. Full stop.

"Good morning, Art." He assists me into the car and offers a grunt, which I take to mean "Hello," before climbing into the driver's seat. It looks like we've reverted back to single-word responses, even though last week, he finally seemed to be on his way to warming up to me.

After adjusting the driver's mirror and his seat, he reaches for the ignition to start the car, but stops short. "Bollocks, I forgot the key." He rests his forehead on the steering wheel. "This. Is. Not. My. Morning," I hear him murmur under his breath. Sighing, he opens the car door and starts to climb out.

"Wait," I shout.

He freezes, slowly turning to stare at me as if he's forgotten I'm in the back seat. "It's push to start. You only need the key fob to be in the car, which I'm pretty sure you have since the car is unlocked and we're sitting in it."

Tapping the pocket of his suit jacket, he reaches inside and slowly pulls out the black key fob. His ears, cheeks, and neck flush a deep shade of cherry-red, reminding me of a nutcracker doll. Wordlessly, he settles himself back into the driver's seat and slams the door closed. A moment later, the engine hums to life.

"Do you need a coffee?" I ask. "I can have a cup brought down from the kitchens, or we can stop by a Norma's Cafe if you'd like. My treat."

He points to a stainless-steel thermos in the center console's cup holder.

"Have you gotten a chance to enjoy any of it?" I make an educated guess.

"No," he grunts.

"Then take your time and have at it. I'm not in any hurry."

"I'm fine."

You don't have to be so stubborn, you know, I think as I roll my eyes. I understand how important that morning caffeine fix is. If you need it, you need it. "Art, it would make *me* feel better if you had the coffee. At least a few sips. I need you to be fully alert. Otherwise, I'll drive."

"That's against protocol."

I wrinkle my nose. Is he being serious? The other agents drink coffee all the time. And to the best of my knowledge, there isn't anything in the agent rulebook about me driving. I have a license. Eddie and Amanda have driven themselves before. Why should I be any different?

I open my mouth to argue, but quickly shut it. As I study Art, I notice purple rings under his eyes and patches of uneven stubble coating his face. Somebody probably didn't get a good night's sleep. It would be easy to push his buttons, but I know when I'm cranky, the last thing I want to deal with a smart aleck. I'll let him off easy. For now.

"I'm pulling rank on you, Art. I'm ordering you to drink your coffee."

Through the rearview mirror, I watch the muscles in his forehead crease and his brows form a deep V. "Fine." Unscrewing the lid, he takes two swigs, replaces the cap, and returns it to the cup holder.

I half expect him to reply with a sarcastic "Happy?" But he keeps his thoughts to himself. A few moments later, we pull out of the palace complex and onto the city streets. The city of London is just beginning to wake up. It's about six-thirty. The tourists haven't yet risen, but the commuters are out.

With the traffic, it takes us about an hour to reach what will soon be my new home in northwest London. My eyes excitedly drink in the locale. I've taken a virtual tour, but this is my first time seeing it in person. Queen's Park is a residential area of the city brimming with character. The budding engineer in me is transfixed by the lovely red-bricked Victorian and Edwardian terrace homes lining either side of the street. A bubble of excitement is building within me. I've dreamed about owning a place like this for so long.

I can just imagine myself walking Lillian down these leafy streets or taking my bike out for a cycle to the park, doing things that everyday people take for granted. I won't be limited by security fences, or cross paths with the hundred or so staff members who work at the palace. It will just be me, my dog, Angela or Art, and whichever one of our neighbors is out.

"Would you mind taking a turn down High Street? I'd like to see the local offerings and shops."

He clicks the turn indicator and circles the block. We pass an antique store, two bookshops, a high-end plant shop, and three different cafés. At the end of the block, across from a cinema, is a pub.

"It's even better than I imagined. I can't wait to get out there and start exploring. I bet I'll be on a first-name basis with the owner of the bookshop, the cinema manager, and everyone at the cafés by the end of the second week here."

Art raises an eyebrow, studying me through the driver's mirror. I read it as *What are you going on about?*

"I'm moving here. I just purchased number twelve." I point to the terrace home at the end of the street. "We're picking up the keys today and doing a walkthrough to see what improvements are going to need to be made to restore it and make it habitable."

He slows the car and parks on the street in the spot near number twelve, then spins around in his seat. I can see the wheels turning inside his mind as he absorbs everything I've just told him. "I need to do a perimeter sweep before you'll be allowed in."

"Art, the space is probably empty. According to the listing agent, it's been vacant for at least three years. In fact, the only person with keys *is* the agent. He's supposed to meet us here at eight-fifteen."

His jaw clenches. "It's proper protocol."

There it is again. The agent who wants to do everything by the book. Where's the chap who joked with me a few nights ago?

"Fine, if you want to do your perimeter sweep, go ahead. I'll wait in the car."

"I can't allow that either. You're not to be left alone in a public space."

"Where else am I supposed to go?" I gesture to the street. "It's either I stay here, or I go with you."

"I didn't think about that." He grits his teeth.

Reaching for his thermos, I hand it to him. "Drink more coffee and wake up," I say. "How about this: I won't tell anyone about not checking out the building before we go inside if you won't." I place a finger to my lips.

He unscrews the lid, keeping his gaze on me. It's the first time I notice his eyes are hazel. A perfect mixture of green and golden-brown. Pouring himself a generous amount into the lid, he takes a few sips, smacking his lips together while suppressing a grimace.

"Do you need something sweet to go with that? It smells strong." I reach into my handbag. "I have a raspberry fig bar." I wave it under his nose.

"No thank you."

"Then I'll leave it here in case you change your mind." I place it inside the empty cup holder next to the thermos.

"I won't."

"Did you have any breakfast this morning?"

He takes another sip of the coffee, raising the lid as if he's toasting me. There's my answer.

"You know, skipping breakfast is bad for your brain health." I relocate the bar so it's in his hands. "Your job performance could also suffer." I rattle off a few more facts off the top of my brain about the merits of breakfast. Some of them are made up, but as long as I sound convincing, I doubt he'll notice.

His eyes continue to tighten until I run out of things to say. He remains quiet, continuing to drink his coffee.

I huff and run a hand through my hair, frustrated by his lack of response. "Gah. Doesn't anything faze you?"

"No." He smirks. A few more moments of silence pass before he sighs and rips the packaging open. He takes a few bites, chews, and swallows. "Thank you, ma'am."

"You're welcome."

Maybe now he'll be a little less grouchy. While Art eats, I unlock my mobile and check to see if the agent has texted me. The green bubble icon is empty, however. It's still a little early. I sigh and rest my head against the seat.

"Ma'am?"

"Hmm?"

"Why this flat?" I open my eyes to see him squinting out the window. "The building is knackered."

"It's not knackered. It's a blank canvas." My lips twitch as I try to ignore the peeling paint, overgrown ivy coating the exterior, and mound of rubbish that's accumulated near the front gate. "You show a building a little TLC and it'll give it right back to you."

"It sounds like you think the building is living."

"It is. It's living history." I nod. "Besides, I've grown up in character properties my entire life, and I can't ever imagine myself living somewhere modern."

"Not a country cottage?"

Butterflies flutter in my stomach at the thought. Art has touched on one of my long-term goals. I'd love nothing more than to own a chocolate-box cottage with a thatched roof somewhere in a small English village. I can picture the original wood beams and a large inglenook fireplace. But those types of properties require a special owner. As much as my heart might be telling me to ignore my head, I'm not at the stage of my life where I can handle it.

"No. Maybe in the future I will, but right now, I have to be practical. I need a space that will suit me while I'm in uni and to figure out how to maintain it before I can make the jump to something like a four-hundred-year-old cottage."

"You're passionate about it," he notes. His hazel eyes are more alert than they were earlier. The caffeine and sugar from the food must've kicked in. The grump is slowly melting away into someone who is tolerable.

"I am. That's one of the reasons I'm going for my structural engineering degree."

"Not architecture?"

"No. I've never had an artistic eye for building design. I'm a problem solver. I'd much rather come up with the systems and configurations to support an architect's designs and work with restoring older properties."

My phone chimes as Art cleans up his rubbish and screws the lid back on the thermos. "The agent?" he asks.

"Yeah, he's about a minute away."

Art steps out of the car and opens my door. "Thanks," I say.

ART WALKS AHEAD OF ME, GUIDED BY THE LIGHT OF his mobile. I've peeked through the photos on the website and knew going into today's visit that the building was in rough shape, but physically seeing it still sends shockwaves through my system. I chew on my lip. Bruce was right. I may have bitten off more than I can chew. And it all could've been avoided if I'd read that darn surveyor's report.

We enter the ground-floor sitting room. The plaster is peeling off the walls, revealing suspicious white patches that could be mildew and cracks. Studying the angles from the corners, I think most of them are going to be cosmetic, but there are still one or two that are worrisome. The floorboards are buckling and have begun to come up from the ground.

There is a large crack in the front window and a pane missing from the lower left corner.

"That's not good," I mumble.

"No." Art joins me by my side and takes a few steps closer to examine the missing pane. "It's probably where the moisture is coming from."

We move deeper into the building. It's dark and stuffy. A cloud of dust floats around the light of his mobile as we explore. The kitchen is in slightly less bad shape, but it's devoid of any appliances, and all the sockets appear to be thirty or forty years old. The entire electrical system will need to be rewired and replaced.

"The garden looks all right. Just overgrown," Art muses.

Through a grimy window, I spy a few patches of light. "It's more of a jungle than a garden." The plants have taken on a life of their own. Vines, weeds, and other shrubs are spilling out from every spare inch of space. We can't see to the back fence, but I know from the map of the property that it's long enough that I'll be able to add a summer house and have a lawn put in so Lillian can run around.

Approaching the stairs to the first floor, I find there is no handrail. Art insists on going up the steps first, and that I hug the wall as we ascend so I don't fall. Each step creaks as weight is placed on it.

"Should I be worried we'll fall through?" he asks.

"No, we'll be all right. The stairs don't let out the type of groaning creak before a piece of wood breaks apart and splinters."

"Uh-huh." He shines the light in my direction. "I didn't realize there were different types of sounds wood can make."

"Take my word for it, there are."

"I will, ma'am."

We turn right and glance inside one of the bedrooms from the doorway. There's an old metal bedframe and a wardrobe.

Faded flower wallpaper is peeling from the walls. The ceiling is covered in cobwebs and yet more disturbing cracks.

I face Art. "You can call me Alice if you'd like."

He glances away from me and becomes intrigued by the wood of the door frame, running his finger along the grain. "That's not protocol, ma'am."

"It might not be, but I'm giving you my royal permission," I urge.

He doesn't speak. Well, he may not be receptive to it, but at least I've put the idea out there. We're making small strides.

"Come on, let's see what else is up here," I say.

We continue our tour. By the time we finish the first floor, we've discovered two additional bedrooms. The stairs to the second floor are narrow, missing a few boards, and also devoid of a railing. Art doesn't let me go up there, but rather films the space for me with my mobile. There's two more bedrooms and access to the eaves of the property.

"Ma'am, it appears there may be a problem with the roof. I felt a draft and there are at least two birds' nests present. The floor was covered in animal droppings. It's a health hazard and needs to be addressed before you can see it."

I add those to my already long mental list of necessary repairs. I have no idea how I'm going to be able to pay for everything. "That's the worst possible outcome. I was hoping I might be able to get away with a simple repair, but I suppose in this case, it'll be better to get it done right."

"Which room do you intend to set aside for the security team?"

I cock my head to the side. Security team? "What do you mean?"

He stiffens. "Ma'am, when you or any member of the royal family rehomes themselves from the palace to an outside property, you're no longer residing in a secured location."

"Okay," I answer slowly, trying to understand where he's going with this.

He fidgets. "That means a protection team officer must be on the premises with you at all times."

"You and Angela will be living with me?"

"Yes, ma'am."

Of all the scenarios that have crossed my mind, having my agents live with me wasn't one of them. In a few months, Art is going to be under the same roof as me. I dry swallow. Oh boy. Things just got a lot more complicated.

Eight

The following day, my father's private secretary exits the study and holds the door open for me. "The king is ready for you, Your Highness."

I straighten my skirt and stand on shaking legs. My pulse is racing wildly in my chest. "Thanks," I manage.

When I enter, Papa is sitting at his desk, scribbling his name on an important-looking document. "Just one more moment . . . and done." He taps the papers together, sets them in the red box to his right, and removes his glasses. As he sees me, a wide smile crosses his face. "Alice." He points to his cheek. I walk around the desk and give him a peck. His beard is scratchy. "You wanted to see me?"

"Yes, sir. I have a few important things I need to discuss with you." I tuck my hands behind my back, proud of how steady my voice sounds.

"As long as I don't have to do any more writing, I'm all ears." He stands and shakes out his hand.

"No, sir, it doesn't involve writing." He takes a seat on the sofa. I remain standing and take a deep breath. "It involves a property."

"Alice, I'll be the first to admit that the trio of listings Amanda found has been by far the best I've seen, but your mum felt you could do better. And I'm inclined to agree with her. It's not a question of location this time. It's the condition of the overall buildings."

"I agree with you, Papa, but the thing is . . . I already bought the one in Queen's Park," I say, my voice squeaky. I brace myself.

Papa sits taller. It takes him a moment to process the words he's just heard. He blinks a few times, then furrows his brows. "Explain yourself."

My father is not a man for excuses. He appreciates when a person sticks to the cold hard facts. That's exactly what I plan to do.

"Last fall, when I first lay eyes on the Queen's Park flat, I immediately fell in love with it. It was one of the few properties I'd seen in my budget that still had most of its original features, like the crown molding, beautiful hardwood floors, and sash windows. I know it's not the prettiest property to look at, but that didn't matter to me. I could see the potential in what the flat could become.

"In hindsight, I should've known the photos might be misleading." My voice quivers, and my body burns with shame. My gaze travels to the ground. "I realized last week when the sale officially went through that I'd made a huge mistake. I never went to go and see it in person, nor did I bother to read the surveyor's report. If I had, I would've realized there were substantial issues purposely omitted from the photos. The flat is in awful shape, Papa."

"Alice, I'm extremely disappointed in you." The disheartened sound of his voice weighs heavy on me. It's worse than anger. He's the person whose opinion matters most to me. We've always shared a special father-daughter bond, and now it feels like I've betrayed him. Guilt swells up in my stomach, squeezing me as tightly as a boa constrictor.

"You made an immensely foolish and irresponsible decision. This is something I can see Edmund doing, but not you. You're supposed to be the levelheaded child."

Papa stands. I risk a glance at him, watching as he walks over to the window, looking out at the gardens with his back to me. "If you'd come to your mum and me and told us this was what you'd wanted, all this could have been avoided. We would've ensured the property was properly vetted. Remember, if a price seems too good to be true, it probably is."

He turns and meets my eyes, and I make myself smaller. There is a tightness around his mouth and deep creases on his forehead. His eyes, usually warm and inviting, are now shadowed, like clouds passing over the sun. "What exactly did you see at the viewing?"

"Nothing but problems. Everything needs repairs and updates to be habitable." My shoulders hunch. "I've spent some time trying to get some quotes from different electricians, carpenters, and roofers. All in, it's likely going to be an additional one to two hundred thousand pounds worth of repairs."

"Do you have the budget for this?"

"Not right now, but if I do things in stages, and learn how to do some of the repairs myself to cut costs, I think I'll be able to get by. My plan is to address the most immediate problems first, all the structural repairs, and go from there. That alone will probably run me about fifty to seventy-five thousand pounds."

Papa closes the gap between us. I feel the weight of his gaze on me. "And how do you intend to secure the remaining funds for the other projects? What if there are unforeseen problems that arise?"

"I'll deal with things as they come. Right now, I think the

most logical course of action is to take out a mortgage or a loan. There would be interest to worry about, but in time, I could pay it back."

"No." He shakes his head. "You will not take out any loans or a mortgage. You're a university student with a part-time job that pays eleven pounds an hour. No bank in their right mind would be willing to take a risk on you even if you're a member of the royal family." He runs a hand along his jaw. "No, Mum and I will lend you the money and we'll figure out how you can repay us later. However, I have several stipulations."

I listen carefully. Papa lays out his lists of demands.

One, they will purchase the neighboring flat, so we own the entire building.

Two, they will have final say over all the work that's done.

Three, in addition to Angela and Art, there will be another security officer on duty at all times to watch the CCTV cameras and conduct bag checks. The garage will be converted into a hidden security office.

Four, a safe room will be installed in case there is a breach of security.

And five, a six-foot-tall gate will be installed in front of the house.

Those are just the ones that pertain to the building. Papa also mentions stipulations like not being able to go anywhere unescorted. In short, living in my flat will mirror my life in the palace. It's like I'm a zoo animal that's being given an upgraded exhibit. It may be shiny and new, but it's still living a life in captivity.

There are no ways around it. I have no leg to stand on since this mess is my own making. Papa's decisions are final. He won't change his mind about any of these demands. He'll likely add to them. So all I can do now is accept them.

"Yes, sir." I nod. "I understand."

"Good. Now that that's been sorted, you can also expect

to start having some more official engagements added to your diary. If you're going to be an adult living on her own, you can expect to work like one too."

"But what about school?"

"We'll work around it. Your studies will always be a top priority."

I squeeze my hands together tightly and chew on my lip. I'd hoped that with the start of uni, I'd be able to slowly begin stepping *away* from public duties. Not beginning the transition to life as a working royal. My gap year travels helped me realize that I want a quiet life. I'm not delusional enough to think I'll ever be completely left alone, but I'd like to at least try and give it a go.

"Do you have any questions for me?"

I open my mouth to argue, but I've used up the allotment of courage I've brought with me. Papa's stern facial expression tells me that for now, this discussion has to be tabled. "No, sir."

"Good." He nods curtly.

"I just want to apologize again."

Papa offers me a grunt and walks over to the intercom, calling his secretary inside. I take this as a signal that my time with my father is over. I mutter a quick goodbye, then make my escape. It hurts that he doesn't ask for his customary kiss on the cheek, but I know he needs some time to calm down.

As I disappear out of his office, his words echo loudly in my mind. *"I'm extremely disappointed in you."* A stray tear escapes the corner of my eye. I know I have no one to blame but myself. I'll learn from this mistake and hope I can prove to Papa I can make something out of this.

BY SATURDAY, MY MOOD HAS IMPROVED, BUT I'M still holding massive waves of guilt inside me. The weather is bright and sunny on this late June afternoon. I'm inside an open-top carriage, seated opposite Amanda and Clara. As we pull out of Buckingham Palace, there's a deafening roar. The streets are brimming with tourists hoping to catch a glimpse of us as we leave the palace for Horse Guard's Parade.

Waving to the crowd, I do my best to place a pleasant smile on my face, despite wishing I could be anywhere else. "I'd give anything to be on a horse like Papa, Eddie, and David. They're so lucky. They don't have to smile. They can focus on their horses. Not to mention, they won't be criticized for what they're wearing." I glance down at my light-blue chiffon gown.

Amanda chuckles. "Now that you're almost twenty-one, I'm sure your dad will give you some type of honorary military appointment. Then you can ride out with the boys in uniform. But if you ask me, events like this are much more fun when you're *with* people. Not riding solo."

"If it makes you feel any better, I can tell you that David was *not* looking forward to being on horseback today," Clara says.

"Neither was Eddie," Amanda adds.

Clara fans herself. "In heat like this, we're lucky we don't have to wear those woolen tunics and tall bearskin hats too."

"I suppose you're right." My gaze travels to the members of the guardsmen lining the Mall who salute us as our carriage moves past them. They're wearing the traditional summer-order scarlet tunic uniforms.

"Which regiment will be trooping its colour today?" Clara asks. Her cheeks color. "I feel silly for not knowing this."

"The second battalion Irish Guards," I answer. "And you shouldn't feel guilty for not knowing. You've been busy." I'm careful not to mention Amanda's suspicions about her expecting.

"I know, but I don't like to make excuses," Clara says.

"Can I let you two in on a little secret?" I start, hoping to lighten the mood. The girls both nod. "Don't tell anyone I said this, but Papa is a bit biased. His favorite regiment isn't one of the footguard regiments. It's the cavalry."

"Because that was the division that he, Eddie, and David all served in?" Amanda guesses.

"Yup. His brother, my uncle Frank, is the odd one out in the family. He joined the navy."

"And which division would you have joined?" Clara asks.

"Obviously the cavalry." Amanda elbows her. "She'd keep the family tradition going."

"Actually, no." I fold my hands and set them on my lap. "Yes, I would've wanted to work with horses, but I would've wanted to make my own mark. If I'd joined the military, I'd have opted for the King's Troop Royal Horse Artillery. No royal has ever served in their regiment."

And it was something I seriously considered too. Becoming a member of the military meant that I would've been treated just like everyone else. I'd be able to do what I love, help care for horses, and serve my country. The only thing that stopped me was that when I considered the future, I saw myself being more fulfilled in the long-term by solving problems with different buildings and structures.

"Wow. I never knew that," Amanda exclaims.

"Now you do."

Suddenly, the carriage hits a rut in the road, and we're jostled in our seats. My breath catches in my throat as I hit the side of the carriage. It stings, but I'll be able to shake it off in a few minutes.

"Apologies, ma'am," the driver calls out from the front. "Everyone all right?"

"I think so," I answer.

Amanda and I recover quickly, but Clara grips the edge of

the door with one hand and holds her stomach with the other. Her face pales and then turns a shade of green. "Ugh."

I exchange glances with Amanda. I really hope she's not going to be sick. Especially when there are millions of people watching.

"Are you okay, C?" she asks.

"I will be." Clara closes her eyes and takes a few deep breaths. "I'm ultra-sensitive to certain smells and sudden movements these days. I might as well tell you two now. I found out two days ago that I'm expecting."

"I knew it!" Amanda exclaims.

Clara takes a few more deep breaths, then sits upright. "I was going to wait until I was further along in case there were any, er . . . complications before we told anybody, but the cat's out of the bag now."

"Congratulations," I exclaim. "I'm so happy for you two."

"Thank you." She smiles. "Theoretically, you'll have a new cousin early next spring."

"I'm going to be Auntie Amanda!" Amanda says gleefully. "You can bet I'll be spoiling your child rotten!" She places a hand on Clara's lap. "I'd hug you, but I don't want to jostle you again."

"I appreciate that more than you know."

Amanda's expression shifts. "Can I tell Eddie?"

Clara considers her request for a moment. "Yes, as long as he doesn't tell anyone else. We're not planning to tell David's mother or the king until I'm into the second trimester."

"I promise." She holds up her hand. "It's just so we can discuss our wedding."

Clara lights up, her normal color returning. "Finally! Have you set a date?"

"We aren't ready to tell any parents yet either. We were thinking about next summer, but nothing's set in stone. Now that I know I have a niece or nephew on the way, if we have to postpone a bit, it's no biggie. Eddie and I can wait as long as needed. I want you to be my maid of honor! And I know Eddie wants David as his best man."

Clara's face grows stricken. "I don't want you to have to wait because of me. If you want to choose someone else, I'll understand."

"Nope." Amanda shakes her head. "We've waited this long. A couple more months won't hurt us."

Seeing the strong bonds of friendship between Clara and Amanda gives me the sensation of a warm, fuzzy hug. These two have known one another for a long time. When I came into the picture, neither of them hesitated to bring me into their circle and treat me exactly as they treat one another. Even though it took me some time to warm up to them, they never gave up on me.

"Amanda?" I say.

"Hmm?" She directs her attention to me.

"Have you considered a Christmas or New Year's wedding? I know when we were younger, it was something my brother talked about. He always thought it would be brilliant to have an ice palace as the backdrop."

"Oh, I'd love that! But it would probably have to be for the reception."

"I'm just putting it out there that *if* you did decide to go for a winter wedding this year, I'm not going to be busy dancing in *The Nutcracker*," Clara says. "By December, I'll be about seven and a half months along."

The carriage makes a turn into the sandy parade grounds. Our conversation circles back to the present moment. The grandstands are packed full of people dressed in their Sunday best. There are three covered tents set up with chairs for us to watch from—one for my father, one for Eddie and Mum, and one for the rest of us.

I may be the daughter of the king, but there is no denying

that my role in the family is changing. I'm not going to be as important in the coming years as Eddie and Amanda. They're the future. The next king and queen. As they marry, start their family, and begin taking on public engagements, the public will focus on them. Not me.

As we climb out of the carriage and walk into the tents, a true smile graces my face. I see a light at the end of the tunnel. Maybe escaping life from the public eye will be easier than I'd thought.

Nine

"You can relax a little," I say to Art a few days later. "I highly doubt anyone who's back here will try and attack me." He's standing with his arms crossed, his eyes narrowed and trained on the people gathered outside our tent.

"You don't know that, ma'am."

Angela rolls her eyes. "Art, come on. You have to admit she has a point. The lads Her Highness is about to meet are all members of the military."

"They could still pose a threat."

I shake my head and give Angela a shrug and an *I've tried to reason with him* look. It's no use. Until we're back inside the safety of Windsor Castle, away from the members of the public and all the military personnel gathered here for the last day of the Royal Windsor Horse Show, he'll be on high alert.

It's the first week in July, and today I'm presenting an award to the winner of the Princess Alice Cup. No, it's not named after me. It's actually named after my grandmum, who was Princess Alice of Wales at the time.

Every year, the members of the two regiments of the

Household Cavalry, the Life Guards and Blues and Royals, spend several months preparing their ceremonial uniforms and horses to the highest possible standard. My brother wanted to enter a few years ago, but he never made it past the preliminary round.

I've been told that the soldiers who participate don't sleep much until the competition is over. And I believe it. From my own experience, I know that taking care of a horse and their tack alone is far from easy. And I don't have a uniform to worry about!

The Princess Alice Cup is one of the few events in my diary that I actually look forward to. It's a relaxed atmosphere where I won't be expected to speak much. Not to mention most of the attendees are fellow horse lovers. They're my type of crowd.

I sigh and smooth down my black-and-white polka-dot dress. As I catch a glimpse of some of the riders exhibiting around the arena's main ring, my body itches to change into the same comfortable clothing they're wearing and join them. Except I know I have to take things slowly.

Just over a year ago, after graduation and before leaving on my gap-year travels, I injured my lower back in a riding accident. I'm fully healed, but I still have some problems when I sit for long periods. Riding is one activity I sorely missed.

Since I've been back home, I've been working on building back up to pre-accident riding activity, minus the jumping. But there have been a lot of days I've had to stop to listen to my body. And that's been a major source of frustration.

"Ma'am, we're just about ready for you," a festival volunteer says as he pokes his head into the tent, stopping short of entering.

It takes me a moment to realize that Art has managed to block his path. Today he's wearing a light-gray suit, crisp white dress shirt, and lilac tie. It's a stark contrast to the normal darker suit he favors. I have to admit, it's a good look for him.

Trying not to be caught staring at him, I rise onto my toes and wave to the volunteer. "Great, I'll be right there."

"I'll, um, let them know." The man swallows hard and dashes away.

Angela walks up to Art and elbows him. "Really?"

"It's protocol."

"What? Scaring everybody away?" She snorts.

"That sounds like something my father would ask you to do." I chuckle.

"No." Art runs a hand through his hair. "You know what I mean." He looks to Angela for help. "We're supposed to be on the lookout for anything suspicious."

"We're on palace grounds and everyone with a volunteer lanyard has gone through a background check to be here. I think they're okay." She places a hand on his shoulder. "I know this is the first public appearance we're working as Princess Alice's protection officers, but that doesn't mean you have to act as if suddenly every person here is a threat. Relax. Do what you've been doing the last few weeks, and everything will be just fine. You know the body language and behavior to look for."

So that's why Art has been acting so off. He's afraid that with so many people around and my making a public appearance, something will happen to me. My heart flutters at the thought of him being concerned about me. Or maybe I'm reading too far into this. After all, protecting me *is* his job.

I glance back at him. His large hazel orbs dart from Angela to me. His posture relaxes slightly. "I guess you're right."

Angela grins. "That's the spirit."

No. It definitely has to be a work thing. He's invested in making sure everything is done by the book. That's the type of meticulous attention to detail that's gotten him this far. Still,

I'll do my best to at least make him feel a bit more comfortable. Trying to lighten the atmosphere, I add, "I heard a rumor floating around that you might be a James Bond type of an agent."

He furrows his brow into a deep V. "I'm not a James Bond. I'm a police officer. Not a member of MI-5."

Angela laughs, but tries to disguise it as a cough. "I don't think she meant it literally."

"I didn't. To quote Amanda, being a James Bond means you have 'super awesome agenting skills.' And that you can handle anything that's thrown at you," I emphasize. "You wouldn't be here if you weren't already one of the best. So listen to Angela. Trust yourself and your instincts."

Normally, I'd be against helping Art inflate his ego, but something inside me is telling me he needs a pep talk like this.

It takes a moment, but I'm rewarded with the slightest upturn of his lips. "The proper term would be 'awesome policing skills.' Not agenting."

"I'll remember that for next time."

Angela clears her throat. "Come on, you two, let's not keep the troopers waiting. Us military folk prefer to do things on time."

She holds the flap of the tent, and Art and I follow her outside to the area where the horses are prepped before they enter the arena. A cool breeze hits my cheeks and brings in the refreshing scent of horses, hay, and mud. Tucked off to the right are fifteen soldiers in camo uniforms chatting amongst themselves, not appearing to notice us. They look to be about my age, in their late teens or early twenties.

As we approach, I hear one of them mutter, "I can't believe the Life Guards took it again!"

"The results aren't official yet, but come on, Baker, you knew it was probably going to happen. The Life Guards have taken the top prize the last couple of years running," his friend replies. "At least we'll probably take fourth through sixth. That's an improvement from last year."

The soldier named Baker winces. "It sounds even worse when you put it that way, McMillian. The Blues can't keep finishing in the bottom half."

McMillian shakes his head. "You're taking this way harsher than the guys in the actual competition. If you want to change things, maybe you should enter next year."

"Me?" Baker laughs sarcastically. "Yeah right. You've seen the state of my kit. I can't even perform well enough during a regular inspection to earn enough points to become a Boxman when we're at Horse Guards. There's no way I'd ever humiliate myself and enter the Princess Alice Cup."

"Never say never," McMillian teases.

Suddenly, one of the soldiers in a red riding helmet spots us and alerts the others. They abruptly stop talking and snap to attention.

I hold up my hand and offer a half wave. "Hello."

"Ma'am," they answer nearly in unison, dipping their heads toward me.

"It's nice to meet you all. I hope the prep for the competition today wasn't too rough."

"No, ma'am," they answer.

Hmm, getting them to relax might be a bit tricker than I thought. What would my brother do? He'd crack a joke.

"Are you looking forward to having some more free time now that this is all over? Or just being done with the constant polishing?" I ask.

That elicits a laugh from everyone. The ice has started to melt.

⁓

LLATER THAT EVENING, I'M BACK IN THE COMFORT OF my flat. As much as I would've loved to spend the night in Windsor, I have to be at work at six a.m. Working in the stables may only be a part-time job I do on the weekends, but it's something I take seriously. I hate being late, and if I can help it, I try to never call out. I was hired to work. Not to show up whenever it suits me. I may be a princess, but I'm also a highly dependable worker.

Knock. Knock.

Odd. Who would be stopping by so late? Padding over to the door, I open it a crack and peer out. "Art!"

"Ma'am." He inclines his head, his cheeks flushing a light pink.

My eyes widen. I have an avocado face mask on, my hair is still damp from a shower, and I'm dressed in a ratty old T-shirt of my brother's and a pair of plaid pajama shorts. Fantastic. Well, Bruce has seen me like this before. Now I suppose it's Art's turn. I'm not ashamed of being comfortable in my own home, but I do feel a bit like Elphaba from *Wicked* with the green skin.

Crossing my arms against my chest, I lean against the door frame and ask, "What can I do for you?"

"It's eight p.m."

I cock my head to the side. Okay. Is he checking up on me? Did Papa put him up to it?

"This morning, you requested for the security office to send someone up around this time," he says.

"I did?" Just then, my chocolate-and-white springer spaniel barks and comes bounding excitedly from the bathroom to the door, still damp from her bath. Her coarse fur brushes my bare legs as she stops directly in front of us. I spy a gleam in her eye and shout, "Lillian, no!" But it's too late.

She shakes. Fur and water droplets go flying, landing on Art and me. Lillian barks gleefully. "I'm so sorry!" If my face weren't covered in a mask, he'd notice it's burning bright-red. Art's trousers are coated in white dog hair, as if he's rolled around on the ground.

He stares for a moment, then shrugs. Kneeling down, he offers his hand to Lillian. She sniffs it, and promptly lies down on the ground, exposing her belly. "Your dog is just being a dog. My next stop is my flat. I'll just change when I get home."

I release a breath.

"What's her name?" He glances up between belly scratches.

"Lillian."

"Cheers, Miss Lillian. I'm Art. It's nice to meet you."

I watch as my hyper spaniel totally relaxes as if she's bewitched by Art. He seems to know exactly all the right places to scratch. Who knew he was such a dog charmer!

That's when I remember and slap my palm on my forehead, covering it in clay. "I forgot. I did ask for someone. I'd planned to take Lillian for a walk after dinner."

Art uprights himself, brushing his hands off on his trousers. "Is that what you still plan to do?"

Lillian's tail wags rapidly. She's stirred up by her new friend. If I have any hope of going to bed early tonight, a walk is a must. "Only if you don't mind."

"I don't."

"I just need to change. Give me a few minutes."

"Take your time, ma'am. I'll be here with Miss Lillian."

With the speed of an Olympic sprinter, I scrub my face and throw on my jeans and a shirt. Outside, humidity lingers in the air, making it one of the rare times during the British summer that it's still warm enough to go out without a jacket. Lillian tugs on her lead and heads directly for her favorite bush to mark near the car park.

"I didn't think you'd still be here," I tell Art. "I thought you and Angela would've headed home a while ago. You put in a full day."

"I was finishing the report on today's outing." He slides his hands into his pockets. "Angela left an hour ago."

"Why'd you come up instead of sending one of the evening security officers?"

"The lads were just clocking in. I offered so they didn't have to rush."

"Of course. That makes sense." I don't know the exact procedures, but off the top of my head, I know they have to sign out their equipment and receive a briefing.

"I could ask you a similar question, ma'am. Don't you have a member of staff who tends to your dog?"

"I do, but whenever I've been out all day, I like to try and spend at least a little time with her."

Lillian signals she's ready to keep going, finished with the roses. Art and I resume our walk around the courtyard.

"You're a good owner."

"Thank you." My body warms at his compliment. "Sometimes it doesn't feel like it, since I was gone for a few months, but I'd like to think I'm at least responsible."

"Don't worry. You are, I can tell. How old is she?"

"About four and a half years. I've had her since she was a puppy. Her mum is my parents' dog."

Art nods. I'm tempted to ask him if he has any pets, but that might be a little too personal for him, and I doubt he'd tell me much. I wrack my brain and try and come up with a few safe, neutral topics we can discuss, but I draw a blank.

Luckily, he chooses that moment to speak. "I always wanted a dog growing up, but my parents didn't think my younger brother, or I were responsible enough. So the only pets we kept were fish."

I bite back a gasp of surprise. This is one of the first pieces of personal information Art's shared with me. It feels like it's a watershed moment in our relationship, but I'm likely reading way too much into this. Pets have a way of helping people relax. And since Art's going home right after this, he probably doesn't realize he's letting his guard down. "What kind of dog would you have gotten, given a choice?"

Lillian stops and elects to do her business on a bed of newly planted flowers. The gardeners will be none too pleased when they see the state of it in the morning. With any luck, they'll think it was a squirrel, fox, or some other wild animal.

"Hmm . . . I don't know." He strokes his chin. "I've never given it too much thought. I'll have to get back to you on it. For now, let's say a rescue dog. There're never enough comfortable homes to go around for them."

I agree with him wholeheartedly. The longer I speak with him, the more pieces of the puzzle come together. Art is not the man I thought he was. Outwardly, he may be a protection officer who plays strictly by the rules, but inwardly, I'm finding him to be a softie. At least, that's my latest theory. There are still many layers to uncover.

After I clean up Lillian's mess, we walk in comfortable silence along the side path that runs parallel to Green Park. Beyond the iron gate, I spy the silhouettes of a few people strolling through.

"It seems busier than normal," I muse.

"The summer concert series begins tonight in Hyde Park. I think it started at eight."

"Any idea who the headliners are?" I joke.

"The briefing book mentioned Coldplay, but I skimmed over the other acts." He stops walking and freezes. His eyes widen and his breathing quickens. "You, er . . . didn't want to go, did you?"

It's almost as if he's panicked about it. Why would he be? I shake my head. "No. There're too many people and I have an early day tomorrow. I work six to three at the Kensington Stables."

A look of relief passes over his face.

"If *you're* interested in going, we can head back now. I've kept you long enough."

He shakes his head. "Thank you, ma'am, but no. I'm like you. I don't enjoy places with too many people."

I wonder if it's because of his experiences as a police officer, because he's antisocial, or a combination of the two. He doesn't volunteer any more information. I decide not to probe.

Turning tail, we head back for the palace. Lillian's pace is slowing. She's ready for her last meal of the day and bed. Just like me. I cover a yawn with my hand.

Art walks me to the palace's main doors. "Good evening, ma'am. Arthur." Bill, one of the night guards waves to us.

"Cheers, Bill," I say. "Is it you and Killian tonight?"

"Yes, ma'am."

"Then I know I'm in good hands." I wink.

Bill chuckles. "Do you need me to sign anything back in for you, Arthur?"

"No. I took care of it all earlier." He shoves his hands back into his pockets. "I'll leave you here, ma'am. Have a good night. Bill." He nods to the guard.

"You too." I wave as he walks away toward the staff entrance.

Bill scratches Lillian's ears. "That rookie is certainly devoted to his work."

"Oh?"

"Arthur insisted on being the one who accompanied you on your walk with Lillian tonight." He shakes his head. "Killian and I assured him we could manage just fine, but the young man wouldn't take no for an answer, even though he'd already clocked out." Bill slips my spaniel a treat from his pocket, then stands. "I guess all rookies feel they have something to prove."

I spend a few more minutes chatting with one of the palace's long-time officers before heading up to my room. Thoughts of Art swirl around my brain. He insisted on being with me even though he was already done for the evening? Why? Does he feel that he has a lot to prove? Or is it something more?

Unlocking the door, I slip Lillian's harness off her and watch her pad over to her food and water dishes. I lie down on my bed, intending to replay some of the day's moments in my head, but as soon as my head touches the pillow, I fall asleep. Figuring out my personal protection officer will have to wait another day.

Ten

"Welcome back to Charlie's, ma'am. We're honored to have you as our guest today. If you'd please follow me, Mr. Walsh is expecting you," the maître'd says as he leads me through the main dining room to a private room in the back of the club. It's Tuesday afternoon the following week, and time for my date with Eric.

Falling back a half step, I joke to Art, "Did you need to do a perimeter sweep?"

"No, ma'am. Angela did it." His tone is short and clipped.

I don't understand why he's changed so much from the other night. Haven't we gotten past this? I don't think he's hangry. I make a mental note to myself to ensure that both Angela and Art are treated to whatever they want for lunch.

"Here we are, the Garden Room." The door opens, and I'm greeted by the scent of fresh flowers. There are dozens of arrangements incorporated into a living wall, with a water feature as the centerpiece. It's one of my favorite rooms in the club.

I wonder if I could create something like this in my own flat. The only tricky bit would be figuring out how to incorporate the plumbing into the wall. I'd need an existing connection to the water main. I can't see my parents approving the extra cost of adding it since it's only for aesthetic purposes. If I did a smaller-scale project, I wonder if I could use the external plumbing from a fish aquarium.

I store all those thoughts away for later. At the only table in the center of the room is Eric. He stands up so quickly that his chair topples over. I bite back my laugh.

"Alice, you made it!" he says.

"I did." I smile.

"Ma'am, I'll be just outside the door if you need me," Arthur murmurs flatly before he leaves me.

"Okay," I say without turning around.

I approach the table. Eric quickly picks up his chair and rushes around to the other side, beating the maître'd to pulling out my chair for me. "I've got it," he insists.

"Thank you," I tell him.

"You're welcome."

"Here are your menus. If you don't see anything you'd like, please let either myself or your server know—"

Eric abruptly cuts him off. "We've been here before. We know the drill."

I frown. There's no need to be rude about it. The maître'd clenches his jaw, but remains professional. Just before he departs, I touch his arm. "Sorry, but can you please see to it that my detail receives lunch too? Charge it to my brother's account, please."

"Of course."

"Thank you so much."

I reach for my water and take a long sip. It's refreshingly cold and infused with fresh cucumber.

"How have you been?" Eric unrolls his napkin and places his utensils on the table.

"Busier than normal. We've had Trooping the Colour, the

Order of the Garter Ceremony, the Royal Windsor Horse Show, all packed into the last two weeks. At least after this, we'll have some breathing room as things slow down. How about you?"

"Nothing that exciting. Just work. I reviewed accounts and spent this past weekend helping my dad on his narrowboat."

"Oh, is he a keen sailor?"

"Not exactly." Eric reaches for his water. "Dad retired a year ago. Mum was so fed up with him lazing about the house that she told him to find a hobby, or she'd divorce him."

My mouth drops open. "What?"

"Oh, don't worry, it was an empty threat. Mum would never divorce Dad." He chuckles. "But he did read Mum's threat as permission to buy an old narrowboat. He's always talked about wanting to learn how to sail. That type of vessel is supposed to be one of the most user-friendly for novices like him."

"Uh-huh."

Eric shares a little more about his parents with me. Like him, his dad was an accountant, while his mum is an IT consultant. He tries to be polite and ask about my parents too, but there isn't much I can share with him that isn't already public knowledge. Not to mention he knows my brother better than most people from their time in the army.

From the vibes Eric is giving off, and based on his friendship with Eddie, I think I can trust him, but I'm still nervous about it. I've been burned before. After graduation from sixth form, some of the girls who were in my class sold stories and information about me to the tabloids. I thought I knew them well enough that they'd respect my privacy. But apparently not. Money has a way of getting people to reveal where their true loyalties lie.

"Hiya, I'm Elise. I'll be assisting you this afternoon." The arrival of our server gives us both a moment to collect our thoughts. We order drinks—a gin and tonic for me, and a whiskey sour for him—and the potato wedges and artichoke dip appetizer to split.

"Hold on a moment," Eric says. The server stops and returns to the table. "You know what, we'd like to order our entrees now too, so you won't have to interrupt us again. When the dishes are ready, just leave the cart here, and we'll help ourselves."

The server's eyebrows twitch, but like the maître'd, she doesn't say anything. "Yes, sir."

"I'll have my usual order. The culinary staff will know what that is. Just tell them it's for Eric Walsh."

"And you, ma'am?"

"I'd like the club sandwich and an order of chips, please." I shoot her a silent apology. "Sorry if this is any trouble for you."

She nods to me and swiftly leaves the room.

"Eric, you didn't have to be so rude to her."

"The waitstaff is paid well for what they do. All I did was make a request." He brushes me off, picking up his water glass.

I bite down on my tongue and remain silent. I don't want this date to get off to a bad start, but Eric is not doing himself any favors with me.

"So how did you end up wanting to become an engineer? It seems like it's an ambitious degree."

"It is," I admit. "When I was a child, I always loved reading about the ancient Romans. I was fascinated by how they had to literally invent solutions to solve problems, like carrying water over large distances. First, they had to come up with the arch, a shape that was strong enough to support the weight of the water. Then, they needed to invent concrete, a material that was light, yet strong. But the best bit was the maths they came up with to calculate the angles of the rises and falls of the . . ."

It's easy for me to get carried away about all this. Heat floods my body, and I abruptly change subjects. "Er, sorry. The short answer to your original question is that I love the idea of how I'll be able to use my skills to solve a complicated problem." Reaching for my water glass, I take a long drink. The cold water soothes my throat and helps lower my burning body's temperature a degree or two.

"Don't apologize," Eric says. "It's refreshing to see that you're going for a degree doing something you love." Hearing him say that helps quell some of my earlier concerns about him. "There were a number of blokes in my accounting program that were only studying finance because it's a lucrative career. I'm sure most of them are miserable in their day jobs."

"Are you one of those chaps?" I ask curiously.

"Guilty as charged. I followed in my father's footsteps because he wanted me to take over his firm." He sighs. "Given the choice, I would've preferred to do something with photography."

"Oh, what type of photography? Portraits? Landscape? Animals?"

"Landscapes, specifically up toward Scotland. The moors and dales are my favorite places to hike through and capture during the early morning."

That sounds so romantic. There's a lightness in my chest. I can picture the golden rays of the sun casting a soft glow on a field of lavenders. When Eric shares a part of his authentic self with me, I find him charming. But in my head, a red-flag alert is still blaring. How can a man be so rude to the waitstaff and yet so sweet to me? I'm so confused. Just what type of a person is he?

We chat a little more about how he got into photography

and how he's recently started to teach himself how to edit and retouch images with professional software. By now, we've finished our appetizers and moved on to our entrees.

"What about you, Alice? Tell me a little more about what you like to do in your spare time when you aren't in the public eye," Eric says, popping a chip into his mouth.

"If you were to ask Eddie, he'd tell you I'm predictably boring. I spend most of my free time reading, watching SearchTube videos to get ideas for DIY projects, or riding my horses."

"None of those are boring, especially when it concerns horses. I assume you have at least one?"

"I have two. They're both Irish Sport Horses. What about you? Do you keep any horses?"

"I do, actually. He lives at my parents' home in Kent. I have a ten-year-old Norfolk Trotter, but he acts like a spoiled two-year-old."

We share a laugh and fall into an easy conversation about horses, becoming so engrossed in our discussion that three hours pass by in a flash.

Eric glances at his watch. "Whoa, we'd better get going if we're going to have time to squeeze in a ride! It's nearly three."

"Already?" I blink a few times in shock.

"Uh-huh." He runs a hand through his hair. He's rolled up his shirtsleeves, exposing a pair of tanned forearms. It's a good look on him. I'll have to add that to the list of things I find attractive in a guy—a man who rolls up his sleeves. "Amanda arranged for us to take a ride around the Rotten Row at Hyde Park. Is that something you're still interested in? Or would you rather we stay here and keep chatting?"

I chew on my lip. As tempted as I am to stay here, I've had enough sitting for one day. My back is a little tight, but a little riding is something I will never say no to. Unless my body is screaming at me to rest. "Riding would be brilliant."

"That's what I'd hoped you say." Eric signals to our server for the check. "Why don't I take care of this, and you can get a head start on changing. There's supposed to be some riding clothing waiting for you with the club's concierge."

Amanda has really thought of everything. I'll have to thank her the next time I see her. I thank Eric for lunch and practically skip out the door. This date may have started off a little rough, but it's gone better than I could have hoped. And now we're going riding. I can't imagine a better way to spend the afternoon.

Maybe I was wrong about Eric earlier. He's been easy to get along with. Nothing is forced. There are way more positive takeaways so far than negatives. At this rate, he's well on his way to earning a second date with me, which I can't believe I'm even thinking about.

When I push the door open, Art jumps to his feet from a chair. A book drops from his hands. "Ma'am."

Reaching down to pick it up, I glance at the title. "*The Layman's Guide to All Things Engineering*. Doing a bit of light reading?" I joke.

"Yes." He can't grab the book from my hands fast enough, shoving it under his arm as if he's hiding it.

Angela appears in the hallway with two coffees in hand. "Your Highness. Are you finished with your luncheon?" She offers a coffee to Art.

"Yes, we are. We're planning to go for a ride next."

Angela nods to Art. "This one is on you, mate. Horses and I don't mix unless they can fly."

It doesn't dawn on me until then that unlike Bruce, I doubt either of my new agents has any riding experience.

"Is it possible to ring Bruce and ask him to meet us?" My old agent has increased the amount of time he's spent away from me in favor of sending Angela and Art out in the field, but he's still technically in charge for a little while longer.

"Not needed. I can ride."

I turn my attention toward Art. He's standing stiffly, as if it's the last thing on Earth he wants to do. He's opening and closing his left hand. I wonder if that's one of his nervous habits.

"Can you canter?"

Angela snorts as she sips her coffee. "He'd better be able to. He was with the Met's mounted patrol before he transferred over to the protection side."

Art was a mounted police officer? He's never said anything to me. I glance away as my cheeks warm. I feel like that's some-thing I should've known. Then again, he isn't one who volun-teers much information to me. Not that he's supposed to. Technically speaking, as he might say, it's not proper protocol. I manage a smile. "Brilliant. You can borrow one of my horses. I'd hate to leave Sefton behind in the stables."

"Yes, ma'am. I'd better go grab my kit from the car."

Art departs and leaves Angela and me alone. We walk up the stairs to the member services desk, which houses the club's concierge.

"Art is full of surprises. What else is he hiding?"

"A lot." Angela laughs. "But don't bother asking me about them. They're his secrets to share, not mine."

"I doubt he'd ever willingly share them with me."

"I don't know, I bet he would. You're already getting him to actually speak to you quicker than any person I've met."

"I am?" I blink, surprised.

"Mm-hmm. We've been partners since we entered the training academy, and it took about six months for me to be able to hold a decent conversation with him."

We pause a few feet from the concierge desk. "Is he quiet around the rest of the security team too?"

"Yes." Angela lowers her voice. "Some of the daytime shift call him the human robot behind his back."

I exhale sharply. "Are you serious? That's horrid." He's quiet, but he's by no means a robot. He has lots of different expressions; it just takes some time to discover them. Like when he needs coffee, he grunts. When he's hangry, his tone is clipped. When he is embarrassed, the tips of his ears and back of his neck redden.

If I ever hear someone using that nickname, they'll find themselves receiving a dressing down from me that would rival one from Papa. If there's one thing I refuse to tolerate, it's name-calling. Words are far more powerful and hurtful than people give them credit for.

"I agree with you one hundred percent. Art may not be a man of many words, but he's absolutely brilliant at his job. He's one of those people who notices when the slightest thing is amiss, like the time there was a suspicious package left in front of HQ. Some officers walked right by it, but not Art. He noticed it straightaway and called in the experts. He even recently set the department's new bench-press record. If I were in your shoes, Art's the man I'd want protecting me. Your father personally selected him for you."

"Do you hold any department records?"

"Distance running." Angela smirks. "None of the lads can keep up with me."

I high-five her. "I'm lucky to have you on board too."

We reach the concierge desk, and I pick up the clothing that's been left for me. As I step into the changing room, I wonder just what type of riding kit Art will be dressed in.

Eleven

The short ride over from Charlie's to Hyde Park is filled with a discussion on show jumping.

"I competed in it on and off as a teenager, but it's never something I intended to pursue professionally. After I took a bad tumble last year, I had to give it all up while I was healing. I'm only just getting back into riding now," I tell Eric.

"I'm so sorry. I remember hearing about your injury in the news," he says.

"That's in the past now. I'm just glad it's fully healed." What I don't add is that I'm still in the process of getting back to being able to take long, enjoyable rides for pleasure. Forget the jumping. I shift my attention back to him. "Eddie's told me that you have to learn how to do a few basic jumps near the end of phase one of the cavalry's riding course."

"Yes." Eric groans. "It's the week that we all dreaded. Our bums were sore for a solid two weeks from all the falling."

"That's rough," I sympathize. "I didn't learn to jump until I had a few years of experience under my belt, and I still found it challenging. I can't imagine learning to jump after only four weeks."

"There's a reason it's considered the military's toughest course."

"It makes me see things from a whole new perspective." According to my brother, many of the lads who take the course have no experience with horses. They only have a matter of weeks to learn everything from the ground up. It's definitely one of those situations where you either sink or swim.

The car pulls into a spot near the Hyde Park stables off Bayswater Road. I climb out and stretch, ignoring the dull ache in my spine. It's a feeling I've gotten used to. Eric slides out from his seat at the same time as Art. That's when I notice their attire for the first time and forget all about my physical discomfort.

My mouth goes dry. Both Eric and Art have changed into black riding breeches. Heat sears my body as I drink it all in. I didn't realize how attractive I'd find both men in the form-fitting trousers. They're intended to fit like a second skin and leave little to the imagination. Now I know, this is my gateway drug. Where Eric has long, lean legs, Art's are brimming with muscle. It's like comparing a footballer to a hockey player.

"Here's the keys, Angela. I'll text you when we are heading back." Art pops open the boot to grab his helmet.

His voice brings me back to reality.

"Take your time." Angela leans against the car. "I'll just be reading my tablet near the Serpentine."

"Understood." He closes the boot, tucking the helmet under his arm.

"Have fun kids," she teases.

I need to stop staring at the blokes. I hope my face isn't too beet-red. I clear my throat. "Right. Uh, I'm guessing that Amanda arranged to have my groom bring over one of Eddie's horses for you, Eric. Just to warn you, they can be a little spirited."

He puffs out his chest. "That's no problem for me. I can handle anything you throw at me."

I almost miss it, but I swear I hear Art mutter under his breath, "We'll see about that."

I wonder if something happened between Art and Eric when I was with Angela. My eyes dart to Eric. He's relaxed and chatting about how the cavalry exercise their horses on the track we're about to ride. He knows it well. I doubt he's heard anything Art may have said.

My security guard, on the other hand, is moody. His jaw is clenched and he's carrying his shoulders high. Maybe a ride is just what he needs to relax. I know it does wonders to help me clear my head when I'm stressed.

As we reach the stables, the scents of hay, leather, and horses hit my nostrils. I'm home. From the stall closest to the door, a dapple mare has stuck its head out as far as it will go and neighs as if she's shouting at me to hurry up and get on with greeting her.

"Athena." I jog over and rest my head against her muzzle. It's coarse and wet. The horse butts her head right back against me. "How's my girl? I hope you didn't make any trouble on the way over." I find the soft spot on the side of her neck, just above her front leg, and scratch it.

"She's been no trouble at all," Danny, my groom, responds, placing down a bucket of water.

"Oy, Danny. It's good to see you." I hug the man tightly. He has been working in the royal stables for as long as I can remember. He's the one who taught me how to ride.

"The feeling is mutual, Princess."

I release him. Art clears his throat. I've already forgotten about the men I've brought with me. Oops. I make myself an inch smaller. "This is Art and that's Eric. They'll be riding with me today."

"Nice to meet you both." Danny appraises them before

returning his attention to me. "In addition to Athena, I brought Sefton and Poseidon with me."

Hearing his name, Sefton, my bay gelding, pokes his head out a few stalls down to see what's going on. He blows out air in jealousy, wanting his turn with me.

"I'll come see you in a moment, boy," I reassure my horse. "Brilliant, thank you, Danny. I'd like Art to have Sefton and for Eric to ride Poseidon."

"Yes, ma'am."

"Is Poseidon that massive black-and-white fellow down at the end?" Eric asks.

"Indeed, he is. He's in a right mood though," Danny says. On cue, he stomps his hoof impatiently on the ground.

"I've dealt with moody mounts. Leave him to me; I'll show him who's boss." Eric claps his hands together.

His words rub me the wrong way. Horses aren't supposed to be shown who's boss. They're not creatures who can be forced to do anything. They'll win every time if you challenge them. It's about building a trusting relationship and rapport with your mount.

Danny furrows his brow, not liking Eric's boast either. "If you two will come with me, I'll show you where the tack is. Your Highness, I left Athena's gear near her stall."

"Thanks, I see it. I'll take care of kitting her out after I greet Sefton."

The men follow Danny while I head over to my brown beauty. The gelding neighs softly when I open the stall door. I scratch the sensitive skin under his jaw. "I need you to be your charming, handsome self today for a good friend of mine. His name is Art. Do you think you can do that for me? I'll bring you some apples next time if you do," I whisper.

I helped raise Sefton from the day he was born from my aunt's favorite dam. I can still vividly remember helping Danny bottle-feed him every two hours when his mum wasn't able to produce enough milk. He's my big baby, and we've always shared a close bond. Sefton can read my moods well.

Art clears his throat. I glance over my shoulder. He's holding the bridle, saddle blanket, and saddle all with one arm. Those are heavy! His arms must be ultra strong. I notice his sleeves have been rolled up to the three-quarter mark. My throat goes dry. Compared to Eric, he's much tanner and brimming with muscle.

"What if *I* offered him an apple?" he says softly. He joins me inside and carefully places the tack on the ground, approaching us with slow, even steps. He holds up a hand for Sefton and allows him to sniff it.

"You'll be his best mate for life if you do."

Reaching into his jacket pocket, he produces a green apple. Like a puppy who has wide eyes for a tennis ball, Sefton's eyes immediately go to the sweet treat. Art holds his palm flat at hip level. Not wasting any time, my greedy horse gobbles up the apple in two bites.

When he starts sniffing around for more, Art holds up his hands. "That's it for now."

Sefton blows out air, then nuzzles his head against Art's chest. My heart warms. It's one of the most precious things I've ever seen. My two favorite boys.

Wait. I freeze. No. Art's not a boy. I mean, he is . . . but he's more of a man than a boy. And he isn't *mine*. He's the security officer who's here to protect me. Nothing more.

"I need to get over to Athena. Otherwise, she might think I've abandoned her. She's just as processive of me as Sefton. I'll, er, see you in a few."

Not waiting for an answer after making my excuses, I flee the stall for the safety of Athena's. I remind myself that I'm on a date with Eric! My thoughts need to center on him. Not on Art. I agreed to this date. I need to see it through and be fair to him. Clearing my mind, I busy myself with locating Athena's curry comb, and begin brushing her in soothing, rhythmic strokes.

❧

WE MOUNT UP AND TAKE A LONG SCENIC LOOP through Hyde Park. Our plan is to eventually end up riding on Rotten Row, one of the most exclusive riding tracks in London.

It's a beautiful afternoon. The sun is out and warming our backs with its radiant rays. It's probably about twenty-five degrees Celsius, and luckily, there's little humidity. Eric is directly across from me, while Art is trailing us.

I've let Eric do most of the chatting so far, and try to push myself to contribute to the conversation every so often. In all honesty, I'm starting to find that he is a little *too* talkative. When I ride, I enjoy soaking in my surroundings and listening to the sounds of nature. Not idle chatter.

" . . . I was hesitant to go see *Mrs. Doubtfire* on the West End, but actually, the cast did a stand-up job and measured up to the film. At least in my opinion. Is that a show you've seen?"

"No, I haven't."

"Oh, well if you do, the bloke in the lead role was fantastic. He was believable as . . ."

I enjoy seeing an occasional show on the West End, but it's not something I can usually do on a whim. Being in a very public space means I have to have a full security team. All my movements require advance planning, and like a dance, have to be carefully choreographed.

" . . . we could go and see it on a future date if you're game for it," Eric suggests.

"I'll keep that in mind." I try for a non-committal tone.

"The security office usually needs at least two weeks' notice though."

"Blimey, that long?"

"Unfortunately, yes. We'd probably have to buy out a few rows of seats."

"Hmm, that's a lot. What about if we went to a dance club? There's this place down in SoHo that has themed nights similar to the *I Love Lucy* dinner at Charlie's."

"If it's a place my brother or another member of my family has been to before, that's definitely an option. Otherwise, it's just like the theatre. The security office would need some time to scope it out and approve it."

"Blast, it's not Eddie's cup of tea. I doubt he's ever been there. I guess that's a sign we should stick to outdoor activities. We could take a trek to Wales or up to Scotland and go rock climbing! I learned how last year. We could get up early and do an easy four- or five-hour hike to . . ."

I bite my tongue and don't mention I'm scared of heights and that I'm not overly fond of long hikes. Short ones, yes. But five hours long? That's a hard pass from me. If I didn't get the sense before that Eric enjoys high-energy activities and keeping busy, I do now. That's one major difference between us. I'm happy to give those things a go, but they're not overly enjoyable for me.

Come to think of it, all the things he's suggested so far have been activities he enjoys. He hasn't even asked me once if I had any ideas for future dates. A part of that is my fault. I haven't been offering any suggestions.

". . . and that reminds me, there's also this wine bar in Shoreditch. We could take a tour of the cellar and spend the evening sampling different flights of reds and whites. My mate did that with his girl after they went to tour this vineyard in—"

I interrupt him. "Actually, I'm not much of a big wine

drinker. But if we were to go out and sample something like chocolates, that could be fun. My cousin has an acquaintance who just opened a small confectionery shop in Marylebone that I've been eager to visit. I can show you the website if you'd like."

"Sorry, but that's a big no from me. I don't eat sweets. I have a pretty long list of food intolerances I have to be mindful of."

"Oh, I'm sorry." I stare down ahead at the trail.

"It's fine, you didn't know." He waves me off.

"I'm surprised you didn't mention it at lunch."

"The chefs at Charlie's know me and what I can and can't have. It slipped my mind until now." Eric shrugs.

That's funny, because if our roles were reversed, I wouldn't want to take a chance. I'd remind the waitstaff or the chefs every opportunity I had to make sure there were no costly mistakes.

Eric continues on. "I only found out when I turned about thirteen. It was an uphill battle to figure out these allergies. I had the worst rashes, like the one on my bum." He recollects in vivid detail all the reactions he's had to different foods. While it's interesting, it crosses the line of sharing too much information with me. In fact, it's probably the last thing a man should share with a woman on their first date. I was positive things were going well, and we were headed down the right path to a future date. Now, I'm not so sure.

Art is close enough to us where I'm sure he can hear every-thing we're discussing. I glance around to see what he thinks. His face is hard, yet when he sees me looking, he rolls his eyes. I giggle softly to myself. I'd better stop Eric before he goes any further.

"Alice?"

"Hmm?" I return my attention to him.

"How are your racing skills?"

We've reached the dirt track of Rotten Row. It's dry today and the horses are kicking up a small layer of dust. To our far right, there's a trio of kids learning how to ride some ponies.

"They're above average. I can keep up with my brother when we race."

"In that case, how about we have a little friendly competition?" Eric grins. "You against me. Winner gets to plan our next date."

"I don't think that's a good idea. I'm not physically ready to try anything past a canter yet. Not to mention, I don't think we should tempt fate with Poseidon. He's behaved so far, but once he gets galloping, who knows."

"Ah, come on, Alice, let's have a little fun. Besides, I told you earlier, I can handle him. See if you can catch me—let's say one time around the track!"

The hairs on the back of my neck rise. I watch in slow motion as he foolishly tugs on Poseidon's reins and kicks him into a gallop. "Eric, no!" I shout a moment too late.

The thoroughbred horse has been itching to be released from a slow walk and do what he was bred to do. His strides immediately quicken, and soon, he's in an all-out sprint.

"What does that fool think he's doing?" Art barks.

"Come on, we'd better get after him. I don't trust him to stay on the horse!" Reluctantly, I urge Athena into a canter.

The blood leaves my face as I am transported back to Windsor, the day of my accident. I'd been doing some routine jumping practice with Athena. We'd cleared the first two gates of the practice course without any problems. She was maintaining good time and pace.

We turned for the water jump. I brought my elbows in and positioned myself in the saddle for the jump, only instead of sailing over the gate with ease, Athena slipped and skidded to a stop, rejecting the takeoff. I was so surprised that I froze. I had no chance of correcting myself until it was too late.

I remember hitting the ground and feeling like I was lying on a bed of red-hot coals. I couldn't breathe. All I wanted to do was pass out. It felt like it was an eternity before Danny came to help me, but it only ended up being about a minute. At the A and E, X-rays later revealed that I'd fractured my tailbone. Talk about a long, slow recovery. It took twelve weeks before I could comfortably sit. I couldn't even think about riding again for a few months after that.

I've been lucky that that's the worst injury I've had. It hasn't deterred me from riding, but ever since, I've been more aware and cautious. Seeing Eric being so reckless makes me break out in a cold sweat. He's taking a huge risk on a horse he doesn't know. Is he as seasoned a rider as he claims, or was it all for show? I hope for his sake it's the former.

He's flying around the track a good half a lap ahead of us. Athena is starting to tire. I slow her pace. I don't want her to get injured because of something foolish Eric has decided to do.

"Stay here, ma'am. I'll be right back!" Art and Sefton fly past me as he kicks him into a gallop, and they continue their pursuit of Poseidon. Sefton has always been a faster runner than Athena.

From the quarter-mile mark, I watch as Eric turns his head to try and see where we are.

"Don't! Stay focused!" I cry, forgetting he can't hear me.

Poseidon picks up speed and continues as if he's in the Kentucky Derby, trying to set a track record. My heart beats wildly in my chest; it's the only sound I seem to hear.

Art and Sefton are gaining on him. "Stop!" he shouts. "If you care about your safety and the horse, stop!"

"I'm sorry, girl; I'll make this up to you later." I squeeze my thighs and urge Athena back into a canter until we reach the blokes. I can now clearly make out the backs of Eric and Poseidon. Even through the screen of dust, it's easy to read how tense Eric's body is. All the muscles in his arms and upper body are straining to hold control of the horse. Poseidon is slowing, but decides to try and buck the rider off his back.

Eric fights tooth and nail to stay on as Poseidon continues to fight him. Art reaches them first, and like an Olympic diver gliding into the water, he stops, vaults off Sefton's back, and makes a run for Poseidon to help Eric regain control of the horse. This is a delicate operation. One wrong move could spell a serious disaster for both men and horses.

I arrive at the scene a minute later, jump off Athena, and grab her reins. Both of my horses are breathing heavily. I pat them on the back and speak to them softly, reminding them both how good they are. We walk to the edge of the track, as far out of harm's way as we can get. I can't look. I'm too terrified at what I'm going to see. All I know is after today, I don't think I ever want to see Eric again.

Twelve

Peeking around Sefton's back, I see Art's holding on to Poseidon's lead while walking the horse in a wide circle. The men are glaring at one another. Poseidon is bathed in sweat. Danny is going to be livid when he sees the state Eddie's horse is being returned in.

"I have him!" I hear Eric shout. "Release the reins."

"No."

"You're going to do the horse more harm than good if you don't let him cool down," Eric insists.

"I know what I'm doing," Art grunts. "Why do you think I'm walking him in circles?"

"I can walk him around the track just fine, thank you very much!" Eric counters.

"You've proven you can't be trusted!"

"Yes I can! Ask Alice. You're just the hired help. Nothing you say or do matters."

Eric's words are as sharp as the tip of a penknife. Did he not see that Art just risked his own life and limb to help him? I'm seething. As if it weren't bad enough when he didn't listen to me warning him not to race Poseidon, now he's verbally attacking Art? I won't stand for it. Enough is enough. Time to take out the rubbish.

I'm boiling mad. I'm like a porcupine puffing up to extend its quills toward an enemy. All I can see is red. "Art. Is. Not. Hired. Help," I start in a deadly tone. My eyes narrow. "He is a royal protection officer. His words and actions matter a *great deal.*"

I have Eric's and Art's full attention. Both sets of eyes are on me. Repositioning Athena and Sefton's reins, I walk through the gap between my horses and harden my glare. "You've crossed the line, Eric. You deliberately put yourself and my brother's *favorite* horse in danger. How dare you!"

"I thought it would impress you," he sputters.

"Impress me? Impress me?" If I were a robot, I'd be shooting lasers at him to get my point across that it did the opposite of impress me. It repulsed me. "All you've managed to do is show me how immature and reckless you are! This date is over. I don't want to see or hear from you again. Get off Poseidon and get your worthless bum out of my sight!"

"You heard the princess." Art's tone is so icy.

"I paid for your lunch, and this is the thanks I get? How am I going to get home?"

"I'll have my brother's private secretary reimburse you for your expenses by the end of the day. As for getting home, you have two legs, a phone, and a brain, don't you? Take a taxi, catch the Tube, or order a rideshare. You'll think of something."

To show him I mean business, I assume a power stance, lifting my chin and straightening my posture. It's a trick I learned from my cousin David. A lot of officers in the military do it as an intimidation tactic.

"Everyone warned me not to get involved with the Ice Princess, and they were right. You're hot, but you have zero personality. I only agreed to a blasted date as a favor to

Amanda. Never again." He dismounts from the horse. "What a waste of time."

It takes every ounce of strength in me not to cringe and cry. I've had insults hurled at me before, but Ice Princess is the worst moniker of all. It's the nickname the media gave me when I was fifteen. I've always been shy when I'm in public. It's gotten much better since then, but I still don't possess the same natural gift for public speaking as everyone else in my family, and prefer to avoid being photographed.

I can talk to friends and family for hours just fine, but for some reason, anytime I had to interact with the public, my mind would draw a blank, and I wouldn't know what to say. It was like I drank a vial of water from the pool of forgetfulness.

I'd use short, clipped answers for the questions I was asked. I avoided being photographed whenever possible. The papers ran headlines like "Our Very Own Frozen Princess" and "An Icy Outing." The one that cemented the nickname, though, was "The Ice Princess: Will Her Frosty Facade Ever Melt?"

Last year, when I disappeared from the public view while my back was healing, the media had a field day running stories about me. The nickname returned with a vengeance. The stories upset me so much that it got to the point where the palace was forced to come out and make an official statement about what had happened. It gained me public support and put a temporary end to the stories, but it still felt like I'd been scrubbed raw with how my privacy had been invaded.

Eric marches off the track, kicking dirt as he retreats.

"Good riddance," Art mutters as he continues to walk Poseidon. "Ignore what he said."

I've tried to grow a thick skin, but sometimes it's still like ripping off a scab and exposing the raw healing skin that's underneath. I take the back of my hand and wipe it against my eyes.

"Ma'am, use these." Art presses a travel-sized packet of tissues into my right hand.

"Oh, thank you."

He grunts his reply, watching me carefully as I open the pack, take one from the top, and pass it back to him. "I hope the bloke's phone dies and he loses his wallet. He deserves to have to walk back to whatever sewer he crawled out from," Art says.

I can't help myself as I conjure an image of Eric wearing a cheesy rat costume, a long tail tucked between his legs, and I start to chuckle.

"Ma'am. Are you okay?" Art's voice is soft.

"I'll be fine. I've been through a roller coaster of emotions over the last couple of minutes and it's all hitting me now." I fan myself.

"Do you want to talk about it?"

"That's not in your job description," I joke lamely.

"No, it isn't. But right now, you look like you need a friend." His voice drops so low, I can barely hear it. "We can be friends, can't we?"

I'm filled with a rush of excitement, like a kitten opening its eyes for the first time and seeing the big, expansive world around it. "We can," I answer, trying to keep my voice even. "You know, friends offer hugs to one another too."

"Is that what you need right now?"

"Yes."

Closing the distance between us, Art shuffles Poseidon's reins into his left hand, and awkwardly raises his right arm for a half hug. Knowing Athena and Sefton will be all right on their own for a moment, I drop their leads and hug Art tightly with both arms.

He stiffens momentarily, then relaxes, patting my shoulder with his right arm. His shirt is damp with perspiration and a layer of dirt, but I still smell the clean sandalwood scent of his cologne. His body is rock-solid. Closing my eyes for a moment, I take a deep breath. He feels so right in my arms. I never want to let go. I choose to savor the moment.

This will probably be the first and last time I'll ever receive a hug from Art. Protection officers aren't supposed to do this. If it weren't for Eric, he would probably have never offered me a hug in the first place. If there is one good thing that came out of today, it's this. After a few long moments have passed, I reluctantly force myself to release him. I don't have to step away from him. But I must.

My body is buzzing. Hugging Art is like having been given a taste of the forbidden fruit. I suddenly want more. I can't lie to myself any longer. Art's started to grow on me, grumpy exterior and all. I know him well enough to know now that he's not as tough as he likes to seem. I've started to develop a deadly crush on him.

"You're quiet, Princess. Tell me what you're thinking." His voice is softer and more tender than I've ever heard it.

I'll tell you what's going on in my head. I'm thinking that I want another hug and that I should've gone on a date with you instead of Eric. However, as much as I might wish those things could come true, it's impossible. The best I'll ever be able to do is fantasize over what could have been.

"I'm sad," I admit. "I thought he'd be different. I should've known the red flags from earlier would lead to something like his stupid behavior with Poseidon." I shudder. "I'm lucky you were here to save the day."

Poseidon's breathing has evened out. Art strokes his neck as the massive horse brushes his head against his shoulder. "Don't let your time with that man or his words get into your head. You have loads of personality. I should know, I've witnessed it firsthand, like on the day we went 'round your flat."

That's *not* the reason I'm sad, but there's no point in

correcting him. I can't tell him I'm melancholy because I wanted a longer hug and I'm starting to develop feelings for him. I stay silent, not trusting myself to speak for a moment.

"I state the facts as I see them." He focuses on Poseidon. "You were extremely diplomatic with Mr. Walsh. Far more than he deserved. Having listened to his running commentary back there, he didn't give you much of a chance to contribute to the conversation. He didn't give you a proper chance to show him who you are. It's his loss."

I chance a glance at Art through my eyelashes. Since the restaurant, he's become more relaxed. This soft man underneath the exterior is what's drawn me in. I've caught glimpses of it over the past few weeks, but it's the longest he's let it show.

"You know, Princess, this is just my opinion, but it doesn't seem like you had much in common with him to begin with. So in that regard, the problem was him, *not* you."

He has a swoon-worthy deep baritone voice. I wish he used it more often. I could listen to him speak for hours on end. It's calming and sends a rush of giddiness from head to toe. He's trying so hard to make me feel comfortable and to ensure I'm not reading into Eric's words. *Compassion. That's another quality you have in spades, Art. If you keep this up, I'm going to be in big trouble of losing my heart to you.*

I wish the stupid non-relationship rule didn't exist, I think bitterly. But I know why it's there. I've heard the security staff discuss it before. A protection officer needs to be able to think clearly and never risk having their actions clouded by personal judgments. Relationships cause messes. It's easier to ban them than take any chances. In their line of work, it could be the difference between life and death.

Sefton nicks my shoulder, reminding me he's standing right beside me and taking me out of my thoughts. "Thanks, Art."

He clears his throat. "Come on, let's start back. The horses need some water and electrolytes."

We decide it's best if Art rides on Poseidon and I ride Athena, leading Sefton. It's an unusual way of riding, but I've done it before.

"Do you mind helping me up into the saddle?" I ask in a small voice.

"I would've thought a seasoned rider like you wouldn't have any trouble mounting without a block." He adopts a teasing tone as he adjusts the girth strap on Poseidon's saddle.

"Normally, it wouldn't be a problem, but the muscles in my lower back have tightened up," I admit.

Art stops what he's doing and narrows his eyes. There's no need to tell him about my back injury. I'm sure it's in my file. "How long has it been bothering you?"

"Since the chase with Eric."

"Why didn't you say anything?" He grimaces.

"Stubbornness? Pride?" I chuckle. "Actually, I didn't start to notice it until after Eric left."

"On a scale of one to ten pain wise, where are you at right now?"

"Four?"

"Do you think you can make it back? If not, we can call your groom to come out here."

"I can manage," I insist.

Art passes me Poseidon's lead, then walks over to Sefton's saddlebags and pulls out a small black pouch filled with medical supplies. Rummaging around, he locates a bottle of paracetamol. "Take two of these. Do you have a water bottle with you?"

"No."

From Sefton's other bag, he removes a metallic water bottle.

"You're always prepared. The riding kit in the car, now the medical kit. Were you a Scout as a child?"

"I was."

"I knew it."

"But that's not why I have all these supplies."

"Oh?" I pop the lid and take the two pills as directed before returning the bottle to its rightful owner. "Thank you."

"Not to be grim, but we're warned when we're doing our training to always be prepared for the worst-case scenario. If we're traveling outside the palace and will be gone for the day, I always have my riding kit, an emergency kit, clothing, and a few other items on hand that come with us just in case."

Reading between the lines, I think he probably means weapons and communication equipment. Papa's and Eddie's teams have an entire van that goes with them. This doesn't surprise me too much.

"Does Angela keep a bag too?"

"Yeah, she does. She manages to fit everything in a small backpack. I don't know how she does it." He glances at his watch. "Those meds will likely take about ten to fifteen minutes to take effect. Would you rather wait, or can you ride? I don't want you to be in pain."

"I'd rather crack on and see to the horses."

"You're sure?" His hazel eyes bore into me, as if he's attempting to read my mind.

"Uh-huh. All I need is a boost up to the saddle."

Art walks over to my left side. "I have a fun fact for you," I tell him. "Do you know why riders always mount from the left?"

He pauses and shakes his head. "I don't. Why?"

"I learned from my brother that nobody mounts from the right because back in the cavalry days, soldiers used to keep their swords on their left hip. Mounting on the left ensured the sword wouldn't get in the way."

"Huh, interesting. I never knew that."

"Now you do." I take a moment to compose myself. "I'm ready now." I allow the horses' reins to drop from my hands for a moment.

"I'll lift you on the count of three. One. Two. Three." Practically one-handed, Art smoothly lifts me to his shoulder level. He doesn't buckle under my weight or even make a grunt. He just does it as if lifting people is something he does every day.

"Thanks." I swing my legs over the side and stabilize myself.

"You're welcome." Jumping off the ground, Art settles himself in Poseidon's saddle. He pats the inside of the horse's neck. "We'll ride at a leisurely walk. If you need to take any breaks, I expect you to tell me." He shoots me a knowing look. "I don't want you suffering in silence."

I mock salute him. "Yes, sir."

He snorts. "There's a heating pad you can sit on when we get to the car."

"Thanks, but I may not need it."

"We'll see about that."

He's probably right. I doubt I'll be good for much for a day or two. My back is going to be sore for a while.

We settle into an easy, relaxed pace filled by the sound of the horses' clip-clops. This is how I prefer to ride. "Art, how old are you?"

"Twenty-four. Why?"

"I'm just curious," I say quickly.

"Most people think I look older than I am."

"It's the constant frowning and the beard. When you smile, you come across as younger." I shimmy in my saddle.

"Doing all right?"

"Uh-huh. Trust me, this is nothing compared to when I first started back a few weeks ago."

The frown has returned. "I remember reading the report. It was the coccyx you fractured?"

"Yes. My tailbone." My voice becomes soft, and I avert my eyes from him. It feels strange and almost embarrassing to have such an intimate detail shared with a man who's around me all the time, but I know the security office put it in there for my own safety.

"Have you looked into having an orthopedic saddle made up for you? It's like a normal saddle, but the divot is supposed to help relieve some of the pressure from the injured areas."

"I didn't know that was an option." I blink in surprise.

I've gotten used to the nagging, dull pain that radiates up and down my lower back every time I'm bumped up and down in the saddle. Riding is one of the things that gives me the most joy in the world, and I'd never give it up. But if there were a way to make it so my bum didn't hurt . . . that would be a game changer.

"They are. One of the patients I worked with during my physical therapy module in Manchester had a similar injury to yours. I'll see if I can find the details of it in my notes on my day off."

"Thank you, I'd appreciate that." My insides warm, as if I'd drunk a glass of mulled wine. I'd forgotten Art studied kinesiology at uni. "Did you ever consider going into PT instead of joining the police force in London?"

"Until my second year, yeah, I did."

"What changed your mind?"

He takes a few long moments before answering. "Two reasons. I struggled with dealing with patients who didn't want to listen."

"I can see that." I grin as I picture a student Art telling a patient exactly what was on his mind. He isn't the type of person who would sugarcoat how someone is doing. "And the second reason?"

"I figured I could help people better as a policeman than a PT."

I've confirmed it. Underneath the suit is a man with a big, squishy, teddy-bear heart. *Don't worry, your secret is safe with me.*

"Thanks for sharing with me."

He shrugs. A comfortable silence envelops us. I use the time to sort through my thoughts and ensure I commit the image of Art in riding attire to memory. Although the date with Eric ended so poorly, at least it wasn't a total washout, and I got to spend a little time with Art getting to see what lies beneath the man who always keeps calm and carries on.

Thirteen

Jenna, my best friend since childhood, asks me to have lunch with her in Covent Garden a few days later. It's now mid-July. She's in her final year of studies at the Westminster Ballet School's Upper School and one of the most talented people I've ever met. I'm sure she's going to become the next rising star in the Westminster Ballet company, although she's modest and will tell you otherwise.

We're seated outside at a restaurant that's near the London Transport Museum. A set of tall shrubs hides us from view, but we can still see the crowds of tourists working their way through the many stalls of the Apple Market and Jubilee Hall. A street musician plays an acoustic guitar, providing a fun and lively atmosphere.

Angela is on duty today and has taken the table across from us. She's rereading one of the *Bridgerton* novels on her tablet, before the latest telly series drops later this week. She's tried to convert me to watching it too, but as I've told her, I refuse to until I've finished the books first. They're always better than a telly series. At least, that's the stance I'm taking until proven otherwise.

"Spill the beans, Alice! I've been dying for the details all week! How did it go?" Jenna asks.

"It was an utter disaster," I admit. Thinking about Eric still leaves a bitter taste in my mouth.

Jenna's hazel eyes widen as she stirs her bowl of gnocchi around slowly. "I'm sure it wasn't as bad as you're making it out to be."

"No, it was. Trust me."

She arches her eyebrow in challenge.

"Okay, maybe my date with Eric didn't start off as a disaster, but it certainly ended that way."

"Tell. Me. Everything."

I lean forward in my seat and speak in a low tone. "It all started with a casual lunch together at Charlie's. We picked up the conversation right where we'd left off at the *I Love Lucy* event . . ." I don't leave out any details. Jenna listens with rapt attention. ". . . then after I told him to leave, Art and I rode back to the stables and took care of the horses."

"Blimey, I can't believe he did that. How did Amanda react?"

"She was mortified and kept apologizing. I still feel semi-guilty that all that effort she put into the date was wasted." I reach for my water glass.

"And Edmund? Did he go into protective older brother mode?"

"Uh-huh. Eddie was like a volcano. He marched into his office, slammed the door shut, and ripped Eric to bits over the phone. Even with the door closed, I could clearly hear everything he said. I've seen him get angry once or twice, but this time, even *I* was scared. Needless to say, they're no longer friends."

Jenna lets out a low whistle. "I would *not* want to be on the bad side of your brother. Or your father. They're both downright terrifying."

"Agreed." I take a heaping bite of my lasagna and chew slowly.

"Where do you go from here?"

"Amanda is begging me to give her another chance. She's promised that if I agree to another date, she'll make sure the bloke is properly vetted before we go out, but I don't know." I sigh. "I'm not too keen on another date anytime soon after the experience with Eric. What do you think I should do?"

Jenna takes a moment to study me. "I think you should tell Amanda exactly what you're telling me. I think you just need some time to process and move past the whole experience. Say you'll keep her offer in mind for the future, and when you're ready, you'll let her know. I know it wasn't easy for you to agree to a date in the first place."

Jenna was one of the few people who was able to get through to me when I hit rock bottom after the media storm. She's the one who suggested I travel during my gap year.

"There's something else you're holding back. Isn't there," she states more than asks.

"There is." I never have been able to hide anything from her.

"Well, get on with it."

I glance in Angela's direction. She's still engrossed in her book.

"This is a state secret. It has to stay strictly between us."

She zips her lips closed and holds up her hand to show she promises.

"There *is* somebody I like, but it's complicated." On cue, the guitar busker begins to sing Taylor Swift's "Lover."

"Who?" she whispers.

"Arthur," I admit in a barely audible tone. I can't believe I've just said his name aloud.

"Your personal protection officer?" she mouths to me.

"Yes." I cover my face with my hands.

"Oh, Alice. It had to be him?"

"I know. I'm in so much trouble. I see him every day and it's a battle of my wills to keep my mind focused on what I'm doing. He's in all my thoughts, and lately, all my dreams."

Last night, for instance, I dreamed about Art and I going for a ride together in clothing from Jane Austen's time. The top hat. The form-fitting jacket. The breeches. All the Regency-era clothing fit him so well. He was just like Matthew Macfadyen, my favorite Mr. Darcy. Everything in the dream seemed so real. I could smell the lavender of the field. Feel the damp morning fog upon my skin. We were just about to kiss when my alarm went off.

"And you can't tell anyone or else he'll lose his job," Jenna says.

I nod, hunching my shoulders. "I'm caught in an ugly catch-22."

"All things aside, let's say there weren't any restrictions holding you back from telling Arthur how you feel. Are you convinced he's the right lad for you?"

I lift my head slightly, "I'm about sixty-five percent sure."

Jenna finishes her meal and pushes her plate to the side. "Then it seems to me that we need to figure out a way to get you to be one hundred percent sure."

"How am I going to do that? And what happens if I *do* become a hundred percent sure? Or if he doesn't feel the same way I do?"

"We tackle one thing at a time. First, we need to be sure about you. Because if you don't end up really liking him, then there's no point in worrying about the consequences. I know you said you weren't keen on going out on another date, but in this case, I think it's a necessary evil to help you confirm to yourself where your heart stands."

"I was afraid you were going to say that." I push my plate aside; I've suddenly lost my appetite.

"I promise you won't have another experience like last time. I have two lads in mind who I *know* would be complete gentlemen to you if you were to go out with them. One of them is a dance classmate of mine named Alfie, and the other is a friend from school named Oscar. Both are the type of blokes who would make you feel more like you're hanging out with a friend rather than out on an actual date." Jenna locks eyes with me. "There's no pressure. This is your call. *If* it's something you decide to do, just send me a text."

My head is telling me to listen to Jenna's advice. I've only been around Art for a few weeks. My feelings in that time have grown from wanting him out of my sight to counting down to the moments we're able to spend time together. There are still so many things I don't know about him. Is he even single? Would he even consider dating a woman like me?

The muscles in my stomach clench. What if he sees me as too young? As a child? Or maybe he considers me an entitled brat. I mean, he's told me we're friends, but was he just saying that? Or did he mean it?

I hear his voice in my head from last week. *"I state the facts as I see them."* My pulse increases. Art wouldn't lie about being my friend. He doesn't mince his words. He says exactly what he means. Could our friendship grow into something more?

I lick my lips. "I'll do it." Butterflies flutter inside my stomach. I vow to myself here and now that this time, I'm going to be in control of the situation. I'm going to ensure I put myself out there and test my heart. I have to know . . . Is what I'm feeling the beginnings of love? Or is it just a passing infatuation?

Jenna reaches across the table and places a hand on mine. "You've made the right decision. My father is fond of both Alfie and Oscar. If you need a character reference, he'd be happy to provide it for them."

Hearing Jenna say that her father approves of them takes a

small weight off my shoulders. I value the words and opinions of Dr. Evans equally to those of my own father. "I trust you."

~

ON THURSDAY, ART AND I TRAVEL TO MY FLAT TO see how work on it is progressing. It's been about two weeks since my parents gave the green light for construction to begin. The timeline for the entire project is supposed to be twelve weeks, which I think is ambitious. In my opinion, it's more of a sixteen-week project. But I'll leave that in the hands of the project manager.

"Ma'am, I'm not letting you go in there without the proper safety gear." Art shoves a hard hat, safety glasses, and a yellow construction vest into my hands.

"I wasn't planning on *not* wearing any. That's why I wore steel-toed boots today." I point to my feet. "I'm going to be an engineer; these items are going to become my uniform. You and Angela better get accustomed to it too."

"Mmph." Art closes the boot of the car and places his own helmet and glasses on his head, and a vest over his suit jacket.

"Um . . ."

"Yes?" He cocks his head to the side.

"You may want to remove your jacket. There's a lot of dust floating around, and I'd hate to see it get covered with bits of debris. It looks expensive." He's wearing another black blazer today, but this time with a light-blue dress shirt and a silver tie. Blue's quickly becoming my favorite color on him. I love how it accentuates the flecks of green and gold in his eyes.

"It's just a men's basic blazer from Primark."

"Hmm, I had you pegged as a Savile Row gent."

"Those are too expensive for my pay grade. I do have some suits that come from there that I inherited from my grandad, but those are reserved for special occasions, like my first day on the job. I generally prefer things that come from M and S. That way I won't feel guilty if they get messy or destroyed."

"Smart."

His lips twitch.

"Going back to the jacket, even if it's a less expensive one, it's black and it'll show any speck of dust that lands on it. Do you still plan to wear it?" I challenge.

"Yes, it's against the regulations to be dressed so casually."

"We're not living in the Regency era; I doubt anyone will mind if you show off your shirtsleeves." I snicker. "I won't tell anyone if you don't."

"That sounds like something Angela would say." Art sighs and rubs the back of his neck. "Ma'am, I can't."

"Can't or won't?"

"Can't. There are some things like these"—he opens his jacket and reveals a radio wire and black leather holster attached to his belt—"that need to be kept discreet."

The laughter dies on my lips and my face sobers. Although we may be joking with one another, at the end of the day, Art is a police officer. That means like all the officers assigned to the protection division, he's armed, and the tools of the trade he carries with him need to be kept out of plain sight. "Oh, of course." I clear my throat. "Let's, er . . . go in."

Art doesn't let the awkwardness throw him. He moves on. "I'm curious to see how the flat's changed since the last time we were here. What have you signed off on?"

We walk through the front gate and past a large skip filled with rotting wood, plaster, wallpaper, and other items that have been gutted from the structure. I hear the sound of hammering and drills, and men shouting to one another.

"The builders were supposed to clear away any material that was rotten or deemed unsalvageable and start on replacing the roof, pipes, and any other damage to the weight-bearing walls. I'm hoping to keep most of the layout the same as the original footprint, but with an expanded kitchen and bathrooms."

The project manager greets us in the main sitting room. He's eager to show us all that's been accomplished. We spend a few minutes making small talk, then begin our walkthrough of all the ground-floor rooms as he explains what each contractor is working on.

The interior is barely recognizable. The rooms have all been stripped back to the joists. There are exposed wires and pipes everywhere I look. I'm a little shocked at seeing the flat in such a state. This wasn't the plan.

"I'm sorry, Mr. Gregory, but why has so much of the plaster been removed? We talked about restoring the building, not stripping it bare."

The project manager removes his hat and scratches his head. "Apologies, ma'am. It was my understanding that you'd received and read last week's report."

"I haven't." I pinch my lips together. "It must still be sitting in my father's office." I'll have to sort it out later.

"Last week, unfortunately, once the crew began stripping away the old wallpaper, they discovered there was more water and structural damage than was originally expected." The muscles in his forehead crease. "In this room, for instance, three of the four walls were infested with damp. We had to remove everything so we could clean the mold and install a waterproof membrane to prevent the same problem from occurring in the future."

My heart sinks as he continues explaining the countless problems he's encountered in the kitchen, and the remaining rooms on the ground floor. It hurts to know that so much of the charm and character I'd fallen in love with has been taken away. If I had known many of the original features couldn't be saved, I would've invested in a different property. Well, it's too late now.

"Please try and save as much of the flooring and crown molding as you can," I urge.

"We will, ma'am. I promise."

As we leave the building, I slowly remove my gear, tucking the vest and glasses into the hat under my arm.

"I know you're disappointed, ma'am, but it's not the end of the world," Art reminds me in his deep voice. He clicks the security lock on the car door. "By the time the new plaster is laid, and the walls are painted, you won't be able to tell the original materials from the new ones. Mr. Gregory is a master craftsman for a reason."

I manage a nod. My thoughts are swirling inside, like a jigsaw puzzle, trying to piece together and make sense of what we've just seen. "Maybe not, but I'll know," I say softly.

We slide into the car, and Art starts the engine. We pull away from the flat. "Why is using the old material so important to you?"

"When you replace the old with something new, you lose a piece of the structure's history. In my flat's case, it was somebody else's home before it was mine. It guts me to think that the floors where a child might've taken their first steps, or the walls where somebody might've marked how tall their children had grown, are being ripped out and discarded. Even if the people have long passed on and we'll never really know exactly what happened there, I'd like to try and honor those memories by preserving the spots where they occurred. They add heart to the home. It's silly, I know."

"I don't think it's silly. What you're describing makes perfect sense. You see yourself as a caretaker of the building, more than an owner."

"Exactly." I lower my head to hide the flush I'm sure is appearing on my face. Art is beginning to understand me on as deep a level as Bruce. Yet another reason I'm falling for him.

"I understand why you might be frustrated, but I think

your judgment is clouded. You're focused on what's being lost, not on what is being gained."

"What do you mean?" I ask.

"If it were anybody else, they might've walked through the flat and decided to gut everything and start fresh. But you, Alice, have decided to work ten times harder to do what you can to restore the flat. You're giving it a second life it might otherwise never have had."

My breath hitches. Art has called me Alice. It's the first time he's broken that formal barrier between us. It's like my veins are being infused with an IV of hot fudge. I'm filled with a warm, fuzzy feeling. I want him to say my name again. I'm so tired of being called ma'am. Your Highness. Princess. *Call me Alice, please*, I mentally beg.

"I never looked at it like that." A silly smile tugs at my lips. "Are you turning into Mr. Positivity?"

I'm rewarded with a flicker of one of his own elusive smiles. "That's another secret that can stay between us, ma'am."

"Nuh-uh. No more ma'am when we're in private. You *finally* called me Alice, so that's the name you're going to stick to."

The tips of his ears redden, and he grips the steering wheel tighter. "It was a slip of the tongue, ma'am. I didn't mean for it to come out."

"Well, it did, and now you can't take it back. You *have* to call me Alice. In fact, I'm ordering you to do so. Forget whatever the rules say."

"Ma'am . . ."

"Arthur . . ."

"Your Highness . . ."

"Arthur . . ."

"Princess . . ."

"Arthur . . ."

He groans.

"I can keep doing this all day." I chuckle. "I have a lifetime of practice bantering thanks to my brother."

"You're really not inclined to drop this?"

"Nope. I tried for *years* to get Bruce to call me Alice. This time around, you and Angela *will* be converted to my ways." I don't mention Angela gave in a few days ago. She didn't even fight me about it. She shrugged it off and said she'd go along with whatever I wanted since I'm technically her boss.

Art shakes his head. "Fine. You win."

I dance in my seat. "Victory is mine."

"For now," he says in a silky, sure tone.

Clicking the car's turn indicator on, Art pulls into a car park, settles into a spot, and turns off the engine. I've been so distracted by bantering with him that I have no idea where he's taken me. He exits the car and goes around to open my door.

"Thanks."

"I just need to exchange this jacket for one in the boot. Give me just a second, then we'll pop up into the shop." He slips the garment off his shoulders and wrinkles his nose. "You were right about the dust."

The dress shirt fits snugly across his broad chest. As he moves his arms, his biceps and pecs pop. I dry swallow. I knew he was fit after seeing him in riding trousers, but now I have a complete picture. And it's one I won't forget anytime soon. I take a moment to imprint this image and add it to my mental photo gallery. At this rate, I'll have to open an entire wing dedicated to him.

"Is something off?" he asks, noticing my staring as he slips a fresh black coat on and buttons the top button.

"No, er . . . you just have some dust on your bum," I fib.

"I do?" He frowns and looks behind him. Using his hands, he brushes off the non-existent specks. "Is that any better?"

"Loads."

"Good because I don't have a place to change my trousers."

The tips of my ears burn, and I cough. "Where are we exactly?"

"A shop in Kensal Town."

"Arthur."

"Ma'am."

"I thought we went through this." I rub my temples.

"We did." He closes the boot and gestures around us. "We're no longer in private; therefore, you are ma'am, Your Highness, or Princess."

"Fine." I hold up my hands in defeat. "Round two goes to you."

"Thank you."

"Now would you mind sharing where we are?"

"I did. Kensal Town."

It's clear he won't be giving me an answer anytime soon. I'll just have to follow his lead and see where we end up.

Fourteen

I practically press my nose against the glass window of an antique shop with a bright-red awning just off High Street. A shiver of excitement runs along the length of my spine. "Oh. My. Goodness. This has to be ten times better than a Disney amusement park." I'm bouncing up and down on my toes.

There are rows upon rows of doors, lamp bases, and chandeliers. There are chairs, tables, door handles, windows, and even a few kitchen sinks. It's as if there is a helium-filled balloon inside my stomach, ready to burst. I have to go in. I can't wait a moment longer.

"Excited much?" Art chuckles.

"Beyond excited," I squeak. I give him the best impersonation of a puppy dog I can muster. "Can we please go in?"

"Yes. The entire reason I brought you here was so you could shop for your new home. Angela mentioned you had some Pinterest boards for inspiration. I thought perhaps you might find something here. That is assuming you're looking for period furniture."

Without thinking about what I'm doing, I wrap my arms

around him in a big hug, pinning his arms by his sides. He staggers backward two steps into the shop's window. His body is firm. The fabric of his jacket is soft and smells of fresh detergent. "I am! Thank you. You're the absolute best and the world's most amazing officer." I glance up at his hazel-brown orbs, dancing in amusement.

"Can I have that in writing?"

"If you want."

"You know what, a video recording is better. That way people can't claim your note is a forgery."

"Whatever you want."

I feel the warmth of his body radiating through his suit. For a few moments, I envision myself leaning in. His strong arms would wrap themselves against my body, pulling me closer to him. He'd tell me I'm beautiful. Then I'd expose the nape of my neck to him, and he'd plant a slow trail of kisses up it until he reached my mouth. His lips are so full and a lovely shade of cherry-red.

A dog's bark, however, brings me back into reality. A woman walking a white highland terrier gives us the side-eye as she passes us, pretending not to be nosy. I'm reminded that we're standing in a very public place where anyone can see us and recognize me. We can't afford to have somebody snap our photo and sell it to the tabloids. I pull back and release Art. He adjusts his tie while I straighten my jumper.

I don't need to look at my reflection in the window to see how I probably look like a mess right now. I imagine my hair is wild and my face a bright, lipstick-red. My body feels like I've been standing next to a wood-burning stove for an hour or two while wearing two or three thick woolen jumpers. I study the sidewalk, trying to regain control over myself. That was too close. The sooner I put Jenna's plan into action, the better. I'll arrange a date with one of her friends for later this week.

Art clears his throat and pulls the door open. A bell chimes. I lift my chin. "Ali—ma'am. If you would."

We enter.

"Cheers and welcome." A woman with curly, short strawberry-blond hair approaches us. She's wearing retro eyeglasses with a pearl strap, a red-and-white checkered dress, and has a black cardigan draped over her shoulders. If I had to guess, I'd say she's in her mid-thirties.

"Hello," I say in return.

"How may I help you two today?" Her eyes flicker directly to Art, ignoring me as she drinks him in. A feral cat inside of me wants to growl that he's off-limits, but that's way outside of my bounds. Especially since he isn't my boyfriend. He's just a friend. And my bodyguard.

"We're just looking," he answers curtly. The playfulness he exhibited earlier has disappeared. The mask is firmly in place.

To my satisfaction, disappointment flickers behind her eyes. I add, "I'm doing up a flat and I may need some reclaimed items, like doors, when I move into the next phase of the project."

The saleswoman focuses on me. "Oh my! Princess Alice!" She curtsies. "I . . . I . . . I'm sorry. I didn't recognize you at first, Your Highness." She immediately shifts into business mode. "As you can see from our stock, we have a wide selection of items. I'm sure we have exactly what you're looking for. What period is your flat?"

"Victorian," I answer tonelessly, attempting to disguise my annoyance.

"Mmph. That happens to be the majority of our inventory. Our Victorian and Edwardian collections are going to be located in our basement. What you see out here is more contemporary." She signals for us to follow her. We cross the sales floor and over to a set of stairs tucked into the back wall of the shop. We're the only customers inside. "Feel free to have a browse. If anything catches your fancy, do let me know. We'll be happy to hold any items for you."

"We will," Art assures her. He places his hand on my shoulder and gently urges me forward. Something tells me he can't wait for us to be alone again downstairs. I can't say I blame him. The saleswoman is making me uncomfortable too.

Once we're out of earshot, I joke, "Do you need to scout the floor before I'm allowed to explore?"

"No. I checked out the lay of the land last week. I wanted to bring you here as a surprise. Today just seemed like the right time."

The fact that Art knows I'd like scavenging through items other people may consider to be junk sends my heart into a flutter. "How did you discover the shop?"

"By chance. Angela and I have been tasked with putting together some reports and maps for the office about your new neighborhood. Once I discovered this boutique, I immediately knew I had to bring you here."

"Well, you're right. We'll probably be making *multiple* trips here in the near future if their stock is any good."

"I don't know what to look for, ma'am, but if you ask me, I think their stuff is pretty decent."

"Oh, it's more than decent. You may never get me out of here."

Art glances at his watch. "You have about three hours until they close."

"Only three hours? That's barely enough time to scratch the surface," I whine.

"Then you'd better crack on with it." He smirks.

Similar in layout to the ground level, items are sorted by type. My eyes are darting every which way. I'm overwhelmed with how many things there are. I decide the best way to tackle this conundrum is to take a lap around the room and see what calls to me.

I glance over my shoulder at Art. "I'm right behind you. Don't worry about me," he says.

Taking his words to heart, I rub my hands together and begin my treasure hunt.

~

ART'S A GOOD SPORT ABOUT IT ALL. I END UP spending the entire three hours meticulously taking photos and recording the tag numbers of every single door, chandelier, lamp, electrical socket cover, and other items I'm interested in. I decide to hold off on making any impulsive purchases until I've had some time to have a think over how I want the interior to look, and the first phase of construction is complete. I'll pop some of the photos from today into Photoshop and play around with a few different renderings.

As much as I want to buy everything I saw today, that's not realistic. I *do* have a budget. I'd originally set aside ten thousand pounds, but I'm hoping my parents *might* be willing to chip in a few extra pounds to my loan. Either way, I know I can't have everything I want all at once. This is a long-term project. I'll buy things over time. The kitchen and sitting rooms are my top priorities since those are where I'll be spending most of my time.

"Do you think she hates me?" I mutter to Art on the walk back to the car park.

"Who?"

"The sales associate. She kept the shop open an extra half hour for us and we walked out of there without making a purchase."

"We told her when we arrived, we were browsing." He shrugs.

"I know that's what you said, but to me, that implies that we'd buy something. Especially being in there that long." I rub the back of my neck. "They're a small business. I feel like I'm cheating them."

"Ma'am, I wouldn't worry two bits what she thinks or about not making any purchases. The shop has been in business for over a hundred years, and I'm sure it'll last another hundred just fine. Besides, if they were in a dire situation, their prices wouldn't be so premium."

He clicks the key fob and the doors unlock. I place my hands on my hips. "How do you know that?"

"While you were busy making a spreadsheet, I had plenty of time to google the prices of similar pieces of furniture." He's smug. "I wanted to make sure you weren't being taken advantage of."

"And?"

"Considering we're in London, everything I saw looked to be comparable to items in other UK shops. They're at the upper end, but within range."

A sudden thought hits me. "Do you think they'd raise them even more because of who I am?"

"There's always that probability." His lips thin. "But if they decided to pull a trick like that, you have photographic evidence you could use to call them out on it."

Climbing into the car, he turns over the engine and exits the car park. "Where would you like to go, ma'am?"

"It's Alice. We're alone," I remind him.

His eyes soften as he glances at me in the mirror. "Where to, Alice?"

My stomach does a somersault at hearing Art say my name. "All that shopping has made me hungry. How about we pick up some takeaway for dinner. I'll even let you pick where we go, my treat."

I hope he takes the bait and doesn't fight me over dinner. We missed lunch because of me. He was so patient. This is my way of paying him back.

He hesitates a few moments, an internal battle of wills playing out inside him. "I'm a man of simple tastes. How about Pret?"

"Sounds brilliant." I clap my hands together.

Art locates the closest Pret a Manger by checking the map on his mobile. "We're about ten minutes away." A cool female voice on the navigator directs him to exit the car park and turn left.

"Do you already know what you want? Or should I load the menu and read it off to you?" I ask.

"No need. I'm getting the Swedish meatball hot wrap and the smoked salmon protein pot."

I stick out my tongue. "Those do *not* go together."

"Maybe not to you, but that's my usual order. What are *you* planning to have?"

"The chicken salad sandwich and maybe a side of soup."

"Good choice. They had a tasty butternut masala one the other day. The seasoning is just right on it."

"Are you getting a dessert too?"

"No." He wrinkles his nose. "What they have on offer isn't made with the right crispness. Take their chocolate croissants, for instance—the outer shell should flake off in your hands when you pick it up. The interior should melt in your mouth when you take a bite. They don't tend to proof their dough long enough."

Art sure knows a lot about baking. "You're making me hungrier with all this talk about chocolate croissants. Now I want one. It sounds delicious."

"If you *must* have something sweet for dessert, I'll take you to a proper bakery when we finish our meal."

"Deal," I say. "So, how do you know so much about baking?"

"It's a hobby of mine."

I sit up taller in my seat. "You bake?" That explains it.

"I do.

"Oh, that's dangerous information," I tease. "Now that I know you bake, I may order you to whip up a batch of fresh cookies or scones."

"It would be my pleasure, Alice. Except I'd have to use your kitchen."

"What's wrong with yours?" I ask, cocking my head to the side.

"It's tiny."

"Are you just saying that? Or is that an excuse to get out of it?"

"I'm a decent baker." We stop at the signal, and he glances back at me. "I applied and was accepted to be a contestant on *The British Baking Championship*."

I can't believe it. Getting onto *The British Baking Championship* is extremely difficult. The competition is stiff. All the contestants who appear on the program could be star bakers in any of London's top Michelin restaurants. "Art, that's amazing! When are you going to be on the telly?"

"I'm not. I declined the offer." The signal changes and he returns his focus to the road. "I had another opportunity come my way that I couldn't pass up."

My mouth opens and closes. Turned it down? That doesn't make any sense. Why would he do that? "Art, no." I'm gutted for him. "Can you ring the producers and tell them you've changed your mind? I'm sure we could sort some leave out for you."

"No, it's too late." He shakes his head. "I was told by the network I'd have to reapply if I was interested in appearing in a future season. Anyway, it worked out for the best. I would've had a terrible time working with others and being filmed all the time. I'm a private man. I can't imagine anything worse than sharing my life with the world. I only applied in the first place to see if my skills would make the cut."

"How long ago was this?"

"About six months, give or take."

I start to connect the dots. I know Art has been with the protection division for nine months. If I'm doing my math correctly, the timing of his refusal roughly coincides with when Bruce and the security office began looking for his replacement. He didn't do the show because of me.

"Art," I start, but he interrupts.

"No, I know where your mind is going. I want you to know that I had plenty of time to weigh all the pros and cons. I even talked it over with Angela. I stand by my decision. Not doing *The British Baking Championship* was the right call. I enjoy working with you, Alice. I wouldn't give this up for anything."

Does he really mean being with me? Or is it that his time here could be the stepping stone to something bigger and better? If he bides his time, I wouldn't be surprised if he's offered a better position in the future, like protecting my brother or my father. If he's around long enough, he could even become the head of the security office someday.

"Your destination is on the right in one hundred meters," the cool female voice says.

Art slows the car and pulls into a spot near the front of the shop. I agree to wait in the car with the doors locked while he runs in and places the order. He's bending the rules by letting me be alone. I hand him some cash.

As I sit in the car, I have a few moments to mull over Art's words. *"I enjoy working with you, Alice. I wouldn't give this up for anything."*

We're securely in the friend zone by now, but I want us to be something more real. He's beginning to open up to me in a way I never thought possible. The more I learn about him, the deeper I'm falling for him. I enjoy being around him too. A little too much for my own good.

Pulling out my mobile, I open the text message app and begin to type.

ALICE

Hi, Alfie, my name is Alice. I'm the friend Jenna was telling you about. Are you up for getting drinks sometime? I'd love the chance to get to know you.

I read the message over one more time, then click Send. Closing my eyes together, I lean against the back of the seat. There. I've done it. I've reached out to Jenna's friend. If I were one of the characters in the books Angela likes, I'd be told I'm doing the sensible thing. However, as I look through the glass of Pret and watch Art checking out at the till, I'm filled with sadness. My heart belongs to him, and I don't think that's likely to change anytime soon.

Fifteen

A knock sounds at the door. Art pokes his head inside the private room of the pub I've booked for the evening. "Ma'am, I have a Mr. Alfred Moore asking to see you." His forehead creases and his tone is flat and coldly professional.

"That's my date." I stand from the table. "Send him in, please."

"Ma'am." His shoulders hunch and he continues wearing the frown he's had on his face all morning.

"Good luck and have fun." Angela winks. "Leave Mr. Grumps to me."

"What are you going to do to him?" I ask, genuinely curious. He's been moody all day.

"I'll tell him he can be the one who gets to stay outside the door and babysit you two. I'm hoping if he's away from the crowds and noise of the main pub, he'll loosen up."

"Is it social anxiety?"

"I think so." Angela nods. "He's come a long way, but loud places like this don't help the situation."

The door creaks open and a tall, slim guy enters, holding up a hand to wave. "Cheers Alice, I'm Alfie."

He's got a bright smile on his face and carries himself with a loose easiness about him. I immediately like him. "Hi, Alfie. It's nice to meet you."

"Jenna's told me nothing about you." He pushes up the round black glasses perched on his nose. "I can't wait to fill in the blanks tonight."

"Likewise." I let out a nervous chuckle.

"I don't know about you, but I'm feeling incredibly awkward right now." He lets out a deep sigh. "I haven't been on a proper date in ages."

"You're not alone. I'm feeling awkward too."

We share a laugh, and the tension flees the room. Angela discreetly disappears as Alfie approaches me. He's dressed casually in black jeans, a heather-gray T-shirt, and white trainers. He has wavy brown hair and almond-brown eyes with thick lashes.

"I hope it wasn't too much trouble for you to meet me here," I say.

"Not at all." He slides his hands into his pockets. "It was a nice walk from the dorms in Covent Garden."

"You didn't take the Tube?" I ask, knowing he's spent all day taking dance classes and in various rehearsals. If it were me, I'd be exhausted, but I guess he isn't like us regular humans. He's a dancer, and that means he's well-conditioned and in excellent physical shape.

"Nah. I figured it would've taken me the same amount of time walking here as it would going through the stations."

We share another laugh. He's right. Some Tube stations like the Covent Garden one are deep underground. It might've taken ten minutes of walking and riding escalators to reach the train and another ten or fifteen minutes when he arrived in Mayfair.

"Are you in the mood for some drinks?" I ask.

"Sure." He grins. "Shall we go grab them from the bar?"

"Actually, I'm not allowed to. One of the agents you passed on the way has to do it." I hold my breath to see how he reacts. From experience, I've learned that the reality of who I am doesn't tend to sink in until there's something I can't do that normal people do.

Alfie shrugs. "Would you be okay if I ordered both our drinks, then, and saved them the trouble?"

That's thoughtful of him. A sharp contrast to Eric. "Only if you're sure."

"Sure, I'm sure." He flashes me a cheeky grin. "What can I get you? I'm probably gonna order a pint of whatever's on tap."

"I'll have a gin and tonic, please."

"On it. One pint and one G and T, coming right up."

I tap the pocket of my jeans and retrieve my card holder. "Here. The first round is on me."

He pushes my hand away. "Nah, Alice, I got it."

"How about I cover something for us to snack on like an order of chips."

His gaze travels up to my eyes. "Are you going to continue to insist on paying for something until I agree to it?"

"Yes." I nod.

"You're the opposite of my sisters." He snickers. "They make me pay for everything. But if you insist, you win." He accepts the fiver.

"How many sisters do you have?"

"Five. All older."

My eyes widen. "Wow. That must've been interesting growing up."

"Oh, it was. I'll tell you all about it when I get back."

He slips out the door, and I sit down as Art pokes his head into the room. "Everything going all right, ma'am?"

"Yeah, so far so good. He just stepped out to grab drinks. Why?"

"I just wanted to make sure the bloke was behaving himself and you didn't ask him to leave." The muscles in Art's neck relax. "If you have, it'll be my pleasure to refuse him entry when he returns." He cracks his knuckles.

"Oh, he's been a gent so far." I chuckle.

Art, however, frowns. "First impressions can be misleading."

He's right. I trusted Eric when I first met him. I liked him right away too. But meeting Alfie this time feels different, especially since he's Jenna's friend. I'm more willing to trust Jenna's judgment than Eddie's. She knows me in a way only another girl would. "Don't worry, if there's any problems, you'll be the first to know. Does that satisfy you?"

"For now." He marches back to his post outside the door, mumbling under his breath.

I shake my head. It's funny how things have changed. A few weeks ago, if Bruce had tried to pull a stunt like that, I would've been annoyed that he didn't trust my judgment. With Art, however, it's another story.

I *like* this overprotectiveness. He's feisty and almost— almost—comes across as jealous. Not that that's possible. I shake the thought away, reminding myself Art has a job to do. He's probably worried about my security in such a public place. The faster we're back at my flat in St. James's, the sooner he'll be back to his normal self.

Alfie returns a few minutes later with drinks and a piping-hot order of chips. I stir the ice around in my glass and let it cool the drink.

"So, five sisters?"

"Uh-huh, five *older* sisters. I was the surprise baby of the family." Alfie settles into his seat and explains to me that as the only boy, he grew up being spoiled rotten.

"I can relate. Being the girl and the youngest means that compared to my brother, there's a lot I was able to get away with that Eddie was never allowed to."

Growing up, it made me feel special that Papa and I had such a close bond, but now that I'm older, my perspective has shifted. I carry so much guilt over it. As the future king, Eddie has always had the weight of the crown on his shoulders. I can remember that Papa always treated my brother like a miniature soldier. He received lectures on how to act, dress, walk, and speak as the heir to the throne.

It's not all that surprising that he chose to act out by partying and going to clubs. Eddie craved freedom and the ability to be a teenager. Except when your father is the king, there's no room for mistakes. You're expected to be perfect. It's difficult for the public to imagine us as people, like them. But we're human. We can and we do make mistakes too.

If I had to guess, I think Papa learned with Eddie that his children shouldn't be raised with the same old-world, hands-off approach that he, Auntie Charlotte, and Uncle Frank were given. We're only four years apart, but our childhood experiences vastly differed. I count myself lucky that in spite of this, my brother has turned out to be a kind, caring, annoying, yet compassionate man. I hope I can live up to being half the person he is.

Alfie takes a few chips and savors the taste, and I decide to move the subject away from discussing my family. "You're in your final year at the ballet school, right? Do you hope to join a company?"

"We have another two weeks left before graduation. I'm excited, but it's bittersweet. I've been with the school since I was eleven, and now it's all coming to an end. Unfortunately, I didn't earn a spot with the Westminster Ballet, but I did earn an apprenticeship with a company in Stuttgart, Germany."

Oh, he's moving away soon? And to another country.

Why did Jenna set us up for a date, then? She must've known. I'm disappointed, but at the same time, I'm genuinely happy for him. From Clara and Jenna, I know that for a dancer, getting into a company isn't always a guarantee. "Congratulations!" I raise my glass to him and toast him. "That's brilliant."

"Thank you." He clinks his pint against mine. "I'm excited to start my professional career."

"Are you nervous about moving to another country?"

"No. I lucked out. One of my sisters happens to dance at the same company. I'll be moving in with her, and hopefully, she'll start teaching me some German. Luckily, a lot of the company is made up of dancers from around the world. Most of them speak English."

"That has to be a relief."

"It is," he admits. "The only major thing I'm worried about is getting around the city and communicating with people outside the company."

I nod in understanding. "I think if you're living there, you'll pick up the language quickly. Being immersed in a place really forces your brain to adjust."

"I hope so." He sighs. "You're starting uni soon too, aren't you?"

I finish chewing my chip and nod. "I am. I'm starting at Imperial in about a month and a half."

He lets out a long whistle. "Imperial. That's a difficult school to get into."

I duck my head. It was difficult. I worked my bum off to get top marks on my A-levels. I didn't want anyone to think I'd been awarded special treatment to get into uni. I applied just like all other UK students do. "It was either going to be Imperial, York, or St. Andrews."

"What made Imperial your top choice?"

"It had the stronger degree program, and I enjoyed the vibe of the campus when I did a visit."

"That's important, especially if you're going to be spending three years there. Are you going to do the dorm experience too?"

"No." I puff out my cheeks. "The powers that be decided it would be wasteful since I already live in London." The exact words the PM used were "a waste of valuable taxpayer funds." Mr. Carrington refused to hear what I had to say about the topic.

Alfie takes a sip of beer from his pint. "But was it something you *wanted* to do? Given the choice?"

I play with my glass. "It *would've* been nice to get to know some people before fresher's week." It's the first time I've admitted that to anyone. I'd hoped to be able to go through the same experience as my cousins. They made brilliant friends with their dormmates.

"Having lived in a dormitory the last three years, I can tell you that it's not all it's cracked up to be. Aside from living close to school, you're not missing out on much. I still have to do my own washing up, food shopping, and share a tight space with two other blokes. Our rooms are tiny. There is no privacy."

Hearing him say that makes me feel slightly better. Privacy is a big concern of mine, especially given my past.

"Not to mention you don't know who you're going to get as a roommate. Sometimes it works out well, and other times it doesn't. I know people who've had it both ways. There were plenty of my classmates who didn't dorm and they made friends just fine. I bet the same is true for you and you'll get to know the people in your classes well."

Alfie shares a little about his own roommates, then asks, "Have you ever lived away from your family?"

"Uh-huh. I was a boarder at the Wiltshire Girls Academy from the time I was ten until last year."

"Then you've already done the dorm experience," he says.

"Huh, I guess I have. I never thought about it that way."

"Did you enjoy it?"

"No, not especially." I play with my glass. "It might not have been so bad if my school hadn't been all girls."

"Growing up with sisters, I've heard stories about how cruel girls can be to one another." Alfie's large eyes appraise me. "I can tell you firsthand that bullying isn't just done by girls. It happens with boys too. Until I decided to become a full-time student at the Westminster Ballet School, I attended a local comprehensive in Surrey and I was bullied mercilessly."

My chest tightens. "Was it because of dance?"

He nods and gives me a sad smile. "Eight- and nine-year-old boys aren't mature enough to understand that even though social media and the internet paint dance as a feminine art, it isn't just for girls. It's for everyone."

I wince. "I'm sorry for you too. How did you get through it?"

"I tried to give up ballet completely, but I was miserable. It was the one thing I enjoyed. My grades dipped and I grew really depressed. Luckily, my sisters stepped in and helped me sort out that I shouldn't have to give it all up. I needed to be surrounded by people who weren't so close-minded. So my parents decided to pull me out and let me enroll full-time in dance school. That change in environment made all the difference in the world."

As I listen to Alfie speak about his past, a warm, fuzzy feeling runs through my chest. Here is a man who's not just surviving, he's thriving. There is so much I can learn from him. He inspires me to share a little bit of myself with him, even though we've just met.

"Our stories are a lot alike. I had some problems in my last year of school. I was bullied. All I could do was pretend I lived in a bubble, and it didn't bother me, but in truth, it did hurt. I spent a lot of time alone."

"Alice, I'm so sorry you ever had to go through something like that."

"I just wish there had been someone like you I could've talked to. It would've made a huge difference."

"Me too, Alice. Me too." He reaches for my hand and squeezes it. It's a small gesture, but brings me so much comfort.

~

AROUND TEN, ALFIE AND I SAY OUR GOODBYES AND I am driven home by Art and Angela.

"You two looked pretty cozy with one another when you walked out. Do you have plans to see him again?" Angela grins, glancing back at me from the front seat.

I stare out the window at the darkened streets of London. The shops are closed, yet the there are still plenty of tourists out and about, especially as we pass Piccadilly Circus. "Alfie was great. I liked him a lot. We agreed to keep in touch with one another, but if we go out again, it'll only be as friends, not a date."

"It's for the best, ma'am," Art mutters.

"I agree."

Toward the end of dinner, Alfie admitted to me what I'd suspected earlier. He isn't looking to get involved in a relationship right now. His focus is on starting his new life and career in Germany, and I can't say I blame him. He agreed to go on a date tonight because Jenna kept talking me up to him. He wanted to be open-minded. A part of me was relieved to hear him say that. I like him, but in a friend sort of way. We didn't have that zing or chemistry between us that I feel when I'm near Art.

One good thing that did come of dinner was our discussion about bullying. It was like a weight being lifted off my shoulders when I was able to talk so openly to another person who's gone through what I have.

Throughout the evening, I couldn't help but wonder about other people who are being bullied and whether they feel invisible and helpless. If I can, I'd like to find a way to help them and bring awareness to it. Maybe it can be my platform. I made myself a mental note to speak to my brother for some advice.

"Are you going to go on any other dates this week, ma'am?" Angela asks.

"I don't think so. Maybe I'll try again in another two or three weeks. For now, I'd rather focus on enjoying the remainder of the summer."

Art remains silent. My gaze travels to him. He may not be scowling, but he's still clenching his jaw. What's on his mind? He was in a much better mood once Alfie was gone, and leaving the pub relaxed him. But now we're back to square one. Why are his moods so unpredictable?

"Have you finished reading the second *Bridgerton* book yet?" Angela asks.

I turn my head. "No, um, I haven't really been in the mood for romances lately. I've been on a fantasy kick. There's this amazing series involving dragons and a school in—"

"You're killing me." She groans. "I need you to finish them so you can watch the series. There's nobody else I can talk to about them."

"What about me?" Art deadpans.

"You?" Angela and I say at the same time.

"Yes, me."

"You've watched the series?" Angela asks.

"Yes," he mutters. "All three seasons, so you'd get off my back about it."

"Why are you only telling me now?" she demands. "We could've been talking about this all week."

"Because I've only just finished," Art mutters.

"See, Princess, you need to catch up to us cool kids."

"What do you think, Art? Should I give up on the books and go directly to the series?" I tilt my head to the side.

"Yes. I think you'll enjoy seeing all the sets. It may even give you some inspiration for your flat."

"Oh, how is that coming along? Do you have any progress photos?" Angela asks anxiously. "You know how I love interior design!"

"The construction team has moved on to demolition on the first and second floors. They're in just as rough a shape as the ground floor. At this point, I'm losing hope that much of the original flat will be left by the end of all this."

"I'm sorry to hear that, Alice. Are they still on track to finish by September?"

"No, it's looking more like December, if we're lucky." I unlock my mobile, opening the Pinterest app. "Here's the latest renderings I've come up with. Art helped me find some brilliant furniture pieces to play with." I hand her the device, noticing his gaze watching me through the rearview window. A thrill runs straight to my core.

The date with Alfie made clear to me that I'm eighty percent sure I like Art a lot more than I should. I'm likely on my way to one hundred percent, and everything is starting to become more real. Because when I do get there, I don't know if anything can come from it. Protection officers can't date princesses.

Sixteen

A week passes. The following Monday, I meet with Mum for brunch. We do this at the beginning of every week to discuss and organize our schedules for the following one. It's hard to believe that we're nearing the last week of July.

"Morning, Mum." I give her a kiss on the cheek as I enter her sitting room.

We're taking our meal out on the terrace. There's a warm breeze. On the grounds below, a series of white tents have been erected on the main lawn. Like an army of ants, servants and gardeners are running around making sure everything is perfect for this afternoon's garden party.

Mum is still dressed in a long-sleeved athletic shirt and Lululemon leggings. She's just come from her Pilates class and hasn't bothered to change yet.

I sit down at the table and pour myself a cup of tea. "How was class this morning?"

"It was fine. It was just your aunt Lottie and me." Mum sips her tea. "I wish you'd consider joining us sometime. You might find that Pilates helps relieve some of the pain in your back."

"It's gotten better with the physio exercises." I take a plate and load a few pieces of fruit onto it. "Everything's healed. The muscles just need time to adjust. I don't think I need to do anything extra for it."

"You should be back to full health, not have good days and bad days." She pinches her lips together. "I don't like seeing you in pain."

"It's barely noticeable unless I overdo it. The doctors and therapists said I'm doing well with my coccydynia. It'll go away in time. I just have to be patient." Mum has been on my case to join her and Aunt Charlotte for a class since I arrived home. "If it'll make you happy, I'll *try* it next Monday—but that doesn't mean I'm committing to it regularly."

"That's all I ask." We each serve ourselves some eggs, sausages, and yogurt. "Has your father spoken to you about the Japanese state visit?"

"No." I shake my head. "What's happened?"

"Unfortunately, it looks like it's going to have to be canceled. The PM has ruffled quite a few feathers, and the Japanese government took offense to it."

"Yikes." I almost feel bad for him. "How is he planning to smooth it over?"

"Prime Minister Carrington was on the phone with your father earlier this morning. He wants us to step in and help mend the fences between London and Tokyo."

"Uh-huh." I cut my sausage in half. "What does he want Papa to do?"

"Send Edmund to Japan."

"I'll give it to the PM; that's not a half-bad idea. Eddie is popular. Would Amanda be going with him?"

"No." Mum sighs. "They're not married yet. It wouldn't be proper for her to travel on a behalf of the crown. Hopefully, they'll figure out *when* they're going to get married sometime this year. Everyone, including me, is getting tired of waiting."

"I'm sure they will," I say casually, trying not to let on that I know they *have* been discussing it. "Well, if Eddie has to go alone, I think he could manage the visit just fine."

Eddie is easily distracted. It would've been much better if my brother would've been able to bring his fiancée with him. But when it comes down to something important, he always rises to the occasion.

Mum places her napkin on her lap. "Yes, I'm sure your brother could *if* he were going."

"Mum?"

"Your father thought it would be better if we sent you instead of him."

My fork clatters onto the plate. "Me?" I sputter, trying not to panic. "But I'm not nearly as important as Eddie. Even David and Clara would be better to send. The public loves them. If it's good PR the PM is after, I should be the last choice." They don't need the Ice Princess.

Mum's eyes harden. "That's where you're wrong, Alice. You are the daughter of the king. You *are* just as important as Edmund."

"But I still don't understand. Why me over Eddie?"

"For two reasons. One, your father believes this is the perfect opportunity for you to step out of the shadows and shine. You're bright, well-traveled, and have impeccable manners. If there's anyone who can be trusted to smooth over a delicate situation it's you."

"And the second reason?"

"He thought you'd enjoy seeing all the architecture."

I have to hand it to Papa; he's found reason to make it difficult to say no to this trip. We're in uncharted territory. I've never been on an important solo trip before. There is a lot at stake. With my past history with the press, there is a risk I could mess this all up. On the other hand, the reward of seeing a mixture of ancient and modern buildings in Asia up close would be worth putting in a few public appearances for.

Mum watches me carefully.

"You and Papa have me. I can't turn this opportunity down," I say with resignation. "I'll do it."

"Brilliant." Mum's lips twitch. "The press release already went out about an hour ago. Papa and I will also consider this your first payment for the flat renovation."

My jaw drops open. "What if I'd said no? Would you have sent Eddie instead?"

"It never occurred to us you'd refuse." Mum chuckles.

I shake my head. My parents' gamble is paying off. This visit is to going to mark my first official engagement as a working royal. Talk about trial by fire. I had hoped I'd start with something smaller, like an appearance at the Chelsea Flower Show or a garden party. I blink slowly. At some point, I really need to tell them my true feelings about my future. "When is the trip planned for?"

"You'll leave in four days. You'll be there for a week."

"Is there a briefing book being put together for me?"

"Yes, you'll have it by the afternoon," Mum says.

"Great," I muster.

Mum moves on to discussing the plans for the afternoon's garden party. I pick up my cutlery again and push some of the fruit around my plate. It's hit me that I'll be expected to give a large number of speeches and be photographed twenty-four seven from the moment I step off the plane. I've lost my appetite. I'll need to study the itinerary to see where I'll be going and whom I'll be meeting. Then I'll review their biographies to make sure I have something appropriate to speak to them about. Not to mention putting together a suitable wardrobe.

If you've ever seen *The Devil Wears Prada*, there's a scene midway through the film where Miranda, the editor of *Runway* magazine, has her assistants whisper information about whom she's meeting into her ear. They spend all day studying their briefing books to memorize the names and faces of their guests. That's exactly what I try and do when I'm at social gatherings with important people. It may seem like overkill, but it's saved me once or twice in the past.

With a state visit, the stakes are high. I need to start studying as soon as possible. I won't let my parents down. Especially when they are trusting me to handle an already delicate situation. I've met the emperor and empress once before, and from memory, they were both kind and spoke English brilliantly. However, going into their home country, I'll need to have a few words of Japanese prepared. It's the polite thing to do. Especially since I'll be their guest.

I'd better start caffeinating myself. It looks like I'll have a few long nights ahead of me. But when I see the temples and old-world grandeur of Japan, it'll all be worth it.

Seventeen

I rest my head against the car door, careful not to mess up my elaborately styled hair. I've sprayed it with three times the amount of normal hairspray to combat the early August Japanese humidity. Without it, my hair would be ultra frizzy.

"Do you want me to wake you when we arrive at the Imperial Palace, ma'am?" Art asks from the seat beside me.

"No, I'm just resting my eyes. There's no chance of me falling asleep. I downed an entire can of Red Bull before we left the hotel so I could get through the banquet tonight."

"Not coffee?"

"No. It won't last long enough. I needed something stronger. The banquet's going to be at least four hours long."

"Which means we won't be back before midnight." Art sighs, glancing at me with concern. "Ma'am, would you like me to see about canceling your morning engagements so you can have a lie-in? You've been working nonstop since we arrived."

"I'm exhausted, but I feel like it would come across as a massive insult to our guests if I cancel anything. The main reason I'm here is to make up for the PM's mistakes. We only have to get through two more days. And tomorrow shouldn't be too bad. We're finally doing some sightseeing in Kyoto between engagements! I promise I'll sleep when I'm on the plane home."

We've been in Japan for four days, and from the moment the plane touched down at Narita International Airport, it's been all cylinders firing. The scheduling office in London somehow miscalculated the time change. All the dates were off. Instead of having a day to recover from jet lag when we arrived on Monday morning, after a fourteen-hour flight, I was faced with a full day of events, including lunch with the prime minister of Japan.

Tuesday, Wednesday, and today haven't been much better. It's almost as if the planning offices in London and Tokyo couldn't agree with one another on what events were the most important, so they decided they'd squash their schedules together and hope everything worked out for the best. It seems like every minute of the day is accounted for. I'm either in a car on my way to meet with government leaders, or attending a reception held in my honor. I haven't been able to do much sightseeing.

At first, it was difficult to be under so much scrutiny. The press and photographers are everywhere. However, unlike back at home, the members of the Japanese media have been extremely polite and respectful. I've even had a few of them bow and say "Thank you" to me after snapping a photo. It's helped me relax into my role and served as a reminder that not all members of the media are out to get me. Now that we're a few days in, I feel that I've finally gotten the hang of things. Some of the frost has melted away from this Ice Princess.

Today is Thursday, and I'm off to a banquet at the Imperial Palace. I've had little downtime to myself, which is fine. I can handle this knowing that it's temporary. I'm more worried about the toll it's taking on Art and Angela. They've had to be up ready to go before me every day and haven't been able to call it a day until I'm in bed. I'll wager they're only averaging four hours of sleep a night, like me, but both of them tell me they're fine every time I check.

"If you ask me, ma'am, I don't think canceling one or two engagements would be insulting."

Art's right. Events at home get called off and rearranged all the time. I *could* have my morning cleared, and it probably wouldn't bother anyone, except me. Clearing my day tomorrow would be the easy way out. Being raised by a father who is a military man at heart, I've always been taught to keep calm and soldier on. It's probably why I'm so stubborn. I'm not giving up if I can help it. I refuse to let anyone down on my first official engagement.

"I can do this," I urge, picturing Kyoto's temples, castles, and forest landscape that I've seen in all the photos of the city. It'll be my reward for all the hard work I've put in.

A few moments of silence pass between us. "Do you promise you'll let me know if you change your mind?" he asks in a tone so quiet, I almost don't hear it.

"Mm-hmm." I open my eyes and turn my head slightly to the left. My thoughts go to my bodyguard. It's one of the rare occasions Art is sitting in the back seat with me. He looks incredibly handsome tonight in a form-fitting black tux. Every time I see him, I lose my breath a little bit.

Angela is riding in the car ahead of this one with the three other temporary members of my expanded detail. She also looked elegant in a long, sequined dark-green evening gown. I've been meaning to ask her where she hides her weapons and radio. She has to be using something like a thigh holster. Or maybe she plans to rely on hand-to-hand combat in the rare event there's an attack.

"Do you need me to quiz you on any of the people you'll see tonight?" Art asks.

"No. Thankfully, I can give my brain a little bit of a mental rest. I'll probably be seated next to the emperor's eldest daughter, Princess Kaori, or by the empress. They're both easy to talk to and we actually have quite a few interests in common. I like them a lot."

"The princess is around your age, isn't she?"

"Yeah, she is. She's twenty-one and has been attending uni in the States the last three years. I'm hoping maybe we can pick up where our conversation left off on Monday. We were talking about roller coasters."

"Roller coasters? Are you both wild thrill-ride seekers?" he jokes. The laugh lines around his eyes and his mouth crinkle. I lick my lips. It's like he's playing a game with me. It's the one expression I find irresistible on him. I rip my eyes away from his mouth and focus on an interesting spot on my clutch.

"No, nothing like that. They actually make me motion sick." I laugh. "Kaori is working toward a hybrid civic and structural engineering degree. She hopes to become a theme park attractions designer. I was curious about the different programs she's been using to render the 3-D models of her designs in the computer."

"Huh, I'd never really considered designing roller coasters could be a full-time career. That sounds like a brilliant job." Art crosses one long leg over the other. His shoes are polished to perfection. I can't stand it any longer and lift my chin to meet his gaze. He's still smiling. My insides are beginning to melt like an ooey-gooey ice cream sundae.

"Doesn't it?" I say enthusiastically. "Kaori is so passionate about it; she lights up like a Christmas tree. I don't have any doubts she'll be snapped up by a top design firm when the time comes."

"Aren't members of the Japanese imperial family not allowed to hold jobs?" he asks.

"They aren't. In the long-term she's planning to resign her title. She can't inherit the throne. And if she marries, she'll become a commoner. In her words, she'd like to make her own mark and do things on her own terms, rather than be subjected to antiquated standards."

"She sounds a lot like somebody else I know."

I decide not to answer him.

Art's eyes linger on me. They're overly large, and in this lighting, the color of a warm butterscotch. My sundae is melting faster the longer we're seated next to one another. I hope we're almost at our destination. "There's something else on your mind—you can tell me anything, you know. Whatever you say to me is confidential."

"That's what Bruce used to say." He's beginning to be able to read me with scary accuracy. It's been a long four days, and even after having a Red Bull, my brain is still mentally exhausted. I lower my shields and open myself up to him. "I know I shouldn't be comparing myself to Kaori, but when I'm standing next to her, it's hard not to. She knows exactly what she wants to do, and the path she needs to follow to get there. Me? I have no clue what I'm doing. I feel like an imposter. I'm registered for the structural engineering course at Imperial because that's what I'm interested in. But I'm not too sure what I'll do with it.

"Then there's all this royal stuff to consider." I take a deep breath. "Everyone expects me to start taking on more responsibility now that I'm an adult. While I'm at uni, it's fine. My schedule is light. But what happens after? I don't know if I want to give up on my dream of becoming an engineer. I *think* I might want to live a quiet life. I loved being an anonymous person during my gap-year travels. I *hate* the spotlight;

speaking in public makes me queasy. That's why I come off as being so cold."

For the first time ever, I've said what I've always felt aloud and shared it with another person. It's no longer this deep, dark secret I have to hold back and pretend doesn't exist. With Art, I'm free to be me. Plain old Alice. He sees me. Not just a girl with a title. I lick my lips.

Being so exhausted and near Art in a tux is testing me in every possible way. I'm trying hard to keep a tight grip on the emotions that are swelling inside of me. It's like there's a seed that's been planted that's yearning to break free of the soil to reach the sun.

Art stays quiet for a second. "I know you hate the lime-light. I see it every time someone points a camera at you—your eyes have this tiny bit of panic in them that you try to hide."

I manage a nod. He knows me. Even my brother and Jenna haven't ever noticed. They think my time with my thera-pist has helped me conquer all my fears. But it hasn't. At least not completely. I'm dying to let him know exactly how much his little observations mean to me.

"When it comes to your future, I don't think you should worry too much. You haven't even started uni yet. Everything will fall into place when the timing is right," Art says.

I suppress a wince. I don't want to appear young to him. I want to appear mature—a woman worth dating. Not a first-year student.

"Look at me. I've changed my mind about what I wanted to do a number of times. I jumped from wanting to attend culinary school to being a physio. And I didn't end up doing either of those things. I became a police officer instead."

My eyes widen. I never knew he'd considered culinary school. "What stopped you from becoming a baker?"

"Fear." Art stares out the window and takes a moment before continuing. "I *love* baking. It's the way I relieve stress.

It's something I did growing up with my mum and my nan. I was afraid that if I chose to bake professionally, I'd lose my passion for it, and that's a risk I wasn't willing to take. So I held back and decided to follow a different path."

My lips twitch as I picture the normally perfectly turned-out Art standing in a kitchen with his mother, coated in a light dusting of flour. He wears an apron over the tux. His jacket has been removed, and the sleeves are rolled up to his elbow. I picture discarded bowls and measuring utensils spread out over every square inch of space as he rolls out a dough, the muscles in his arms rippling from the effort. My pulse increases. I chew on my lip. I. Must. Keep. Myself. In. Check.

"Do you think you made the right move?" I ask.

"For where I am right now in life, yeah, I think I did. For the most part, I'm pretty happy. I know if something changes, I can always go back and change careers." He clears his throat. "For what it's worth, I think you're *exactly* where you need to be right now too. Have you thought about having a proper chat with your parents on your thoughts about being a working royal?"

"No. I've been too afraid to." My voice is shaky. I try picturing my parents. Try thinking about anyone other than Art right now.

"Well, when you get home, I think it's a conversation you should make a top priority."

"My father is going to disown me." For a moment it works. I imagine the scowling face of my papa.

"Ali, I've seen you interact with your father. You two are close and he loves you. If you decide to just be Alice Wales, I think your father will still love and respect you. I *highly* doubt he'd ever disown you. I think that right now, everything seems ten times worse because you're exhausted. After a good night's sleep, things will seem better. I promise."

All thoughts of my father disappear as Art starts to reach

for my hand, but stops himself, setting it on his knee instead. I inhale deeply. He's playing with fire. Is he feeling the same intense spark that I am? My fingers itch, longing to touch his hand. "You know exactly what I need to hear."

"I'm always here if you need me, Alice."

Hearing my name on his lips sends a wave of pleasure through my body. I stare at them again. They're so full and the perfect shade of pink. I watch as he blinks slowly. My breath quickens, and suddenly, the urge is so unbearable, I can no longer fight it.

The car has stopped. I unbuckle my seat belt. I know I only have seconds before the door will open. "Art." I twist my body toward him.

"Hmm?" He turns his head.

Leaning forward, I give in to my body and press my lips to his, stealing a kiss. His eyes are wide with surprise, and he freezes. His lips are just as soft as I've imagined them to be. His cologne is like catnip, sending my senses into overdrive. I don't want to stop. This is the moment I've dreamed about for weeks. I want my lips to stay locked with his forever.

Except we don't have forever. The door opens. Immediately, I spring apart from him, and dash out of the car and up the steps to greet one of the palace stewards. I don't risk looking back. I'm too afraid. I can't believe what I've just done. Everything between us has just changed.

My entire body burns with shame. I didn't think anything of the consequences that kiss could have. I lost a grip on my emotions and now I might have ruined everything. Stupid. Stupid. Stupid.

Eighteen

My mind relives the kiss over and over again during the course of dinner. I'm seated at the high table with the imperial family. I engage Princess Kaori in conversation as best I can, but my heart isn't in it. It's sitting back in the car with my protection officer. Or rather, wherever he is now.

As I scan the room, I hope to catch a glimpse of him. All I see is a sea of men in black tuxes and women in colorful kimonos.

"Ali-chan, are you all right? You've been quiet tonight," Princess Kaori says. Her large, almond-shaped brown eyes appraise me, full of worry.

"I'm fine. Just tired."

"I heard you've been making the rounds all over Tokyo. My mother was impressed by how much you've done already."

"I'm supposed to take a day trip to Kyoto tomorrow too."

"You'll probably have to get an early start." She nods knowingly. "Do you want to leave the banquet early? I can ask my father to start wrapping up the event." She leans closer and whispers into my ear, "He looks like he's fighting to stay awake. My parents are normally in bed by eight-thirty."

We both glance at the emperor, who hides a yawn while he speaks to the mayor of Yokohama. It's about ten-thirty in the evening. Dinner began at seven.

"Actually, Father may thank you." Kaori giggles.

Her offer is tempting. I'd love to be able to escape to the solitude of my hotel room and dissect everything that's happened so far. But on the other hand, when I make my leave, there's no way I'll be able to avoid Art. Can I pretend it didn't happen? What if he's told Angela? Would she tell my father? Would Art be fired on the spot because of me?

"If you could make it happen, I promise I'll make it up to you the next time I see you. I'm beginning to have a headache, and I think sleep might be the best thing for me."

"It doesn't help that we're in the middle of a hot, humid summer too. Make sure you drink plenty of water and stay hydrated." Kaori signals for one of the servers and exchanges a few words with him in Japanese. He relays her message to the emperor, who looks toward us with a grateful smile. "Give Father five minutes."

"You're a lifesaver, Kaori."

"Women in STEM need to stick together. Let's stay in touch. We may even be seeing one another sooner than you think."

"Oh?"

"My parents are considering sending my middle sister, Fumiko, to a boarding school in Wales. She wants to improve her English. The two of us may be visiting the UK during our spring holidays to check it out."

"Let me know; you're welcome to stay with me. I have a new flat I'm working on."

She grins. "I'd love to see it."

We chat for a few more minutes until the emperor stands

and the room falls silent. He gives a short speech thanking everyone for attending, bids farewell to me, and takes his leave. Dinner is officially over. I fight a wave of dread.

Angela is one of the first people to find me as everyone makes their way down to the front drive of the palace. Trying to gauge her body language, I ask, "How was your evening?"

"The food was delicious. Some of the best sushi I've ever had." She manages a smile, but it doesn't reach her eyes. Her posture is stiff and she's glancing around nervously.

The muscles in my stomach tense. Has Art told her? Does she have a crush on him? Have I ruined their working relationship? What about their personal one?

"And the company?"

"It was awkward," she answers slowly.

I wince. "I'm so sorry . . ." I start.

"Ma'am, there's nothing that could've possibly been done."

"Yes, there is," I sputter. "It's all my fault."

"Ma'am, I knew going into tonight that the security lounge was going to be a boys' club," she says, lowering her voice. "The main office warned me I was going to very likely be the only female protection officer here. And they were right. I was mentally prepared to be ignored. Believe me, it's something I've had to come to terms with since my military days. That's why I brought my Kindle."

I freeze. That was not what I was expecting. Poor Angela. I can't believe it. I mean, I know in many places of the world, it's unusual to have a female bodyguard, but hearing it and seeing it are two different things. "You spent the entire three hours reading?"

"Not all of it, but most."

The three temporary members of my extended detail stumble down the two front steps. Their arms are linked as they sing loudly and out of tune. I recognize it as a popular pub tune. Art trails them. His eyes are narrowed into thin slits, his lips pressed firmly together.

My throat is dry. Is he angry with me? Or the three drunkards? I feel like I'm staring at Godzilla emerging from the sea and walking directly toward us. Every instinct in my body is telling me to flee, but I can't move my feet or find any words.

"Ange, you escort Princess Alice back to the hotel. I'll see to these blokes." His tone leaves no room for negotiation.

Angela flashes him a thumbs-up and opens the door for me. We both climb in and drive away.

"I don't think I've ever seen him so angry," I whisper.

"You'll find out soon enough, but Jerry, Paul, and Brock got into a drinking game with some of their Japanese counterparts. Art tried hard to put a stop to it, but they chose to ignore him. I told him to just let them make fools of themselves and let HQ deal with them, but he's too much of a gentleman to do so."

She shakes her head. "When we're on duty, it's strictly against regulations to drink any alcohol. It wouldn't surprise me if their bums are on a plane back to London first thing in the morning. There's a zero-tolerance policy for misbehavior like that, especially when we're abroad on a diplomatic mission." Angela rubs her temples. "There's going to be so much paperwork to fill out. It'll be another long night for us."

I shudder as guilt floods my system. A zero-tolerance policy. What would Angela say if she knew about the kiss? I gulp. Her hands would be tied, that's what would happen, and Art would probably be on the first plane back to London too. I've mucked everything up.

Angela and Art already have so much on their plates. Trouble from me is not what they need right now. What can I do to help them out? *Think, Ali. Think.* Ugh. Nothing is coming to mind. My brain is fried. I'm so exhausted, and I bet they are too.

That's when it hits me. As much as I want to stick to the planned schedule and had my heart set on seeing Kyoto's architecture, if I cancel tomorrow's engagements, they can have a few more hours of sleep. It stings, but I know it's the right call. Tomorrow can be a "take it easy" day. If Papa were in my shoes, I bet he'd agree with me. He's the one who taught me that a good leader listens to his troops. Being healthy is more important than anything else.

THE WALLS CONNECTING MY SUITE TO ANGELA AND Art's are thin. I hear practically everything they're saying to one another and to the London office. Art's voice is as sharp as a knife. I can sense the anger radiating out from him.

I try playing music, a fan app, and using my supposedly soundproof headphones, but nothing works. I may be exhausted, but my mind is whirling with too many thoughts for sleep to come to me. I desperately need to speak to Art. Alone. But at the rate things are going, that may not happen until we're back in London.

Around three in the morning, I give up completely and decide I'm going to call down to room service and order some midnight—or rather three a.m.—snacks.

Slipping my bathrobe over pajamas—a baggy T-shirt and a pair of shorts that fall to my knees—I tap my knuckles lightly against the connecting door to the adjoining two-bedroom suite. It's yanked open a moment later by Art. He's in a white T-shirt that's stretched tightly across his chest and plaid pajama bottoms. Only he could make those pajama bottoms sexy. I fight to keep from gaping at him.

He places a finger to his lips and gently closes the door three-quarters of the way. Peeling a sock off his foot, he rolls it into a ball and places it on the ground to act as a doorstop.

We're in my room now. Alone. My heart has begun to beat wildly in my chest. He's so close to me. I stop myself from reaching out to touch him.

"Angela just fell asleep. I don't want to wake her."

"I thought I heard you guys both moving around. I didn't know she'd gone to sleep."

Art crosses his arms, the T-shirt straining against his bulging biceps and ripped forearms. My throat goes dry. It's the first time I've seen him in an outfit with short sleeves. There's a tattoo trailing up his arm. It's hard to tell what it is, but I think it's a phoenix. I instantly want to know more about it.

"That was me puttering around the bathroom. I dropped the charger for my toothbrush." His Adam's apple constricts in his throat. "What can I do for you?"

"I, er . . . was just going to see if either of you wanted a late-night snack." I slip a lock of loose hair behind my ear.

"Can't sleep?" He raises his eyebrow.

"No. I turned the telly on, and the commercials seem to be for snacks. I can't stand it anymore—they're making me hungry. I was going to see if I could get some matcha ice cream or something else sweet."

"I'm not in the mood for dessert, but I could go for some curry." He runs a hand through his hair. "We need to talk anyway. Let me just grab my glasses."

He wants to talk. Is that a good thing or a bad thing? His tone is calm. So maybe it's not as dire as I thought? "I'll order the food." My voice squeaks. "What type of curry do you want?"

"Yellow if they have it, with the pork tonkatsu? I'll take a side of edamame and water too."

"Hungry much?" I let out a nervous laugh.

He lingers in the doorway. A patch of pink colors his

cheeks. "I didn't get to enjoy my dinner. I was otherwise occupied. I'll be right back."

He disappears into his darkened room. I hurry over to the telephone and press the room-service button, ignoring the rapid beating of my heart as I place our order. As I hang up the receiver, Art reappears and takes a seat on the bed next to mine.

"It'll be about twenty minutes."

He nods, adjusting his glasses and glancing to the TV, where a giant robot is helping clean up a woman's living room. Neither of us talks for several minutes. I'm more awake than I was earlier. My body is humming with pent-up energy. Is he going to say anything?

Another ad plays, and it's still silent. "I didn't know you wore glasses," I squeak. They're basic black and oval-shaped with thick arms, but they suit him. He reminds me of Henry Cavill playing Clark Kent.

He turns his gaze from the telly to me. There they are again—those bright hazel orbs. All I want to do is stare. "Only at night. I wear contacts during the day."

I pull my knees to my chest and force myself to look anywhere else. "How could you stand to wear them *all* day today? Aren't your eyes burning?"

"You build up to it. I can wear them comfortably for about twelve hours. But tomorrow, I may have to settle for these. I forgot to pack a backup pair. My right contact ripped as I was taking it out."

"They're a good look on you."

"Thanks," he says quietly.

The telly program has begun again. Catchy pop music plays and an announcer with an overly enthusiastic voice comes on. Five new contests are introduced for the next round of the game show. "So I may have this wrong, but I think they have to navigate an obstacle course—"

"Alice," Art interrupts.

I pull my legs in tighter to my body and stare at the pristine white sheet, my chest tightening. "Yes?"

"What happened in the car tonight?"

There's a woodpecker drilling its beak into my ribs. All I hear is the constant, rapid thud, thud, thud. My breathing increases. I've already ruined our friendship. I doubt anything I say can salvage it. I might as well come clean with him. The truth is something he values.

I continue staring at the sheet as my cheeks burn lava-hot. "I kissed you," I whisper.

"Yes. I know you did," he says slowly, his expression unreadable.

"I'm so, so, so sorry. I know I was in the wrong and shouldn't have done it." I look away and begin drawing a few circles on the bed. "You've worked hard to get where you are and to be promoted to the rank of a royal protection officer. I'm aware of just how many hoops you've had to jump through. The security office only takes one out of every fifty people who apply. I never meant to put all that at risk."

"Alice . . ."

"I was foolish. I let my emotions get the better of me. I knew you were off-limits, and I've tried hard to repress how I feel about you. But nothing has worked. Even when I was on dates with other men, all I could think about was you."

"Alice . . ."

I lower my head even more. "Tonight, when you were right there, and you looked so handsome in your tux, I couldn't stand it any longer. It was like a feral animal was inside of me. I gave in to it and kissed you and—"

"Alice!" Art's voice is finally strong enough to get my attention. I hear the sound of the bedsprings moving. Footsteps approach and he settles himself next to me, his legs barely brushing against mine as the bed shifts. He takes a hand and slowly runs it up my arm to my face, causing me to quiver from his light touch. His big hand stops at my chin and tilts it up. Our gazes are locked.

"What you did *was* highly inappropriate. And yes, it broke all the rules. But the truth is . . . I wanted it." His admission comes out raw.

"What?" I sputter, freezing with shock.

"You're not the only one who's been fighting an internal war with their feelings. For the past few weeks, I've suffered in silence as I've watched you go out on dates with other men. It's been pure torture and made me moodier than normal. Sorry if I've been a grouch. It's just that all I've wanted to do is steal you away from the blokes you were with and take you out on a proper date with me."

So that's why he was so grumpy. He wanted me to be on a date with him! He was jealous! My pulse picks up. I look into his eyes, wide and full of desire. They remind me of a tiger who's been silently watching and stalking its prey from behind a carpet of grass. I swallow hard. He feels the same about me as I do about him.

"The hardest part about this job is that we're discouraged from developing any personal relationship with our charges. But ask anyone in the protection division and they'll tell you it's nearly impossible to follow *that* protocol. As I've spent time with you and gotten to know you, I've come to learn that you have such a beautiful, gentle spirit. You're the kind of woman I've always dreamed about finding, but unfortunately can never have because of the rules."

I can't believe what I'm hearing. "Forget the rules. Forget the job. Right now, I'm just Alice and you're Art. We're two people who have been starving to show one another exactly how they feel. So let's stop wasting time. Kiss me," I demand.

In an instant, Art cups my cheeks. "As you wish," he whispers, and presses his lips to mine, demanding access. I let out a content sigh at hearing Westley's famous line from *The Princess Bride.* I run my hands through his hair, sinking them into the back of his neck. He smells so good, like a mixture of a gingerbread latte and honey.

I'm filled with an adrenaline rush. My body is hot and alive. I kiss Art right back with greedy, primal need.

I move my hands down his neck to his back. Through the thin fabric of his T-shirt, I feel all the rock-hard muscles underneath, running my hands over the defined ridges. Art pulls me into him, so our chests are touching. Heat is radiating off his body too. If there were any ice around, we'd melt it before it came within a ten-kilometer radius of us.

When we finally surface for air, we're both breathing heavily. My lips are swollen, and my body is humming in delight. I've never *ever* kissed a man like that! And I don't know if anything will ever top it.

His eyes are locked on to mine. "You, my beautiful Alice, are full of surprises." He runs a hand down the side of my face and tilts my chin up. My body quivers. This time he places a softer, gentler kiss on my lips.

"You know how to make a girl feel special."

"Only you. You're the one I've been waiting for."

"I feel the same way about you."

For the third time tonight, we kiss.

OUR ROOM SERVICE ORDER ARRIVES AFTER EXACTLY eighteen minutes of waiting. We reluctantly break apart to eat. The telly has been turned down low. Art and I are sitting next to one another, cross-legged on the bed. He's enjoying his curry, while I tuck in to my matcha ice cream. "What were you thinking after I ran away from you?" I ask.

"It took me a full sixty seconds to make sense of what had

just happened. I've thought about kissing you every time we've been together, but never thought it would actually happen." He tickles my foot with his bare one. "By the time I was out of the car and had tracked you down, you were busy chatting with the imperial family. I knew you'd be out of reach until after the dinner."

"I thought about you throughout the entire dinner," I admit. "I was terrified I'd ruined our relationship and put your job at risk."

"I'm so sorry you had to go through that. If we'd been able to find a moment alone, I might've stolen another kiss from you." He rewards me with a cheeky grin. "In that moment, you had me on cloud nine and ready to admit my feelings to you. But in hindsight, it was for the best I didn't get carried away because we both know how the rest of the evening turned out." He takes a heaping bite of his curry and chews slowly. "The difficult part is going to be figuring where we go from here."

I sit taller. "You mean you'd be willing to break the rules?"

"Yes, because you're worth it."

My heart races with joy.

"I meant it when I said you were the type of woman I've been waiting for. I know the rules and I'm aware of the consequences. I don't care two bits about them. I'm fully prepared to put it all on the line for a shot at seeing where this thing between us goes."

It's like I'm an overfilled treasure chest and can't help but smile wider than I ever have before. Art is choosing me. Even though there is no guarantee we'll work out. Me. Over everything he's worked for. "I don't know what to say, other than I've never been more honored and excited about anything in my life." I place my melting ice cream aside, scoot as close as I can to him, and rest my head on his shoulder.

He kisses the top of my head and places his curry down.

"If it's all right with you, I'd like to keep everything under wraps and as discreet as possible. We need more time to talk and figure out where we go from here."

"I agree."

He wraps an arm around my body and hugs me to his chest. "We'll have to be mindful of our interactions around others and in public. But when we're alone, we can be more open with one another."

"What about while we're here in Japan? Since I canceled all the events tomorrow, do you think you and I could spend the day exploring Tokyo alone? Maybe Angela could be given the day off. She seemed to think the three drunkards will be sent on the first flight back to London this morning."

"We'll have to play it by ear. I don't know if Ange would be comfortable with us out alone. But if she is, then yes." He sighs deeply. "As far as *those* three are concerned, yes, they'll be on the eight a.m. flight out of Narita International Airport." He winces as he glances at the clock, noticing it's near four. "I should probably make sure they're up, packed, and in a taxi."

"You're nicer than me. I would let them suffer the consequences if they missed the flight."

"I'd love to see that too, except they'd be our problem until they're on that plane." He reluctantly releases me, stands, and stretches. "Try and get some sleep. I'll check on you again if you're not up by noon."

I wave him off. "I'll probably be up by nine."

He collects our plates and utensils and wheels the room-service table out into the hallway. "Thanks for dinner, break-fast, or whatever you want to call it."

"You're welcome. Can I at least have a goodbye kiss?"

He chuckles under his breath. "As you wish."

As his lips brush against mine, I can't help but think he's saved the best for last.

Nineteen

I remember crawling under the sheets and reliving each kiss with Art, but I have no recollection of falling asleep. The next time I wake, it's eight in the morning. Despite only getting about three and a half hours of shut-eye, my body feels refreshed and raring to go. Knowing I won't be able to sleep again, I hop in the shower, and quickly dress in the only casual outfit I brought with me, my jeans and a blue chiffon blouse.

Pulling back the curtains, I look down on the high-end Tokyo shopping district of Ginza. Many of the shops aren't yet open, but there are plenty of people out and about. I see a few people on bicycles. There're men in suits carrying brief-cases and students in the traditional sailor uniform school-aged children wear through high school. I'm stuck by how much Tokyo is both alike and different from London.

A light knock sounds on the connecting door.

"Come in," I whisper.

Art carefully slips through the door and keeps it from making too much noise. His sock is still there. When I get a full look at him, my breath hitches. It's the first and only time

"

he's chosen not to dress in a suit. If you don't count the riding clothing, that is.

Art is dressed in worn dark-wash jeans that conform to his massive hockey-player-sized legs and shapely bum. He's paired it with a faded Beatles T-shirt that hugs his chest. The phoenix tattoo is fully visible, and peeking out from under his shirt-sleeve is another tattoo that I must've missed last night. It looks like a whisk and a chef's hat. For his love of baking perhaps?

"Good morning, Alice."

He joins me by the window and wraps his arms around me. I smell the same gingerbread-and-honey scent as earlier. "Good morning to you too." I rest against his strong chest.

"I heard you get up about a half hour ago and wanted to give you some time to get ready."

"Are the three troublemakers sorted out?"

"Indeed, they are."

"Good." I tug slightly on his arm and look up at him. "Were you able to get some rest too?"

"A little, but what I could really use is some breakfast. Do you fancy going out this morning and doing some sightseeing?"

I inhale sharply. That's one of the best offers I've ever received. Time alone with Art *and* the opportunity to finally see some of Japan's architecture. "Do you mean it? Just the two of us?"

"I do. I spoke to Angela. She was more than happy to be able to have a lie-in and agreed to take the morning off, but she made me promise we'd switch this afternoon. We agreed that the security risk would be low enough to merit one protection officer."

I let out a happy squeal, but Art places a finger on my lips, then points to the door. "Shh. Don't wake her. We can't let on that everything's changed."

I blush and giggle. "Sorry."

He chuckles. "Come on, Princess. Let's get our shoes and we can head out." He releases me.

"It's Alice. And are you going to be able to go like that?"

"Like what?" He glances down at his clothing.

"So casually? Without your, um . . . tools of the trade?"

"Our mission today is to blend in like tourists. I think this is the perfect disguise, don't you?" He winks. "Don't worry your gorgeous head over my 'tools of the trade,' as you're calling them. They'll be hidden on my body. Is five minutes enough time?"

"Perfect."

The moment he disappears into his suite, I do a happy dance that would make Amanda proud. This is my first date with Art! Okay, maybe it's not really a date, but it's the next best thing. I'll take it.

Running to the bathroom, I toss my hair into a messy bun, brush my teeth one more time, and layer on my signature Yves Saint Laurent pink-pearl lipstick. Mum has pounded it into my brain that it's the one cosmetic that should always be worn on a daily basis. Smacking my lips together, I give myself a once-over. I look and feel like a million pounds. For one magical day, I'll finally be able to spend some time with the man I'm falling for.

~

"So what are you in the mood for this morning besides coffee? What do you usually eat for breakfast?" I ask.

We walk side by side down one of the side streets a few blocks from the hotel. I trust that Art knows where we're going, because if he's relying on me, we'll end up walking straight until we hit a dead end. I may be good at problem-solving, but I have no sense of direction. None of the people we pass stare at us. There are no whispers behind our backs. I'm in the Japanese bubble. I'm free.

"Coffee, fruit, and protein. Think eggs, avocado toast, cottage-cheese pancakes, things like that. It depends on what ingredients I have around my pantry and how much time I've allowed myself to whip up a dish. I try to work out right after I've gotten up."

"Cottage-cheese pancakes?" I wrinkle my nose. "Those sound horrid. The texture alone is . . . bleh."

"Speak for yourself. *My* pancakes are delicious." He playfully elbows my shoulder. "I'll make you a batch, then you can decide for yourself what you *really* think of them."

My heart jolts at the possibility of us being together as a couple. I picture Art standing in the kitchen of my renovated flat, happily baking to his heart's content with the top-of-the-line appliances he's picked out. He'll be in jeans and a T-shirt and don a frilly pink apron over his clothing to keep it clean. He'll be my teacher and help me survive on more than the standard uni diet of microwave meals and takeaway.

"Deal." Even if this is a daydream, at least I can pretend it's real.

"What do you like to have?"

"Either cereal or yogurt, granola, and berries. It's like a dessert, but it counts for breakfast."

"Is dessert what you think about most of the time?"

"Uh-huh. It's the first thing I look at on a menu."

"Then it's a good thing I enjoy baking. With me around, you'll have an endless supply of desserts."

I lace my fingers through his and squeeze. "My hero."

"I think we make a left at the next street." He fiddles with his glasses and presses them higher up on his nose. "Yeah, it's a left."

"Can you read what the street signs say?"

"Sometimes. I tried to learn a few things for the trip, but sadly not many of the lessons stuck."

When we turn the corner, the sleek, high-end shops give way to a lovely green space filled with towering leafy green trees, a Zen rock garden, and a koi pond. It's too late in the year for the cherry blossoms to still be in bloom, but if we'd been here a few months earlier, I wager it would've been a sight to behold. A few tourists occupy benches as they munch on their own breakfasts, but otherwise, the park is deserted. We pause as I take my mobile out and snap a dozen or more photos.

"We're nearly there; it's just on the other side of the courtyard," Art says.

"This isn't a park?" I sputter.

"No, it's all part of this office building." He laughs.

"Entryways like these should be mandatory in London," I muse, taking notes of how the structures around us seamlessly use elements of Japan's ancient past and greenery to give the illusion that this building has been here forever.

"I agree with you. Except I don't know if people would be willing to sacrifice the space or the money for it."

"You're right. Space is at a premium in London. But a girl can dream."

A set of glass doors opens with a whoosh. The air is nice and cool. I hadn't realized until just now how humid it is outside.

"Here we are." Art pulls open a door to a cafe with a pink-and-white striped awning. "Ladies first."

Inside, it's a whimsical world resembling a fairy garden. Artificial trees as tall as me are covered in fake moss and bright purple wisteria. Some of the trunks contain holes large enough for an owl to fit into, while others contain medium-sized wooden houses with red-and-white mushroom roofs and toadstool chimneys. All the trees are interconnected by wooden bridges. As I take a closer look at one of the black holes, I'm greeted by a pair of eerie glowing yellow eyes.

"Eek." I jump back, bumping into Art's chest. "What is this place?"

He lets out a deep roaring laugh. "Welcome to one of Tokyo's infamous cat cafes."

As soon as the words leave his mouth, I notice that the ground contains about a dozen different felines who are lined up in a row, eating their morning meal. There are blacks, grays, whites, calicos, orange and whites, tuxedos, and striped tabbies.

"I hope you don't mind cats. I know you're a dog person, but the puppy, owl, and hedgehog cafes didn't open this early. This one was the closest and had the best reviews. All their animals are rescues that are up for adoption."

I rise up onto my toes and peck him on the cheek. "This is brilliant. I'm not just a dog person. I'm an animal person."

"Phew." He wipes his forehead with the back of his hand. "I booked us in for a thirty-minute visit. We can either play with the cats first or eat first."

"Let's eat first, then we can play."

A few minutes later, a hostess seats us at an emerald-green table in the back area of the café, tucked away from the cats. The lighting is much dimmer. The walls are painted hues of dark-green to resemble a forest. Each table contains a glass lantern, lit by a tealight candle. We're left alone with a laminated menu, thankfully written in both English and Japanese.

Art orders a stack of blueberry pancakes and a side of eggs. No surprise. I decide to be more adventurous and have a go with the matcha-flavored ones with some extra whipped cream and strawberries on top. We order a pot of Earl Grey to split.

"Have I surprised you?" He rests his elbows on the table.

"Yeah, you have. I never would've thought to visit a cat café. What made you think of it?"

"I was looking through a list of different things tourists come to Japan for, and animal cafés happened to be one of the top results. I'd had my heart set on taking you to an owl café, but this is the next best option."

"Well, you chose well, I'm beyond excited. I've always wanted to adopt a cat, but I've been too nervous to do it."

"Because of Lillian?" he asks.

"That's part of it." I nod.

"And the other reason?"

"I never grew up with cats. It's always been dogs and horses. I'm nervous about caring for one. If I'm adopting one, I want to make sure I do right by them, so they have a proper forever home."

"I love how thorough you are. You always do your research." His lips curve up. "Having said that, I'm happy to tell you that caring for a cat isn't as much work as a dog. They're independent creatures. As long as you feed them, clean out their litter box, and give them plenty of vertical room and scratching posts, you'll do just fine."

"I thought you only owned fish growing up."

"I did. But I have two cats. Would you like to see their pictures?"

"Yes, please."

Our order arrives as I flip through an album of about five hundred photos on Art's mobile. I'll be the first to admit I never pictured the man as a cat daddy, but here's the photographic proof. Aside from a hundred selfies, he's also captured his two felines from just about every angle imaginable—sleeping, bathing, holding on to a toy with their paws, sitting with their paws tucked in, lying stretched out, exposing their belly. The list goes on and on.

"The orange-and-white striped one is named Peppermint, and the black-and-white one is called Cinnamon."

"You named them after baking spices?"

"Their favorite place to hang out with me when I'm home is in the kitchen. The names actually chose the cats." He takes a sip of his tea.

"Oh, what's the story behind that?"

He places his cup down and shrugs. "Peppermint broke a bottle of peppermint extract the day I got him, and Cinnamon managed to knock a jar of the spice off the counter when I was cooking and tracked it all over the flat."

I giggle. "I love that you chose to turn their accidents into their names." I pour myself a cup of tea and take a bite of my pancake.

"How did you decide on Lillian's name?"

"It's somewhat similar to how your cats got their names. Lilies are my favorite flowers. When Lillian was a puppy, she used to love running through the palace gardens and digging up the flower beds. The flowers she destroyed the most . . ."

"Were the lilies?" he guesses.

"Bingo." I watch in amusement as he expertly slices his pancakes into equal square-sized pieces. "Who watches your cats when you're away or working?"

"Most of the time, they're fine being left to their own devices, entertaining one another. For this trip, though, I asked one of my neighbors to watch them," he says. "What about Lillian? I remember you mentioning that the staff member who normally watches her is on holiday."

"I left her with my brother's dog. She was one of Lillian's littermates."

"That's convenient." I pour a generous amount of syrup onto my pancakes. A habit I picked up from spending time with Clara and Amanda. Americans love their syrup, and as I've learned, so do I.

"Ugh, isn't that a bit much?" Art frowns. "They're already sweet, aren't they?"

"Yup." I make a point to soak a piece of my food into the

thick maple liquid and pop it into my mouth. It's delicious, but a tad too sweet even for my liking. I can't lose face to Art though. I chew and swallow it with a straight face. "Mmm." He shakes his head, choosing not to use any syrup on his, I note. "What made you decide to adopt cats over the dog you've always wanted?"

"I think you know by now that I have a problem with social anxiety." He glances at me through his long lashes. "When I joined the police force, I knew that I needed to find a way to try and work through it. I needed to be able to deal appropriately with my coworkers and the large number of tourists. My mum suggested that getting a dog or cat might help me relax. And she was right. I needed an animal that would work with the tiny space of my flat and my awkward work hours. The internet told me cats were the solution, so cats it was."

"You can't disagree with the power of the internet."

We enjoy swapping more funny stories about what our pets have done before heading over to the cat area.

"You're tense. It's all over your body. Are you scared of cats?" Art asks.

"No," I answer quickly. "I just don't want to mess up with them. They have sharp claws."

"Come here," he says softly. "I'll show you how it's done." He takes hold of my hand and leads me to the center of the room, next to the cat tree. Together, we kneel down on the carpeted floor, watch, and wait.

The cats' bowls have been cleared away. The felines have dispersed themselves throughout the space. Some are bathing, while others are sleeping or watching us with interest. Two full minutes pass, then a tortoiseshell emerges from a darkened hole at the bottom of the tree.

"Hold out your hand. She wants to sniff you," Art whispers. "The key is to act like you would with a horse that you're introducing yourself to. Use slow and deliberate movements, keep your fingers tucked in, and watch its tail."

"Its tail?"

"Yeah, a lot of cats use their tails to talk. For instance, if it's upright, like a question mark, they're happy. If it's whipping quickly side to side, that means they're agitated."

That makes a lot of sense, yet it still seems foreign to me. Dogs are much easier to understand—you can read their faces. Cats, on the other hand, only seem to have one expression.

Art extends my hand toward the cat. It crouches and sniffs it. I watch as its thin tail goes from slowly swishing side to side to upright. A moment later, it begins to purr, and butts its head against my hand.

"That's a good girl." Art beams and scratches under its chin.

"How can you tell it's a girl?"

"Ninety-five percent of all calicos and tortoiseshells are female. Just like eighty percent of orange ones are male. Something to do with the genetics of coat colors." He shrugs. "Limit your petting to the forehead area, back of the ears, or its cheeks. Only pet her body if she does it for you by nudging your hand. She'll let you know what she wants."

"I should call you the cat whisperer."

Soon, more felines surround us, all demanding attention. Art turns out to be much more popular than me. They rub their heads against his hands, elbows, legs, and one even jumps onto his back.

"They must smell Cinnamon and Peppermint on my clothing. They love using my suitcase as a bed sometimes."

He's so relaxed and at ease, smiling as he spends time giving each cat a proper pet. Animals are the best judges of character. It's not lost on me that they see him as a special man. Just as I do. I want nothing more than to spend more time in his arms, kissing.

In the back of my mind, I'm terrified at the thought that when we get home, Art could be taken from me now that we've finally admitted we like one another. I'm more determined than ever to find a way for us to be together. Trying to find another guy to replace him was foolish. Nobody can measure up to him.

For now, however, we'll make the most of all the time we can spend together. Before we're back to reality in a few days' time.

Twenty

The remainder of the morning passes in a blur. When we finish at the cat café, then have a wander around the city, and end up in the area known as Asakusa.

"When I was browsing some of the travel blogs, this area stood out to me. I thought you'd enjoy the architecture," Art says.

Butterflies flutter in my stomach. He has planned this day around experiences that *I* might enjoy. Considering this is a last-minute kind of date, he's certainly put a lot of thought into it.

We start by exploring the famed Sensō-ji temple and the shrines attached to it. It happens to be the oldest in Tokyo. I snap a hundred different photos from various angles and tug poor Art a million different directions.

"Oh, look at the gate . . .and those carvings . . .

" . . . and the steps . . .

" . . . I wonder what the pitch of the roof is and what materials they've used on it . . .

" . . . the paint on those statues appears brand-new. I wish I could ask the type of protective coating they've used . . .

". . . look at the painting on the shutters of the shops! I have to capture that too!"

I turn, and yet again, I've let my feet carry me a little too far from Art. The crowds are dense, and it's like being squeezed into a sardine can in some areas of the temple. There isn't enough space for all the people here. We're literally standing elbow to elbow. Although there isn't any pushing or shoving. Everyone here is extremely polite about it.

"Alice, there you are." Art breathes a sigh of relief. His forehead is creased. "I know you're excited, but please don't wander off without me." He lowers his voice. "The chances of you being recognized and stopped for a photo are high. Your safety is my number-one priority."

My cheeks burn. "I'm sorry." As much as I want this to be a *real* date, Art is really here to do his job.

"I know you are." He rubs the back of his neck. "It's brilliant to see you in your element. We just need to make sure we stay together." His eyes skim the crowds.

"Um, I think I'm ready to move on and find a less popular area. Maybe we can go find some ice cream?" I fan myself. "The humidity has definitely picked up."

My words have the intended effect. He relaxes. "The street food around here is supposed to be excellent. I'm sure there's at least one shop that sells ice cream."

We continue our stroll away from the temple, and the dense crowds.

"My mobile says Nakamise-dori is the name of the street we're after." Art studies the walking map of Tokyo he's downloaded.

When we find it, however, all thoughts of ice cream and food lose their appeal. Although it smells delightful, like a summer barbecue, the narrow street is so jammed with people, it appears that nobody is moving. They're shuffling like zombies. We look at one another and silently agree that no matter how good the food is, it's not worth joining the school of human fish.

We make a U-turn and walk past some businesses that are closed. "At least the shops have attractive shutters," I offer. They contain intricate designs that resemble some of the woodblock prints from the Edo period that one might find in a museum.

"Always looking on the bright side."

I choose not to respond, and instead hum the tune with the same name from the classic British film *Monty Python and the Holy Grail*.

"Are you a John Cleese fan?" Art asks, naming the main actor from the series.

"My father's the fan in the family. One of his favorite shows is *Fawlty Towers*. If I watch telly or a film, it's more likely to be something on home renovations or a rom-com. What about you? Do you spend most of your time watching baking shows?"

"Not especially. I tend to stream shows like *Peaky Blinders, The Office*, the original *Top Gear*, and *Emily in Paris.*"

"Those are all over the place." I snort. A period drama about gangsters. A comedy about working in an office. And a show about expensive cars. "I have to ask, why *Emily in Paris*?"

"For the food that's featured on the show. French pastries are my favorite. Although the dough can be a nightmare to make," he admits. "Aside from that, I like having options. Don't you have days where sometimes you're just in the mood for something different?"

"I do. Usually that means I'm texting Amanda for recommendations. She and my brother have opened my eyes to classic American sitcoms from the 1950s. They're quite good."

"There you go." Art stops and points to a large display of a vanilla ice cream cone. There's a short queue about five people deep. "What do you think? Should we try here?"

"Yes."

While we're waiting our turn, I try my best to study the menu and guess what certain flavors might be based on the photo. They're completely in Japanese.

"What are you having?" Art asks right before we're up to the window.

"I'll try whatever the pink flavor is."

"Konichiha." The cashier smiles and bows.

"Er, this one and that one." Art points to the menu. "Onegai. Please."

The woman cocks her head to the side. "English?"

"Hai. Yes."

"Do you have a ticket?"

Art and I exchange confused glances.

"No?" he says.

"Sou desu." The cashier sticks her head out the window and points to a machine next to the ice cream cone. "You need to buy a ticket. Then come exchange it for your food."

Art's neck and ears color a light shade of pink. "Understood. We'll be right back."

"Okay." The cashier grins and bows again.

"This is a new experience," I muse. "Who knew you needed to buy a ticket to get your food?"

We wander over to the machine and spend a few minutes attempting to use our translating app to decipher the writing, then a woman in a Tokyo Disney T-shirt comes, takes pity on us, and offers to help. That's when we learn it's common for most quick-service locations to use ticket machines. The shops themselves don't typically have any cash on hand. There's always something new to learn.

"How's the matcha tiramisu crepe cone?" I ask Art after we get our treats.

"Brilliant. I'm trying to figure out what they put in this so I can re-create it when we get home. I taste the matcha powder. Marzipan. Lemon. And something else I can't quite put my finger on. What about your Sakura ice cream?"

"Refreshing. It tastes like flowers and cherries. Do you want a taste?"

"No thanks. Do you want some of this?"

"Nope. It's a little too much even for me."

We've found a bench under the shade of a cherry blossom tree. It's late summer and the blossoms have long since faded. But in spring, I can imagine this as being one of the most magical places to view the cherry blossoms. Especially with the Sumida River directly across from us.

"It's so peaceful here. I kind of wish I had my sketchbook. I'd love to have a go at capturing some of the landscapes."

"I didn't know you like to draw," Art says.

"I'm not too good at it, but it's something that relaxes me. I picked it up in sixth form. I spent a lot of time alone. There are only a few people who know this about me, but I was bullied in school." He's shared a lot about himself with me, and now I feel like it's my turn to reciprocate and let him get to know the real me.

"I was always the shy tomboy, and for the most part, the girls in my year just left me alone—which I didn't mind. I had my horses and books to keep me company. But everything got turned upside down the summer I turned fifteen, when the newspapers started calling me the Ice Princess. That whole summer, the media plagued me. And when school started up again in the fall, it got worse. The girls used it as a way to make my life miserable. They'd call me names, act like I didn't exist, or gossip about me nonstop. It felt like I was a ghost—the few friends I had kept away in case they were targeted."

Art listens attentively.

"I was so lonely. My self-esteem and self-confidence were

shattered. When we graduated, I hoped the bullying would end, but unfortunately, that was only the beginning. First, some of my former classmates ended up selling embarrassing stories about me to the tabloids. Then, as if that weren't bad enough, I had my riding accident and disappeared from public view while I healed. It was like a ticking time bomb." I share about how difficult it was when the tabloids ran wild with stories about me until the press office finally broke the news about my injury.

Art reaches for my hand and draws a few circles over the top of it.

"By this point, I was mentally and emotionally on the verge of hitting a breaking point. I'm lucky my family and *real* friends were there to help me through it all. Without them, I don't know what I would've done." I look out at some of the ships passing by slowly in the distance. "It's been more than a year. Talking to a therapist, taking a gap year, and traveling have helped me recenter myself. I'm only now beginning to feel like the old me."

"I'm so sorry that you ever had to go through being bullied and dealing with the media. Nobody deserves any of that crap. I wish I'd been here sooner to help and support you through all of it." His voice comes out raspy and raw. "I have so much respect for you. I don't know any other person, myself included, who would've been able to put on a brave face and continue making public appearances again after an experience like that. I can only imagine how much effort it's taken for you to come on this trip." Art collects our rubbish and places it off to the side. "Come here." He pats the bench.

I scoot in closer to him. He opens his arms and wraps me in them as I rest my head on his shoulder. I listen to his beating heart. It's steady and strong, like a metronome.

"Coming here was difficult for me, but I'm glad I had the strength to do it."

"I'm so proud of you, Ali. But I want you to remember that you always have a choice. If public engagements make you miserable, don't be afraid to tell your parents no. You don't owe anyone anything. You *deserve* only happiness."

I want to melt into his arms and sit with him stroking my forearm forever. There are so few people who've ever asked me what I want. Decisions about my life have always been made on my behalf or in my best interest. To hear him throw all that to the wayside makes me even more eager to grow whatever is starting between us. He cares about me as a person. Not as the princess.

"When I was traveling, I felt so alive and happy just being Alice. Nobody paid me any attention. I was able to have a slice of being normal." I sigh. "The thing is, though, even if I wanted to, I don't know if I'll ever be able to live a quiet life. I'm planning to go into structural engineering, but I also can't sit idle if there are people out there who I can help." I burrow tighter into Art's warm body, taking in the scent of his light lemony cologne.

"I've been kicking around a football inside my head since my date with Alfie. There are so many people affected by bullying. Maybe they feel powerless, they're too afraid to speak up, or they lack the resources to do so. They need an advocate like me to become their voice. If I can help even one person, it's a huge win, and it'll make being in the public eye worth it."

As I speak my thoughts aloud, it's clearer than it's ever been that I *want* to find a way to strike a balance between my duties as a royal and as an engineer. This cause is close to my heart. Unlike other charities I've supported, putting an end to bullying drives me. I have so many ideas for future programs.

Art plants a soft kiss atop my head. "Listen to your heart. It'll guide you to the path you need to be on."

"You're not going to tell me to listen to my head?"

"No, because if I do, I'd be lying to you. And that's not

something I do. My own brain is telling me not to get involved with you, but my heart is shouting from the mountaintops to overrule it. I'm choosing to listen to my heart."

We're starting a very dangerous game. Art knows what we're doing has crossed the line. I hope he really is prepared for the consequences. He has much more to lose than me. I'm going to do everything in my power to ensure that we keep this as quiet as possible. That way if it doesn't work out, Art won't suffer because of me.

"We're a lot more alike than you think. I was painfully shy growing up. It's tied to my social anxiety. I rarely spoke to anyone outside my family. The doctors diagnosed me with selective mutism." He continues to stroke my arm. "I understand exactly what it's like to be ostracized and alone. That was me. I spent more time in the library with books because I couldn't handle being around people."

"How did you learn to overcome it?"

"I had a therapist who taught my parents to use a technique called exposure therapy."

"That sounds like you were made to go out and talk to people to try and get over your fear."

"That's *exactly* what it is. It's like having a child who's afraid there are monsters under their bed. They can look for the monsters, but they won't ever find anything there. It's all in their head. That's how it is with me. My brain is wired to think things are a lot worse or scarier than they are."

Goosebumps appear on my arm. That sounds like me and public speaking. "It's never something you truly get over, is it?"

"No." Art swallows hard. "It's a daily struggle. The ironic thing is that it makes me pretty good at my job. I have a knack for reading body language and being aware of what's going on around me."

"You're amazing." I stare in wonder at the man I've been lucky enough to spend the day with.

We sit in one another's embrace for a while, watching people walk, jog, and cycle past us. I never thought I'd be one to share so much of myself with anyone. Art is different, however. He's a friend, but something deep inside of me tells me he's also the man I've been waiting for. It's almost like how a salmon or a sea turtle knows exactly where it was born and where it needs to go to lay eggs. I've never had such a strong gut reaction to another human. I just know that with him, I'll always be safe. In time, I can only hope this turns into something more. Like love.

"Ah blast, it's nearly two. Angela is going to ring me before I know it." He checks his watch and unravels himself from me. We both stand and stretch. "There was one more thing I'd hoped to do with you, but if we go now, we might not have much time there."

"Oh, what is it?"

His lips twitch. "Do I have it right that you've never been to a proper amusement park?"

"No, I haven't."

"A carnival?"

"No." I shake my head.

"Well, then, this needs to be sorted out. I'm taking you to Hanayashiki. It's Japan's oldest amusement park. It may not be Disneyland, but it has some rides, games, and will give you a taste of what it's like. If you enjoy it, next time, we'll do the real thing."

I chew on my lip. I want to do this, but I'm worried about Art. "Won't there be an awful lot of people there?"

"Probably, but today's adventure can be our little secret. Besides, I'll be there to protect you if anything happens."

I rise up onto my toes and wrap my arms around his neck.

"Thank you." My lips brush against his, melting into his mouth as I take in the moment. Art's kisses are meant to be enjoyed and savored.

Twenty-One

I arrive home Sunday evening and promptly fall asleep. By Tuesday, I'm still a zombie, but a functional one. I sleep much later than normal and take a lazy day, unpacking and catching up on emails and returning calls. By Wednesday, I'm back to normal.

Over the past few days, Art has constantly been on my mind, but I've purposefully gone out of my way to avoid him. We had such a magical time in Japan. However, now that we're back, I know we can't avoid talking about what our future is going to look like much longer.

I send a text to Jenna, hoping she'll be able to inspire some confidence in me. As it stands, I'm being a giant chicken.

ALICE

I did it.

JENNA

You did what? You're being too cryptic. A girl needs more information to go on.

ALICE

I told him.

JENNA

Him who?

ALICE

Art.

JENNA

Oh. Oh! What happened?!

ALICE

I kissed him, ran away, then we talked. He
likes me too.

JENNA

I'm going to need a *much* longer
explanation, in the form of lunch or a video
chat. I won't press you since I know you
have a lot going on.

ALICE

Grinning emoji It's a deal. We'll do lunch
soon.

JENNA

Are you two officially dating now?

ALICE

Not exactly . . .

JENNA

You haven't figured out how to get around
the no-dating rule?

ALICE

Nodding emoji

JENNA

What does Arthur think you should do?

ALICE

I don't know. I've been avoiding him.

JENNA

You won't get any sympathy from me. If you want this to work, you need to fight for him. You'll figure it out. You're the brightest person I know. Love always finds a way.

ALICE

You're right. I have to do this.

JENNA

Yes, you do. I'm here if you need more urging, but the longer you stall, the harder it's going to be. Get on with it.

Swallowing my fears, I close out my message from Jenna and open a new one to text Art. I begin typing, but then I realize whatever I send him will likely go to his work mobile. I'll have to be extra careful with how I word things.

ALICE

Cheers, Art, are you on duty right now? Or is it Angela?

ART

You're stuck with me.

ALICE

Brilliant. I'd like to request the car and stop by the flat this morning. It's been about four weeks.

ART

What time would you like to go out?

ALICE

Is thirty minutes enough time for you?

ART

I'm ready anytime you'd like.

ALICE

In that case, how about now?

ART

I'll meet you out front.

Art's eyes light up as he greets me a few minutes later. He's in a black suit, crisp white dress shirt, and burgundy tie today. "Good morning, ma'am."

"Good morning, Art," I mumble.

I get in the car and secure my seat belt just as he settles himself into the driver's seat. "Off to Queen's Park?"

"That's our eventual destination, but I doubt much will have changed from the last progress report I read. The workers are continuing to find more problems, like a foundation issue. Which is why there were so many cracks between the floors. The latest move-in date was mid-to-late January." I rub the back of my neck. "What I was really hoping for was a private place we could talk first."

He nods in understanding and glances back at me through the rearview mirror. "I can take the scenic route to the flat, or perhaps we could stop by the palace stables and go for a ride? I'm sure Sefton and Athena would be thrilled to see you."

"You always come up with the best ideas." Nothing sounds more perfect than seeing my horses and having a riding date with Art. Yes, I'm counting this as a date.

∼

THE CLIP-CLOPS OF SEFTON'S AND ATHENA'S HOOVES fill the air as Art and I take a slow ride in silence in an area of the Buckingham Palace gardens that's closed to the public. At

Papa's request, it's also an area that's left to grow out like a meadow one might find in the country.

The top of the yellowing grass on either side of the pathway is long and comes up to the horses' knees. In spring, the flowers are out in full bloom, but since we're into the heart of summer, they've reached their peak, and the plants are beginning to die back.

I can still make out traces of pink knapweed, white honeysuckle, purple foxglove, thrift, and the white-flowered grass of Parnassus. I hear the buzzing of honeybees and spot a few butterflies fluttering just above the grass.

Art breaks the silence first. "Alice, are you cross with me?" he murmurs.

"No." I frown. "Whatever gave you that impression?"

"You've been avoiding me. I haven't heard from you for three days. I thought I'd done something to upset you."

"It isn't you, Art, it's me." I let out a frustrated breath. "I've been too scared to talk to you."

"If you've changed your mind about me, I understand." His tone is flat. "We can go back to just being friends and working together in a professional capacity."

"No. That's the last thing I want." I lean my head back and stare at the sky. I'm mucking this up big time. All the words that have come out of my mouth sound as if I'm about to break up with him. No wonder he's glum. "I like you and I want to see where our relationship goes; it's just that everything around us is about to change, and I'm scared of the unknown."

"Change is always scary," he says. "But I don't think it'll alter things between us all that much. At least not right away."

"What about the number-one rule? Bodyguards aren't supposed to be romantically involved with anyone they're protecting." I slow Athena so we're in step with Sefton and Art.

"Okay, you have me there." He takes a moment before he responds. "Hypothetically speaking, as long as you don't mind my being on the clock and the limited locations we can go to when we have our dates, I don't see it as being a conflict of interest until we're officially boyfriend and girlfriend. We just need to be discreet."

"But what about after that? We need a long-term plan." I've created a monster. The stakes are astronomically high. He's all in, risking his career and his future with the protection division. If that's not commitment, I don't know what is. I need to be just as sure about this as he is. I don't care about what happens to me. I'm willing to do whatever it takes for a shot with him.

If I look back, I developed a crush for him early on. He's been on my mind and in all my dreams. I've tried to get him out of my head, but that was a colossal failure. It only served to have me compare the other men I was dating to him. Then there was the kiss in the car. My heart told me to act on my feelings. And I did. It's been leading me to him all along. There's my answer. I'm choosing to listen to it.

"It's simple, really. If things work out, I'll quit or ask for a transfer. If they don't, we go back to being friends. Yes, it may be awkward, but I think we're both mature enough to be able to continue working together."

"And if we're caught?"

"Ali, try not to overthink it," he says softly. "If someone catches us, we deal with it, and find a way to keep seeing one another."

"But—"

He places a finger on my lip, silencing me. "We'll handle things as they come. All you need to know is that I'm all in." He rewards me with a rare Cheshire cat smile. Sefton neighs loudly in agreement. Art runs his right hand down the horse's neck. "That's a good boy," he says softly.

I fidget in my seat. I've gotten used to having him around. I can't imagine Art being reassigned or quitting and not being able to spend all day with him.

"Does your back hurt? We can stop and take a break if you need." He pulls on Sefton's reins and slows our pace.

"I'm fine, just thinking." My gaze travels to the side of the saddle. It's black, without any contrast stitching. My normal saddle is a dark tan. "Huh. This isn't the saddle I normally use."

"Maybe Danny ordered a new saddle for you," Art suggests.

"I doubt it. If there's a problem with my tack, I always try and have it repaired before I go out and buy a replacement."

Sefton and Athena continue in a steady walk until we reach the garden's pond. A trio of willow trees perched along the bank provides the perfect shade from the late morning sun. Art and I climb down and allow our mounts a drink. It's then that I take a moment to inspect the saddle up close.

I run my finger along the material. It's not made of leather, but rather some alternative type of mesh. There's also much more padding, especially toward the rear of the seat where my tailbone sits. No wonder I haven't felt any discomfort today.

"The Orthosaddle," I read aloud from a label I've found.

My breath hitches. I watch Art pretend not to pay attention as he digs an apple out of the saddlebag. A memory resurfaces from the last time we were out riding together. *Have you looked into having an orthopedic saddle made up for you? It's like a normal saddle, but the divot is supposed to help relieve some of the pressure from the injured areas.*

"It was you." I piece it together. "The saddle wasn't Danny's idea. It was yours."

He doesn't answer.

"Did you have this made up special for me?"

His shoulders hunch. "You weren't supposed to find out. I swore Danny to secrecy."

This man is full of surprises. My heart swells. "I want to kiss you right now. Except . . ." I glance around us nervously. "Papa and his horse have a habit of materializing out of thin air."

"Save it for the flat viewing." Art chuckles. "I can't imagine anything worse right now than your father catching us. He'd probably order me to the Tower of London right on the spot."

"Nah, he wouldn't do that. He'd probably give you a stern dressing down, but he'd at the very least give you a chance to explain yourself to him. He may be the king, but he's a reasonable man."

"I'll keep that in mind for the future."

I settle for squeezing his hand and staring longingly into his hazel eyes. In this lighting, the flecks of gold remind me of a thousand fireflies.

WHEN WE FINALLY MAKE IT TO THE FLAT, IT'S around two. The roof repairs have been completed, and the windows have been replaced with efficient triple-glazed models. Work is at a standstill, however, until the foundation is sorted out. I tour the empty ground and first floors, and on the way out, remind the project manager to let me know when we're ready to enter into the next phase.

"Arthur?" We're walking side by side from the flat back to the car.

"Uh-oh, you used my *full* name. What is it that you want from me?"

"Two things."

"And those would be?"

"Would you be willing to help me choose some appliances and plan out how the kitchen will look?"

"Of course, I'd be happy to." He chuckles. "What's the second item?"

I twirl a loose piece of hair around my finger. "Can we treat the rest of today as a date?"

"That depends on what you have in mind," he says.

"What if we did something like an escape-room challenge?"

He stops walking and stares at me. "Does that involve getting locked up in a prison?"

"Not exactly." I hide a laugh with my hand.

"Escape rooms can be held in an actual room or out in the open. From a few SearchTube videos I've watched, it looks like we'd be given a challenge by a game host and then have one to two hours to complete said challenge through a series of mini games."

"Okay, and what types of challenges are we talking about?"

"There are all sorts of different ones. For instance, we could be asked to find an antidote to stop an army of escaped radioactive spiders. Or maybe we'll become passengers stuck in an abandoned Tube station and challenged to figure out how to escape."

He strokes his chin. "It sounds like an activity that would be right up your alley. We'd have to use logic to solve the challenges."

I clap my hands together. "Then we can do it?"

"*If* we can book an experience so it's just us and we're not in a public setting, we can make it a date."

"Thank you." I squeal with delight.

We walk quickly to the car, jump inside, and not wasting a

single moment, share a tender kiss. The private times we have between us are now few and far between. We have to make the most of every opportunity.

Twenty-Two

To my frustration, we aren't able to have our escape-room date until Friday afternoon. Contrary to what I wanted, arranging the date around Art's schedule, finding a private tour guide, and booking the venue solely for our use required advance planning.

We enter a nondescript warehouse in the Greenwich area of London, not far from the famed observatory. The sign above the door reads "Locked in London." I laugh. What a perfect name for an escape room.

"I'm so excited! Aren't you?"

"Thrilled," Art says sarcastically.

I roll my eyes and ignore him. He didn't have to agree to this as a date. I like the idea of doing something outside of the box. It'll help make the occasion more memorable.

It takes a few moments for my eyes to adjust to the dim lighting of the lobby. "Do you feel like we've stepped into the film set of a low-budget American horror film? Because I do," I whisper.

"Yes, ma'am. Low budget indeed."

There's a series of dusty, spider-web-covered mailboxes behind a long desk. Flowers that have been placed in a take-away cup from a Norma's Cafe have long since shriveled and dried up. All that remains are their yellowing stems. An attendant dressed in an ill-fitting, stained bellhop uniform with boxy shoulder pads greets us. His face is covered in a thick layer of white makeup, contrasted with heavy black eye shadow under his eyes, giving him a zombie-like appearance.

"Welcome," he says in a drawn-out, bored tone. "Are you here to check in?"

"Yes," I confirm just as the lights flicker on and off.

The attendant blinks slowly. "Your name?"

"It'll be under the last name Wales," Art says, placing a hand on my shoulder.

"Ah yes, we've been expecting you." From under the desk, he retrieves a ring of oversized ancient brass keys. "Come, come with me." He limps away.

Off the lobby are a series of three doors. The attendant inserts the key into the middle one. It opens with an eerie creek. "Will you be requiring any assistance with your luggage?"

"No. We're fine," Art responds curtly.

"Very well."

He gestures for us to enter. It's pitch-black inside.

"Are you ready?" I ask Art.

"Yes. Let's get this over with."

We shuffle a few steps inside, and then the door slams shut behind us. I reach for Art's hand. A few hairs stand up on the back of my neck. We can't see a thing. It smells of old paper and flowers. A few moments pass, and all I can hear is the sound of my heart racing wildly and our heavy breathing.

"Should I pull out my mobile and use its torch?" he asks.

"No, let's wait a little longer." Another minute passes,

then another. "Escape rooms are about being resourceful, so maybe we're supposed to find a light switch?"

Tentatively, we take measured steps backward until we come in contact with the door. I brush my hand along the wall. It's uneven and bumpy.

"Anything?" he asks.

"Not yet." I chew my lip. "Ow." My hand hits the sharp corner of a piece of furniture.

"Ma'am. Alice. Are you all right?"

"Fine." I shake out my hand. "I just wasn't expecting to have something like a desk be right there." I let out a frustrated breath. "Go ahead and use your phone. There's no point in us stumbling around blindly if we're going to get hurt."

"Mm. This escape room challenge is *not* impressing me so far." The lock screen of Art's mobile flashes the time as 11:20 and he selects the torch icon.

Light floods the space. We've been placed in a circular library room. Floor-to-ceiling bookshelves take up every available inch of wall space, except for the door we walked through and a second door opposite where we're standing. There's a small L-shaped sofa in the center of the room, with a leather-bound journal placed atop one of the cushions.

"Here's the little bugger," Art mutters. The room is filled with the hum of electricity and an overhead chandelier clicks on. "Right. That's one problem sorted. Now what?"

"We explore, starting with that journal."

Crossing the room, we seat ourselves on the sofa next to one another and huddle our heads together. With shaking hands, I pick up the journal, carefully opening it. Inside are a series of handwritten notes and drawings. "Where do we even begin?"

"At the beginning?" Art suggests, subtly brushing his arm against mine. He turns the journal to the first page and begins to read. "It is a truth universally acknowledged that every couple locked in a room must be in want of a way out." He glances at me. "What do you suppose that means? Of course we want to leave the room."

"A truth universally acknowledged . . . Why is that line so familiar?"

"It's a take on the first line of *Pride and Prejudice*."

"That's right!" I snap my fingers together. My attention darts to the shelves of book. "Maybe that means our next clue is in a copy of P and P or another Jane Austen book." I jump to my feet. "See if you can find one."

"As you wish." He bows.

I giggle and playfully push his shoulders. We pick opposite ends of the room and begin scanning the collection of books. There's an eclectic mix of titles ranging from children's fairy tales by Hans Christian Anderson to modern-day biographies on celebrities, like my brother.

"Do you think they picked up whatever books were in the bargain bin at Waterstones or Oxfam to fill the shelves?" I ask.

"It wouldn't surprise me."

I glance over my shoulder. "Any luck yet?"

"I've found *Northanger Abby* and *Mansfield Park* so far. Nothing inside them."

"Keep looking." I kneel down and begin investigating the books on the lowest shelf. It bothers me to no end that there is no order to these books. At the very least they should be sorted by size or title, not haphazardly tossed together. The organizational side of my brain is fighting the urge to do it.

"Eureka! I have it!"

I drop the books in my hands and dart over to Art. "Open it!" I urge.

"It looks like there's a letter." He breaks the seal of a yellowing parchment envelope to reveal a second message in swirly, elegant cursive writing. "The strength of the pack is the wolf, and the strength of the wolf is the pack."

"Wolves . . . wolves . . . what books have wolves in them? *Little Red Riding Hood*? *Twilight*?" I mutter.

"That wouldn't be a quote from *Twilight*. It doesn't sound like something a contemporary author would write."

I place my hands on my hips. "Have you ever read *Twilight*?" I'm genuinely curious.

"Just the first book. And it wasn't for me. A girl I liked at the time was into vampires."

"Uh-huh." I store the knowledge away for future use. I'm beginning to learn that Art is a very well-read man. A man with a brain is something I find incredibly attractive. It's going on the list of qualities that I admire about him.

"What about a Roman fable, like the story of Romulus and Remus?" I suggest.

"No. It's coming to me. I think it's Rudyard Kipling. Give me a moment." Art closes his eyes and scrubs them. "That quote . . . it's on the tip of my brain."

"Oh, could it be *The Jungle Book*?"

"Yes, that's it."

The excitement between us grows as we continue to piece the clue quotes together. It's all Art's brain power at this point. Literature is not my forte, unless it's something science or engineering related. I would've been stuck in here indefinitely without him. Although he may have been grumpy at first, he's relaxed and has even given me a few smiles.

"Two hearts entwined in the glow of the moon—find the answer, and you'll be free." I set the scroll down.

Art runs a hand through his hair. "This one has me stumped. Two hearts and the glow of the moon? Maybe a romance book of some sort?"

"We're so close. This has to be the last clue. Let's search all the titles again." I start on my knees and scan the scattered books with a more focused eye. This clue is different than the rest. It wasn't located inside a book like the others. It was on a scroll inside a hidden compartment under the table. Does that mean it doesn't pertain to a book?

I sit on the floor. My eyes search the decor. That's when I spot a small ornate mirror hanging on the wall. Carved into the frame are two intertwined hearts, reflecting the soft glow of the room's single lamp.

"Here," I say, pointing to the mirror. "This has to be it."

Art reaches for the mirror and carefully removes it from the wall. Turning it over reveals a key taped to the back. He hands it to me, his fingers lingering on mine for a moment longer than necessary. The touch sends a shiver down my spine.

"You did it!" he says, his voice low and husky. He kisses me on the cheek. I let out a satisfied sigh.

"Are you ready to get out of here?" I whisper.

"Yes. Beyond ready. This was fun, but once was more than enough for me."

My stomach grumbles. I'm ready for lunch. We stand and walk over to the door. I place the key inside, hesitating to leave behind stacks of books on the ground. "Do you think we should clean up the mess first?"

"No. Let them sort it out. I'm sure the fee you paid is more than enough to cover them shoving the books and clues back into place."

We share a chuckle. As I move to turn the key, however, it doesn't budge.

"Odd." I rattle it around.

"Maybe that's the wrong door? What about the other one opposite the way we came in?"

I remove the key and insert it into the second door. To my relief, it turns, and we're finally free. We enter into a warmly lit reception area. It's night and day to what we experienced when we first walked in. There are glass windows flooding the room with plenty of natural light. Music from Taylor Swift's latest album plays through speakers. Orchids are tastefully scattered throughout the room.

"Oh, you two have completed the challenge! Well done," an attendant in a green blouse and black trousers exclaims, stepping into the room from the back-office area. "Usually, the Enchanted Library room takes about three hours, but you've managed it in two. How did you find it?"

"Fine," Art says.

"Pardon him. He's hangry." I glance at him and shake my head. "It was fun. It's the first time we've done one of these."

"Is there any feedback you'd like to share?"

"Er, can you have the lights on next time before you shove your players into the room? There was a lot of furniture inside and we would've crashed into it if we hadn't had his mobile."

She frowns. "The lights weren't turned on?"

"No, they weren't. We had to figure out where the light switch was."

"And the books—maybe they could be organized in a more logical manner? It was difficult to find the clues," I suggest.

The muscles in her forehead continue to flex. "They weren't cataloged by author name?"

We both shake our heads.

"Did you two at least receive the refreshments we had made up for you?"

"No."

"I see. It seems I need to have a chat with one of our newest employees about the setup. Now I'm even more impressed that you made it out so quickly. With the state of the room, you might've been here a lot longer if you two weren't so clever." She pinches her lips together. "Please accept my sincerest apologies. I promise the clues and the room aren't normally so disorganized. I'd be happy to offer you a return trip anytime. Your patronage is important to us, Princess."

I stiffen as she uses my title. "Thank you, I'll keep that in mind for the future."

"I hope you don't mind, but is it possible for you to take a photo with the company's logo for our website?"

I wince. Technically speaking, people aren't supposed to ask any member of the royal family for a photo. It's against protocol unless we offer. Today was supposed to be a private date with Art, not me trying out some escape room on a whim. Not that she knows that.

Luckily, Art jumps in and saves me from having to answer. "Her Royal Highness would actually appreciate it if you *didn't* mention today's visit to anyone. It was supposed to be a *private* engagement, hence why she booked the venue for just herself today."

"Oh, er, of course," the attendant sputters.

"What I *can* do, however, is put in a good word about my experience here with my older brother, the Prince of Wales. I'm certain he and Ms. Amanda Collins would *love* to participate in a future event."

"The Prince of Wales? Yes, yes." She bobs her head up and down. "We would be honored to host him."

At least I'm not lying to her. An activity like this would be perfect for them. I can see them wanting to try every room that Locked in London offers. We bid her farewell and dart out of the building as quickly as possible to the car, my fingers intertwined with Art's.

"So, did you have fun?" I ask.

"It was different. Not quite what I expected."

"What was your favorite part?"

"Spending time with you." He shoots me an *Isn't it obvious* look.

"That goes ditto for me." He releases my hand and opens the door for me. "Next time I'll let you be in charge of planning the date."

"You trust me that much?" he asks.

"Yes, I do."

With a smile on my lips, he steals a kiss from me. As we drive away, I can't help but wonder what type of date Art will choose for us. Will he be as adventurous? Or will it be something more low-key? Only time will tell.

Twenty-Three

Two weeks pass, and in that time, Mum manages to squeeze seven public appearances out of me. It's now the end of August. As reluctant as I am to admit it, most of the events I attend aren't terrible. I am asked to pick out a name for the Household Cavalry's new drum horse, visit the opening of a new exhibit at my friend Patrick's Museum of Curiosities, and help Mum present the winners of Wimbledon their trophies.

It's a Wednesday. Angela is off, and Art and I have a rare day alone together. He's decided today's the perfect opportunity to whisk me to a mystery location for a date. I'm eager and curious about what he has planned.

"Are you going to talk to them this week, Alice? You're running out of time before the school term begins," Art reminds me for the nth time.

"I know." I chew on my lip. I've been dragging my feet about confronting Mum and Papa. "It's just that things have been going well, and Papa is finally acting normal around me."

"You're afraid to upset the balance."

"Yeah, I am."

"Could it be that being a working royal is beginning to grow on you?"

"Maybe? I don't know." I stare at my hands, folded on my lap. "All I can say is that right now, I don't *hate* it."

I had it in my head that each appearance I made would involve making speeches in front of hundreds of people and posing for photographs for the press, but as I've come to find out, that's not it at all. Most of my appearances have been low-key, without much press, save the palace photographer.

The people I speak to are usually families with children who live in the local village or community. They're easy to talk to, like when I'm speaking to Angela or Art. I don't have to put on an act and pretend to be Princess Alice. I can just be me.

"I'm so confused. If you were me, Art, what would you do?"

"It's not really my place to say anything."

"Art," I whine. "I thought we were past this. I'm asking you as a friend for advice. *Please* tell me what you think I should do."

"Do you really want to know what I think?" He chuckles.

"Yes," I huff.

"If I were you, I'd finish off your public appearances for this week, then take the weekend and have a long, hard think, weighing out all the pros and cons. Make next week your deadline for how you want your schedule to look during the school year. It'll just get more difficult the longer you put everything off."

Yet again, Art's right. The longer I postpone speaking to my parents, the bigger the proverbial elephant in the room becomes.

"Does that help?" He glances back at me.

"Yes. It does. Thanks."

Art turns down a busy road. One side of the street

contains railroad tracks, and the other side is lined with three-story, red-bricked buildings. Working his magic, he squeezes past a double-decker bus and parks in a spot under a billboard advertising a storage unit. It looks like we're in a residential area.

"Where are we?"

"Queenstown Road on the edge of Battersea."

"Interesting location for a date. What do you have planned?"

"You'll have to wait and see."

Frustratingly, his tone gives nothing away. He steps out his car door and jogs around the vehicle to open mine. It's noisy. All I can hear is the sound of cars honking and trains passing over the tracks, their wheels letting out a high-pitched squeak. He points to a shop that says Corner Café.

"We're getting coffee?"

"Nope, our destination is the first floor of the building."

We enter a side alley, squeeze past the shop's rubbish bins, and ascend two flights of narrow steps. Removing a set of keys from his pocket, Art inserts them into the first door on the right and unlocks it. The moment the door opens, a flash of orange darts past us.

"Darn it. There goes Peppermint." He groans. "Wait inside, Ali, I'll be right back." He doesn't wait for an answer as he rushes down the hall.

I enter the room. My pulse beats with a steady staccato drum. I'm in Art's domain. He's brought me to his flat. He's always joked about living in a tiny place and he wasn't kidding. Everything in this room is compact and minimal. A single bed occupies the space under a small window. On top of the covers, a black-and-white cat is curled up tightly, asleep. I smile —that must be Cinnamon.

As I turn my gaze to the wall on the right, I see the kitchen setup. There's a miniature refrigerator, a microwave, a sink, and a half-sized oven. The only cabinet is stark white. Tucked into the space under the sink is a rolling cart that contains a few dishes and utensils. I'm guessing that must be Art's dining table too, because aside from a wardrobe, all the other furniture in the flat belongs to the cats. There's an oversized cat tree, two scratching posts, feeding bowls, and a litter box.

I'm struck by the fact that this is more of the cats' flat than Art's. He hasn't managed to put any personal touches in here. It's like a room in a youth hostel—sterile and almost depressing. There's no art on the wall. Nor are there any photos anywhere, at least that I can see. If he were to add a plant, a photo of his cats, even a calendar, it would bring a little life and color to the place. I wonder why he hasn't made an effort to do the flat up.

"Sorry about that," Art grumbles, coming back in and setting the large feline down. "This one is an escape artist. If we'd taken him to the escape room, he would've figured it out in less than a minute." He runs a hand through his hair. "So, um . . . it's not much, but this is my flat. For our date this afternoon, I thought it might be fun if we did a little baking."

"Art, I'd love that. Except do you have the room for it?" Peppermint walks straight up to me and is immediately interested in my shoelace. I lower my hand to allow him to sniff it. "I mean, I saw the rolling cart, but you don't seem to have any extra counter space . . . or chairs . . . and, er, do you even have a loo in here?"

Art cackles with laughter. "Everything is put away so the cats don't get into any extra mischief when I'm not home. They're circus artists. And yes, there's a loo. It's through here." He points to the door directly off the entryway. "You just can't open it and the front door at the same time."

Crossing the room, Art reaches under his bed and pulls out a folding table and an ironing board. Next, he opens his wardrobe. Inside, it's organized in a way that would make

Marie Kondo, the queen of maximizing small spaces, proud. He's managed to fit clothing, shoes, a computer, a vacuum, and two stools inside.

"I'm impressed."

"Thanks." He pops open the table and ironing board. "This should give us more than enough counter space. The only downside is that we'll have to make do with my hot plate. I don't have a stovetop."

"You make your omelets and waffles on a hot plate?"

"No, they're made on my waffle iron. But I *can* make them on the hot plate if need be."

Art removes his jacket and rolls up the sleeves of his dress shirt. Fire fills my belly as I see his bare arms. We wash our hands in the sink, and he offers me an apron. I've dreamt often about seeing him in the kitchen, and now, my dream is finally becoming a reality. I'll have to try hard to keep myself in check around him.

"If it's all right with you, I thought we could have a picnic indoors. We'll make some finger sandwiches, mini quiche, Scotch eggs, pigs in a blanket, sausage rolls, scones, potato salad, and either cookies or custard tarts. What do you think?"

The way Art is moving around the kitchen organizing supplies could not be more attractive. It's hard to focus on what he's saying. "Um, could you repeat that?"

He rattles off a gluttony of picnic foods.

"Those sound lovely, but that's an awful lot of food. Do we have the time to make all that?"

"We wouldn't if I hadn't gotten a head start on some of it." Art chuckles. "I made most of the doughs this morning. Whatever we don't eat, I'll save and have for dinner or lunch tomorrow."

"Okay, then, where do we start?"

~

"WELL, I OBVIOUSLY WOULD BE ONE OF THE FIRST contestants voted off *The British Baking Championship*. Actually, I doubt they'd even let me into the kitchen," I joke.

I've long since given up being useful. I'm slow and everything I cut ends up being awkward sizes. Instead, I've settled for being on cat-sitting duty, keeping the felines out of the kitchen as I watch Art in his element. He moves around with the grace of a prima ballerina. He can be preparing five or six different things at once. I have no idea how he's able to keep track of exactly what he's doing. It's one of the most attractive things I've ever seen.

"You aren't hopeless, Ali. Baking just takes some practice." I watch as he takes a brush and glazes some type of sauce over the quiche. "I'm just lucky my nan taught me so much."

"Art, I'm curious, why do you live in a flat with such a tiny kitchen? If it were me, I would've wanted a place with at least two ovens and a massive island."

"I would love to have a place with a large kitchen, but flats like that come with a hefty price tag. When I initially moved to the city, I was on a new hire's salary and it didn't go very far, especially since I wanted to live on my own. This flat was the best I could afford."

"What about after you received your promotion and became my protection officer?"

"Sure." He shrugs. "I probably have enough to move into a much nicer place, but I don't see the point. This flat is functional and that's all I need. I'm usually only home long enough to shower, sleep, and tend to Peppermint and Cinnamon." He sticks the quiches into the oven. "Twelve minutes, then we'll be able to start our picnic."

I sniff the air. Everything he's put together smells divine. "Well, on the nights you're on duty and staying with me, feel free to cook up a storm in my kitchen once I'm moved into the new flat. If you can make this kitchen work, I can't wait to see what you'll do with mine."

"I can't wait either."

"Seeing how much counter space you need here, I think we should have the largest kitchen island possible. And we'll also need at least two ovens and an industrial-sized refrigerator." I see Art's eyes sparkle as I mention all these features. "Like I said, I'll probably leave the appliance and kitchen-gadget shopping to you, since I have no idea what I'm doing."

"Ali, it would be a dream come true." He places a towel over his shoulder and snaps his fingers together. "Which reminds me, I should start searching for a proper pet sitter for my little troublemakers. I can't keep asking my neighbor to watch them when I have overnight duty. Finding the right person might take some time."

I turn my attention from the cats to Art. He's eyes are wide and full of worry, like a proper cat daddy. "Why do you need a pet sitter? Just bring them over with you. What if we did up one of the rooms for them on the second floor? They can have their own playroom slash chillout space."

Ideas and images begin forming in my mind. "We could see about having a custom cat tree made up like the one in Japan. And have shelving for perches at all different heights. Maybe a telly with some birds or squirrels playing. Do you think they'd watch it? If not, maybe an aquarium would be better. Except we'd have to construct it in a way so the cats wouldn't jump on top of it and knock it over. And Lillian will need a proper introduction to them. She'll be happy to have some companions. And the garden—I heard about something called a catio."

"Ali, I can't do that."

I place my hands on my hips. "Why not?"

"One, it's crossing the line to being unprofessional—"

"Art," I interrupt. "Any lines between being professional

and personal went out the door when we agreed to start dating. Look at us now." I gesture to the flat to prove my point.

He blows out a breath.

"Bring the cats with you. It'll make you happy and it'll be the puuuuuuuuurfect opportunity for me to see what it's like to have one as a pet. I'm going to build a room for them anyway, so save yourself the trouble and listen to your stubborn princess."

Art silences me with a greedy kiss. I'm caught unaware and stumble a few steps backward into the wall. Peppermint or Cinnamon, I'm not sure which one, hisses at us, jumping out of the way just in the nick of time.

Art smells so good, like a mixture of brown sugar, honey, and cinnamon. My arms wrap themselves around his neck, playing with the curly ends of his hair. It's grown out over the last two weeks. His cheeks, however, are nice and smooth. He's shaved. For once I don't feel all the scratchiness of his beard. I like it much better this way.

"You. Are. Brilliant," he breathes between kisses.

I giggle. "I would've told you to bring the cats over sooner if I'd known this was the type of reaction I'd get."

"It's a big ask. Not everyone would be as willing and open-minded as you."

"Well, lucky for you, I'm not just any person. I'm Alice."

We stay glued to one another until the timer dings and Art shuffles over to the oven to rescue the tray of quiches. As he puts on the oven mitts and places the tray to cool on the folding table, I marvel at just how relaxed he looks. He carries himself with a lightness. There are a few creases near the folds of his eyes and around his mouth from smiling. He's happy, and it's the first time I've truly been able to appreciate how it makes him look ten times more handsome. I wish he'd let the mask he normally dons slip away and always stay like this.

"Ali, would you mind grabbing the hamper that's on the ironing board?"

"Oh, um, sure." I snap out of creepy staring mode and focus on the wicker basket.

"We'll eat over there." He nods toward a red-and-white checkered blanket occupied by the cats. "Just keep the lid closed until I have some treats ready for Peppermint and Cinnamon, otherwise, they'll try and steal some of the chicken for themselves."

"Have they done that before?"

"Uh-huh. Those two will eat anything given the opportunity."

"I guess it just shows they have good taste. Although, I've never heard of a cat stealing human food. Dogs, yes. Cats, no."

I sit down on the ground and guard the basket. Cinnamon comes over to sniff and investigate the lid.

"Does Lillian beg for table scraps?" Art asks, reaching up to the top shelf of the cabinet.

"Not with me, but if she's around her brother and sisters, yes. My cousin David is the worst offender. The dogs know it too, so they tend to crowd around where he sits. It's gotten so bad that Clara had to ban the dogs from the kitchen. So now when it's mealtimes, they get crated."

Art chuckles and shakes the bag of treats he's retrieved. I watch as the felines' ears preen and they run over to him like a couple of hungry lions, stretching up onto their hind legs to try and reach the item in his hand. They meow loud and mighty.

"Sit," he calls out in a commanding voice.

Miraculously, Peppermint and Cinnamon obey. Their eyes remain glued on him. He opens the bag and sprinkles a handful of what I assume to be freeze-dried meat chunks into two bowls. They wait for him to set them on the floor before they each run over to the dishes and begin to eat. Felines occupied, Art is free to carry the remaining hamper and quiches over to join me.

"Mademoiselle, lunch is served." While I load up my plate, Art dims the lights with an app on his phone and clicks on some soft classical music. "This may not be a proper picnic, but it's the next best thing."

I peck him on the cheek. "Thank you for going to so much trouble for me."

"You're worth any price."

Swoon. Move over Eric, Alfie, and every other man out there, because none of them can compare to the thoughtfulness and generosity of this man. I'm more determined than ever for him to become my boyfriend, and nothing is going to stand in my way.

Twenty-Four

"Hello?" My voice comes out groggy.

"Good morning, sunshine, this is your conscience telling you it's time to rise and shine," my brother's deep voice jokes.

"Eddie," I whine. "Do you know what time it is?"

"It's four-thirty," he snarks back. "You wake up at five to work in the stables anyway. Waking up half an hour early won't kill you."

"I need my beauty sleep. Especially on a Saturday." I groan, half tempted to hang up on him. "What do you need?"

"Can't your favorite brother ring you just to wake you up?"

"No." So that's his game. He's rung to annoy me. I'll find a way to get him back for this when I'm more awake. "Goodbye."

"Ali, wait . . ." His voice sobers. "I promise I have an actual reason for ringing you."

"Well, what is it?" I burrow into my bed, pulling the covers tighter around me.

"The press office received a tip-off this morning that you'll be featured on the front covers of three or four different tabloids."

"Ugh. Will they ever leave me alone?" I groan into my pillow.

"I'm sorry." Eddie sounds sincere. "You don't deserve this, especially with the crap they've thrown at you in the past."

"What rubbish are they running this time?"

"Apparently, there are some photos and a video of you and your protection officer. The new Bruce."

"Arthur?" I sit up tall, suddenly fully awake.

"That's him," Eddie says. "They're claiming you two are in some type of romantic relationship. I'm waiting for Father to wake up before we figure out if it'll be something we decide not to comment on or if we issue a strong denial."

It's like I've been sitting inside a saucepan with the heat turned up as high as it will go. My blood is boiling. I'm seeing the world in tomato-paste red. "Crap!" I toss the covers off the bed. How on earth have the gossip rags placed us together? We've been so careful. Unless . . . are the photos from Tokyo? Or are they of us in London? "Do you know when the photos were taken? Can you send me one?"

"Alice, I don't want you worrying over this," Eddie emphasizes. "We don't know for certain if they're real. For all we know, they could be photoshopped or generated by AI. You know how the gossip rags are with their fake news."

"Don't baby me. I need to know."

"I haven't seen them myself, but it *sounds* like they were taken in London."

That narrows it down. I place my palm on my forehead, trying to recall our dates over the last few weeks. "Eddie, there's something I need to tell you, but before I do, I need you to swear to me that you won't tell *anyone* about it, including Amanda."

"Ali?"

"Anyone," I repeat.

"I swear."

"The rumor is true. Arthur and I are *kind* of dating one another. I like him. A lot. We're taking things slowly. It's only been about three weeks since we made the call, but now . . ."

"Everything's been turned upside down?"

"That's putting it lightly," I huff. "I know you're probably vexed with me for breaking the number-one security rule, but try telling that to my heart. I promise if we decide to become boyfriend and girlfriend, we'll do things the proper way."

"Ali, contrary to what you might believe, I think it's brilliant you found a bloke you like. *Father* may not be too happy about it, but we'll figure something out. He doesn't need to know if the rumor is true right now, per se."

I exhale. It feels like an elephant is being lifted off my shoulders.

"Listen," Eddie continues, "why don't you get dressed and have someone bring you over to my place for breakfast. We can hold a council of war before we speak with Father."

"I *should* be getting ready for work."

"In this case, I think Danny will understand. Odds are Father will want to speak with you ASAP anyway."

"You're right. Okay, I'll come."

"Good. Text me when you're on your way."

I set my phone down and scrub my eyelids. What a horrid way to start my morning. I need to get ahold of Art as soon as possible. I need to speak to him before he sees the tabloids, or anyone contacts him about it. Somehow, I feel that the blow is better coming from me than anyone else.

Pulling out my mobile, I type up a quick message.

ALICE

Good morning. I know it's early, but are you free?

ANGELA

Yes, I am. What's on your mind this
morning, ma'am?

I wince. Art must not be on duty until this afternoon.
Angela has the duty phone. It doesn't hit me until now that I
don't have his private mobile number. There must be a way I
can get it. Except my brain is moving at a turtle's speed. I don't
have the faintest idea of how.

ALICE

My brother has asked me to join him for
breakfast before work. Would you mind
driving me over to Kensington Palace in ten
minutes?

ANGELA

Of course.

ALICE

Thanks! I'm sure there'll be some breakfast
in it for you too.

ANGELA

That would be lovely. The Prince of Wales
always has top-notch offerings.

"ARE YOU HOLDING UP OKAY SO FAR? I KNOW THIS IS
the last thing you wanted to deal with," Eddie says.

"I'm angry, but hanging in there. I haven't had time to
process it all. I knew at some point I'd become the target of the
paparazzi again. I just was hoping the quiet would last a little
longer."

"I'm sorry, Ali. I wish I could do more to protect you."

"You're doing more than enough by being here for me and holding a council of war."

Eddie pours a cup of coffee straight from his fancy expresso machine and sets it down in front of me. "I can make you something else if you'd prefer." He puffs out his chest. "I can do anything a barista can do."

"Has your fiancée verified that claim?" My hand closes around the cup and brings it closer to me, as if I'm clutching a lifeline.

"Well, no." He deflates. "I wanted to surprise her. I've been testing out my creations on David."

I raise my cup to him. "Well, he's a heavy coffee drinker. If he says what you're making is good, that means you're probably doing a brilliant job."

Eddie pours his own cup and takes a seat across from me at the round kitchen table. The shades are still drawn, and Amanda is asleep. It's just the two of us. My brother's dressed casually in a white T-shirt and a pair of navy-blue joggers. He was probably getting ready to go for a run when his plans shifted.

"So, you and the new Bruce . . ."

"Yes." I stare into the mug. "His name is Arthur."

"Arthur." Eddie smacks his lips together and takes a sip of coffee. "What do I need to know about him?"

I lift my chin. "You haven't asked for his personnel file?"

"I have," he admits. "But all it told me is that if he did something stupid, like hurt your feelings and made you cry, I'd have to go after him with backup."

I roll my eyes and hide a smile. That's my protective older brother for you.

"What I want to hear is why you like him. What sets him apart from other blokes?"

"When you first meet Arthur, he's quiet and shy. He doesn't speak much until you get to know him. In fact, he annoyed me so much when we first met that I asked Papa to reassign him from my detail."

Eddie snorts. "And Father said no? He normally gives you whatever you want."

I nod. "Papa said Arthur was the strongest candidate he interviewed, and he wanted me to have the best on my team. He insisted that I wait until the end of summer to decide how things would play out." I take a sip of coffee and let the strong bitterness roll over my tongue. "And I'm glad he did because I would've regretted never giving him a chance. The man I've come to know is witty, an excellent baker, caring, kind, and considerate. He's the first man who's ever *seen* me. He gets me."

"It sounds to me, baby sister, like you're on your way to falling in love." Eddie studies me for several moments, leaning back in his chair. My brother has a knowing look in his eyes. "What you're describing is exactly how I felt when I first met Amanda. She was one of the first people I'd ever met who treated me like a person instead of a prince. It was an out-of-body experience for me."

I nod, thinking back to how much my brother has grown and matured over the last several years because of the vivacious American's influence on him.

"I knew early on that she was special and that our relationship would be different than the flings I'd had in the past."

"How did you know you were in love with her?" I cock my head to the side.

"Instinct? Feelings?" His lips twitch. "The best way I can describe it is that the energy between us shifted. When we were together, everything felt deeper and more meaningful."

As I sit here and listen to Eddie going on about all the little qualities he began to notice and love about Amanda, an image of Art pops into my mind. We've only been on a handful of dates, but my gut instinct tells me that, like Amanda, something about him is different.

I *want* to spend time with him. He's always in my thoughts and on my mind. I'm not at the point where I'm ready to declare that what I'm feeling is love, but I've definitely begun to care for him more than I have for any man.

"Ali?"

"Hmm?"

Eddie's blue orbs look at me with sympathy. "I want you to know, like I said earlier, that I'm happy for you. I'll do whatever I can to help you two out where I can, but you have to know that things are going to get ugly before they get better."

I swallow hard. That's *not* what I want to hear right now.

"We'll have to speak to Father. I'll leave how much you tell him up to you, but either way, Arthur is likely going to be suspended while an investigation takes place."

"Suspended? Investigation?"

"Yes. It's standard practice. Any rumor or allegation has to be investigated and go through the proper channels."

I rub my temples. "There's something I need your help with. I need to get in touch with him. But I don't have his mobile number."

Eddie frowns. "Ali, it would be better if you did nothing. His personal mobile will be subject to the investigation too."

"Eddie, no," I sputter. "I have to get in touch with him and let him know what's going on. It has to come from me." It's all my fault he's in this situation to begin with.

My brother sighs. "It means that much to you?"

I shoot him a *Duh* look. For a man who's been in love before, he can still be dense. "Yes, it does."

"Then I guess we'll have to figure something out. Maybe a message from a raven? Or a carrier pigeon."

"Eddie," I moan. "Now is *not* the time for bad jokes."

He holds up his hands. "I'm sorry. I know this is difficult for you. Leave it to me. I'll come up with a way for you to get in touch with him without using your mobile. It just needs to be done discreetly. In the meantime, you and I need to come up with a plan for Father."

"He's going to be livid." I fold my hands and set them on the table. "Until I have a chance to speak with Art, I'd prefer to respect his privacy and not comment on the dating thing. I just wish I knew *exactly* what photos the papers have."

"We'll find out soon enough," Eddie says grimly.

Twenty-Five

"**T**hese people are absolute scumbags." My father slams his fist against his desk, sending several papers flying to the ground. Franny lifts her head, huffs, then resumes her nap, stretched out on the rug by the fireplace. "If it were within my power, I'd put all gossip rags out of business, then send the lot of them to be imprisoned in the Tower of London. I'm sick and tired of them preying on my family."

"I fully support that," Eddie says, trying to lighten the mood. He's standing behind my chair with one hand resting on my shoulder. "But since you don't have absolute power, like good ol' Henry VIII, maybe you can settle for talking the PM into passing a law to ban the tabloids."

"If only," Papa grumbles, pinching the bridge of his nose. "Carrington won't lift a finger to help. He's only *just* managed to get reelected by the skin of his teeth. He can't risk angering anyone. No. The only thing we can do is issue a strongly worded statement denying the entire affair and hope that does the job."

The muscles in my stomach clench and tighten. I can't

have him deny it because the rumors are true. It physically hurts me that I have to hide and downplay my relationship with the man I've developed feelings for, but I don't see any other alternative.

My eyes travel to the newspapers on the ground. Staring back at me on the front page is a blurry photo of Art and me sharing a kiss just outside the London escape room a few weeks ago. Luckily, since the quality is so subpar, it could be argued that Art was whispering something in my ear. His back is turned toward the camera.

Even if it's his job, Art has worked hard to protect me. It's my turn to repay the favor. "Papa, actually, I'd rather we stay quiet for now." He meets my gaze. "It's always been the policy of this family to ignore whatever is being printed and let the gossip die on its own within a few news cycles. We made a special exception last time, and I don't think we need to again."

"I appreciate what you have to say, Alice, but I'm not entirely convinced this will disappear all that easily. You're a young and beautiful princess. There are so many people out there who have watched you grow up, and now that you're an adult, they're sure to take an unhealthy interest in your love life."

I wince, knowing that everything he's saying is one hundred percent true. What I've always found incredibly strange and awkward is how strangers can feel like they *know* me based on photos, appearances I've made, or interviews I've given.

Over the years, I've received hundreds of thousands of letters—everything from invitations to a child's birthday party to criticisms of how I wear my hair. They're always written so intimately. I found out a long time ago, for my own mental health, it's best if I don't read or see them. The palace correspondence office takes care of the job for me, but every now and then, they'll let me know if something interesting stands out.

"You're probably right, Papa, but can we at least *try* it my way?"

"I'm open to it, but I'd like to hear your take, Edmund." He nods to my brother.

"I agree with, Alice, sir. I think it's worth maintaining our silence. If we issue a denial, it'll set the precedence that the palace comments on the personal lives of the family. Besides, the quality of the photos is questionable." Eddie bends over to pick one up. "It's grainy and difficult to identify who's in the photo. For all we know, this could be a coffee vendor Ali ordered a cappuccino from."

"It's not. There's no mistaking it's Arthur. From the angle the photo was taken from, I think one of the employees of Locked in London must have snapped the image and sold it to the press," I say, picturing the man in the dirty uniform who'd checked us in. I remember the supervisor mentioning the disorganized clues might've kept us there longer. Now we know it was probably done on purpose. I only hope there isn't any video of us inside the escape room.

"If that's how the staff operates, I'm canceling my visit." Eddie crosses his arms.

Papa frowns. "Locked in London? What on earth is that?"

"It's a room you're locked inside of and given a time limit to figure out how to escape from it," Eddie replies.

Papa wrinkles his nose. "Why would anyone find that appealing?"

Leave it to my brother to simplify the explanation too much. "Eddie's forgotten to mention that the way you figure out how to escape is by solving a series of clues and mini challenges. The ones I was given were actually quite tricky. It involved being given literary quotes and piecing together which books it came from."

"I see," he says.

"I don't know how you managed it. When I was looking on their website, that enchanted library challenge looked way too difficult. Amanda and I were going to do the pop culture one," Eddie tells me.

"Alice has always enjoyed problem-solving. I can see where it might be an activity she'd enjoy."

"It was interesting, but once was more than enough for me," I tell them.

Papa nods. "I'm guessing these photos were taken at this escape room?"

"Yes."

"Did you have any of the staff members sign an NDA? Perhaps we can take some legal action against them."

"I'm not sure," I admit. "That would've been Art's domain."

"Would you like me to follow up with him?" Eddie offers.

"I'd appreciate that," Papa says. "Only you'll have to follow up with the security office. The young man in question has been reassigned."

I jump to my feet. "Reassigned?" I sputter.

"Alice . . ." Eddie warns. "We talked about this."

I ignore him. "On what grounds?"

"On the grounds that he might have broken the terms of his employment." Papa's forehead is creased. "All credible claims and accusations are investigated by the security office. It's standard operating procedure."

"I told you," Eddie mutters.

I snap his direction. "You said he'd be temporarily suspended. Not that he was going to be reassigned." I turn back and face my father. "This isn't going to be permanent, is it? Papa, please, I need him back on my team."

"Alice, I understand this has all come as a terrible shock to you, but you must understand that while an investigation is ongoing, Arthur cannot work on your security team. The protocols are there for a reason. I love you dearly, but I will not intervene on your behalf."

"Fine. I understand that, but has he been *permanently* removed from me?"

"That depends on the outcome of the investigation. If he's done nothing wrong, you have no cause for concern."

But that's just it. We have. My heart is sinking. I fall back down into my chair, opening and closing my mouth. No words come out. I'm a ship that's been lost at sea without a lighthouse to safely guide me in.

How thorough is the investigator going to be? Are there more photos of us out there? We knew there was a chance this was going to happen, and now it has. I have to speak with Art. I have to find out if he's all right. I'll find a way to get by, but his entire life is being flipped upside down. Everything he's worked for.

Eddie and Papa exchange worried glances.

"Why don't I ring for some tea," Eddie suggests.

I bob my head up and down. "Yes, tea. Tea is good." My brother disappears into the front office.

Papa walks around his desk and sits next to me. He places a hand under my chin and lifts it. "Alice, I want you to know, I'll do everything at my disposal to try and help the situation along. As much as I don't like it, we'll try it your way. I'll refrain from having the press office issue any comments."

"Thank you, Papa," I whisper. I hug him, burying my face in his coat. The familiar sandalwood scent comforts me.

As we break apart, I hear Art's voice in my head, urging me to use this time to speak to my father about being a working royal. During our last conversation, I told him I'd try and take care of it soon. But I didn't. I postponed it. Again.

I swallow hard. I've run out of excuses. I need to do this now. Otherwise, I have no idea if I ever will. Taking a deep breath, I say, "Papa, while we're here, there is one other thing I wanted to speak to you about."

"Of course." He scoots back half an inch.

"There's something I should've told you and Mum a long time ago." I look down at the carpet. "Everyone else in this family has always taken to attending engagements and making public speeches like a duck to water. But that's never been the case for me."

I explain to my father how much dread and anxiety I have when I'm out in the public eye. I open up about how the last year has been more difficult than anyone has imagined. Even with a brilliant therapist, it's taken me months to be able to piece myself back together.

"I thought when I began uni, I'd be able to finally have a private life, outside of the spotlight, but as I've come to find, these last few weeks actually haven't been *too* bad. I've enjoyed some of my work. It's been enough to make me reconsider where I stand on being a working royal. Plus, there's also a few causes I'd like to support, like helping those who have been bullied. I guess what I'm trying to say is that at the beginning of the summer, I was prepared to ask you if I could step away from all royal engagements, but now, I'm willing to be out there on a part-time basis."

When I finish, I lift my head and watch as he blinks slowly several times. I see Eddie standing silently in the background, arms behind his back.

"Alice, why have you never told your mum and me how you feel? If we'd known, we would've scaled your schedule back."

"I . . . I . . . I suppose I was ashamed of myself. I'm the daughter of the king, and being able to be a working royal is what's expected. Eddie has never had any trouble."

"That's where you're wrong, Ali." Eddie scoffs. "Believe me when I say there's been stretches of time where I've struggled. At one point, there was talk of me being stripped of my duties because of how poor my behavior was."

My eyes widen.

"It's true," Papa confirms.

"But with time, practice, and some positive influences, I was able to turn myself around." Eddie elbows me lightly. "None of what we do is easy or comes naturally. To quote Amanda, we're brilliant at faking it until we make it."

"David and Uncle Frank have both expressed the same feelings as you. I'll tell you exactly what I told them." Papa crosses one leg over the other and glances at us. "You may not have been able to choose the family that you're born into, but you will always have a choice in the life you'd like to lead. Mum and I will love and support you no matter what you decide you want to do."

"If it were me, Ali, I wouldn't rush to make any decisions," Eddie suggests. "You have a lot on your plate right now, especially with your school term about to start up. I doubt it would surprise anyone if you focused on your studies. But if you're halfway enjoying yourself as a working royal, why not ask Mum if you can handpick what's added to your schedule?"

"Would that be possible?"

"Certainly," Papa says.

I take tea with Eddie and my father, feeling a little better, but still torn over the situation with Art. One problem has been solved, but another has emerged.

AN AGONIZING THREE DAYS PASS AND THINGS continue to grow worse. Almost all the big tabloids are running headlines on me. More photos of Arthur and me have surfaced. This time they're from us enjoying a walk through

Tokyo together. There's still nothing concrete that confirms we're in a relationship, but the speed with which these photos have popped up is scary.

In all that time, I've been waiting with bated breath to speak to Art.

"My plan is brilliant yet simple, if I do say so myself," Eddie boasts over video chat.

"Well, get on with it, what's the plan?" The muscles in my face twitch.

"Somebody's grumpy."

"What do you expect? I'm out of patience. I haven't been able to speak to him since all the headlines have popped up. I have no clue how he's managing all this. So excuse me if I'm a little anxious. What's. The. Plan?"

Eddie sighs. "I managed to pull his personal email address from his file to pass on to you. It shouldn't be monitored by anyone and should be safe to send a message to."

I smack my forehead. "You want me to send an email to him?"

"Yes?" He cocks his head to the side.

"That could take ages for him to actually read, assuming he even checks his email. There has to be a better way." I hold the mobile screen closer to my face, staring my brother down.

"Ali, there isn't. The man doesn't have any social media accounts. He's got a mobile number and an email in his personal record. That's it." I open my mouth, but Eddie quickly adds, "And no, I'm not giving you his personal mobile number."

Frustrated, I toss my phone onto the bed. "I'm so sick of all this. At this point, I might as well drive over to his flat."

"How do you know where he lives?" I hear Eddie shout.

"He invited me over for a date."

"You know what, I'm sorry I even asked that."

A light bulb hits me. What's stopping me from going

over? Nothing. So why don't I? All I'd have to do is slip away from Angela. I'd feel incredibly guilty about it, but it wouldn't be all that difficult. I'd just need us to be in a place where I blend in with a crowd and could sneak away. Maybe I could use something like visiting Jenna as an excuse. I could catch the Tube from Covent Garden to Battersea.

"Alice? Are you still there?" Eddie asks. "Alice? Oh, bugger off, you're ghosting me. You try and do something nice, and this is the thanks you get." He raises his voice. "Alice, if you can hear me, I'm sorry it's not what you wanted. I'll see if I can come up with something better, but for now this is the best I can do. Ring me later if you want to talk."

He disconnects the call.

"I'm sorry, Eddie, but good enough is not going to cut it," I mutter. "I guess the old saying is true. If you want something done, it's best to do it yourself."

Twenty-Six

"You're sure you're okay helping me?"

Jenna rolls her eyes at me. "For the millionth time, yes. I don't mind getting into a bit of trouble if it's for a good cause."

"Thank you a billion times over." I hug her petite frame tightly. "Here's the note to Angela."

"Got it. I'll give it to her in an hour or whenever she realizes you're not here. Whichever one comes first. That should give you enough of a head start. Do you know how you're getting to Battersea from here?"

I've studied the Tube map so often, I picture it in my head when I sleep. "I take the Piccadilly Line to Leicester Square and change to the Northern Line for Waterloo Station. Then I catch the South Western Railway to Queenstown Road. Art's flat is a two-minute walk from the station."

"That's an awful lot of changes." Jenna sounds worried. "Maybe you should take a cab or rideshare instead."

"Don't you think the Tube will be faster?"

"No, especially since you've never ridden it before." She shakes her head. "Taking a cab will be about the same amount of time. Not to mention there's less of a chance of you being recognized."

I tap my head, feeling the stringy, stiff ends of the wig I've borrowed from Jenna. I've gone from a blond with shoulder-length hair to jet-black hair that falls to my hips. I've also exchanged the dress I arrived in for a pair of jeans, a black-and-white striped T-shirt, and gray trainers. "I guess you're right."

"So you'll take the cab, then?"

"Yeah, I will."

"That's a relief." She sighs. "You can walk right over to the Waldorf Astoria across the street. They always have cabs waiting.

"Perfect." I grin.

"Promise you'll ring me if there're any problems," Jenna urges.

"Deal." We shake on it.

Jenna and I hold our breaths and wait after she sends a text to her friend Jeremy. A minute later, we hear a knock on the door. As she pulls it open, Jenna occupies the space in the doorway with him, momentarily blocking it from Angela's view. "Good luck," she whispers as I creep past her.

Hugging my body to the wall, I move down the hallway as fast I can and slip down the stairs to the lift. My heart is hammering against my ribs as fast as a Formula One race car speeding down a straightaway. So far, so good. If all goes right, I'll be at Art's flat in thirty-two minutes.

"This has to work," I mutter.

THE MOMENT I'M OUTSIDE, I JOG ACROSS THE STREET to the posh five-star hotel and ask the doorman to hail a car for me. I don't have to wait long, and soon, I'm inside. I just hope I'm far enough away by the time Jenna hands Angela my note.

I wrote:

> Dear Angela,
> By now you may have realized that I am no longer enjoying a girls' afternoon with Jenna. I'm deeply sorry you're finding out this way, but there was something extremely personal and important that I needed to take care of alone. I know I am asking a lot of you, but please trust me when I say I am safe. As soon as the errand has been completed, I'll ring you straightaway.
> Regards,
> Alice

Whether Angela trusts me enough to wait for me to ring her or if she'll report me to the security office, who knows. Either way, yes, I'll be in deep trouble, but to me, it's a risk worth taking. No matter the consequences. Art put everything on the line for me. It's my turn to return the favor.

Twenty minutes later than I'd planned, the cabbie drops me in front of the Queenstown Road Train Station. Walking across the street to the café, I slip into the back alley and ascend the stairs toward Art's flat.

Ring. Ring. Ring. Ring.

I scrunch my eyes closed. I don't need to glance at the screen to know its Angela. Taping the Ignore button, I jog up the remaining four steps and approach the red door of number 4A. With a shaking hand, I lift the knocker, rap it against the door three times, and wait. My throat is dry. My legs are quivering.

Ring. Ring. Ring. Ring.

Ten seconds pass. Then twenty. Thirty. A minute. Two minutes. I preen my ears. I can hear the faint sign of a meow, but no other sounds from within.

I lift the knocker once more. *Tap. Tap. Tap.*

Two more minutes pass. Nothing. Lifting open the mail slot built into the door, I peek inside. Sharp claws swipe at my fingers.

"Ow." I pull my hand back and shake it. There's a small gash and some blood. "Brilliant. Just brilliant." I don't have any plasters or tissues on me. Reluctantly, I use the hem of my shirt. It needs washing anyway—what's a little blood.

Turning my back against the wall, I lean into it and sink down onto the ground. I bend my knees and rest my forehead against them.

Ring. Ring. Ring. Ring.

"Stupid. Stupid. Stupid," I berate myself.

Out of all the scenarios that I've run through my head, Art not being home wasn't one of them. I had one crack at speaking to him and I've failed. After this escape charade, Angela isn't going to let me out of her sight ever again. Well, maybe not forever, but for a very long time. I pull the wig and wig cap off my head, letting my natural hair tumble free. What do I do now?

"Think, Ali. Think."

Ring. Ring. Ring. Ring.

Option one: I could stay here until Art returns. Except there is no telling how long that's going to be. He could be working. Or even out of town. But the cats are around, so that's a positive.

Option two: I could leave a note and slip it through the mail slot. It's probably faster and more personal than an email. The only thing is, I don't have any paper. Maybe I could pop into the café downstairs and grab a napkin to scribble a note on.

Option three: I give up and ring Angela to pick me up. That's likely what's going to happen eventually, but I came all this way and I'm not leaving without making an effort.

So I suppose the clear winner is option two.

Ring. Ring. Ring. Ring.

My head begins to ache. Angela isn't relenting. I decide to answer the darn mobile and let her know I'm almost done. Reaching into my pocket, I grab the device and slide to unlock the screen, mindful of my injured finger. Taking a deep breath, I begin, "Angela, I'm so, so, so sorry. I promise I'm going to spend the next five years making it up to you."

"Princess Alice! Finally! Where are you?" she asks, sounding exasperated.

"I'm in Battersea." I give her Art's address.

"Stay where you are! I'll be there as soon as I can."

"I will." I apologize to her again and disconnect the call. Angela is likely still in Covent Garden. It'll probably take her about a half hour before she's here. I know she asked me to stay where I am, but if I pop down to the Corner Café, it'll only take a second to find a napkin and borrow a pen. A good barista never goes far without one. Besides, technically, it's just the ground floor of Art's building.

Inside the café, I spy several customers sitting at tables chatting, while others are working on their laptops. Nearly everyone has a nice ice-cold beverage. Suddenly, I need one too. I've forgotten just how thirsty I am from the cab ride and all the running around.

"Can I help you?" a cashier asks in a bored tone.

"Yes. I'd like an iced vanilla soy latte please."

"Size?"

"Large."

The cashier pushes a few buttons on the register. "Your name?"

"It's Ali—son," I sputter, momentarily forgetting myself. Luckily, the cashier doesn't seem to notice. She scribbles something on a cup and rings me up. I pay with my mobile. Just as I start to step off to the side, I pause. "Oh, do you have an extra pen I could borrow?"

The cashier wrinkles her nose.

"I promise I'll give it right back."

Wordlessly, she reaches into her pocket and slides a black marker across the counter to me. "See that you do."

"Thanks." Smiling brightly, I dash over to the condiments area and swipe a napkin from the dispenser. I only need one, but they're packed so tightly, I have to grab a wad of them to get any out.

Uncapping the pen, I begin to write:

> *Dear Art,*
>
> *I'm sorry we missed one another. I'm so sorry for everything. You have no idea how much I've been dying to see you so we can . . .*

A person walks up behind me. I hear them coughing. I turn my head.

"Do you mind?" a man dressed in a blue football jersey and black joggers asks.

I blink a few times.

He frowns. "I'm trying to get to the creamer." He holds up a paper cup.

"Oh right. Sorry." I hastily grab my napkins and pen and

step to the side, using the lid of the rubbish bin as my new countertop.

> *. . . talk things out and make things right. I completely understand if . . .*

"Alison!" the barista shouts.

> *. . . you don't want . . .*

"Order for Alison," she repeats.

Recapping the pen, I hurry over and pick up the drink. But the barista holds it hostage, putting out her hand. "Pen first."

"I'm not quite done. I need it for two more seconds."

She slides the drink back toward her, tapping her fingers against the counter. Reading between the lines, I quickly finish writing.

> *. . . anything more to do with me. I hope we can at least still be friends. Please email or ring me anytime. My number, in case you don't have it, is + 44 0712 345678. My email is a.wales@email.com.*
> *-Alice*

Internally, I'm cringing. There is so much more I wish I could say, but I'm out of time. This soddy note will have to do.

"All done."

Like a crocodile snapping its jaws shut, the barista curls her fingers around the marker and slams my drink toward me. The top comes off, spilling some of the coffee onto the counter and my shirt. I inhale sharply.

For a split second, our eyes meet. Hers are cold and give off a *It's not my fault you didn't move fast enough* vibe.

"Hey, lady, I'm ready to order," a teenager shouts from the register.

Without a glance back at me, she stomps off in the direction of the customer. I count backward from five, then use the spare napkins to mop up the mess. I usually like being treated like a normal person, but when someone like her is purposefully rude, it makes me tempted to pull rank and call her out on it. Nobody should be treated like the dirt under someone's feet. Securing the lid on the cup, I take it back over to the condiments counter, find a straw, and toss my rubbish into the bin.

As I turn to leave, I find my path blocked by the man in the football jersey from earlier.

"Excuse me," I say, stepping to the right. Instead of moving, he whips out his mobile and snaps my photo.

"I knew you looked familiar! You're the Ice Princess!"

The blood in my veins goes cold. My face hardens like a stone gargoyle. I need to get out of here as quickly as possible. "Excuse me," I repeat, lowering my chin.

The man continues snapping photos of me. "Aww, come on, Alice, give me a few good shots. I need some cash for tickets to next week's Manchester-West Hamm match."

I move to the left and take a few steps toward the door, reminding myself to stay calm and keep breathing. More people have crowded around us, however. I'm surrounded on all sides by people recording me and taking photos. It's one of my worst nightmares come true. I'm completely vulnerable and exposed.

I can do this. I just can't let them see how nervous I am. I have to become the confident princess I was in in Japan. They'll respect me if I sound authoritative, but polite.

I clear my throat. "Please, I know you may be curious, but I'm here on a private matter. I'd appreciate it if you'd please let me leave and go about my day." Two of the women sheepishly apologize, clearing a space. Muttering a thank you, I make my move.

"Alice," the football-jersey-clad man whines, "come on. I'm a taxpayer. You owe us for the millions of pounds your family costs us." I freeze as he reaches into my back pocket and steals my mobile phone. "I bet this fetches a hefty price with the right paper." He waves the device above my head. "I got what I needed. Now you can go."

I gasp.

"Oy, Joe, mate, come on," someone says. "You've crossed the line. Photos are one thing, but give the princess back her mobile."

"Yeah," another voice chimes in. "You're stealing."

"Bugger off," he shouts. "You're just jealous you didn't think of it first."

"Come on, Joe. I'm not messing around."

"Neither am I!"

The man's friends attempt to grab him and wrestle my phone from his hand. He swings his arm, trying to block them. Things begin to escalate quickly. The next thing I know, the trio of men is engaged in an all-out brawl. Tables and chairs are flipped. The men roll on the floor and shout at one another. There's screaming and some shouting.

My throat closes and my pulse quickens. I'm backing away as quickly as I can when suddenly an arm wraps itself around me and physically carries me outside. I start screaming and kicking, but the person holds firm.

"Ma'am! Alice! It's Angela." I hear my bodyguard choke out.

She only sets me down when we're standing right next the Range Rover. "Angela." I hug her tightly. A few tears escape my eyes. "I've never been happier to see you."

"Are you all right? Have you been harmed in any way?"

"No, I'm fine," I sputter. "I'm so sorry." My chest heaves up and down. I'm still trying to catch my breath.

"Thank goodness. Let's get you in the car. The sooner we're out of here, the better. Bruce has been laying eggs; he's been so worried about you."

"Bruce?"

"Yes. I needed a person with experience to help me out. I knew I could trust him."

She opens the back door, but my feet are glued in place. That's when I suddenly remember. "Ange, they stole my mobile! There are some sensitive numbers in there. What if—"

"Shh, don't worry. We'll activate the kill switch and get you a new device. Your safety comes first." Her voice remains calm and reassuring.

"Princess!" Bruce exclaims from inside the car. "Please don't ever scare me like that again. When Angela called me and told me you'd gone AWOL, I just about had a heart attack."

It's that last comment from the man I've come to see as almost a second father that breaks down my emotional walls and sends down an endless stream of tears.

THE NEXT FEW HOURS ARE A PAINFUL BLUR. I LIE ON my bed with the lights turned off in self-imposed exile. I've always erred on the side that nothing bad could happen to me. I'm just Alice. But the harsh reality is that I am a target.

Today's experience was minor compared to what could've happened.

I can still hear Bruce's words echoing around in my head. *"The threats out there are very real, Princess. I won't sugarcoat it. Every day, there's at least one to two letters or calls the office receives threatening to do you or someone in your family harm. I can't stress how important it is that you take your security seriously."*

I grab my pillow and clutch it tighter to my chest. I've acted foolishly, and once again disappointed the people in my life who are the most important to me. I haven't behaved like an adult. I've acted like a spoiled child. Today was an eye-opening experience for me. I've never been angrier with myself.

Twenty-Seven

On Monday, I receive a visit from Amanda.

"Hey, how are ya holding up?" she asks as I let her in and close the door behind her.

"Fine," I answer, not really in the mood to speak to anyone.

"Ali, it's waaaaaaaaaaaaaaaaaaaaay too dark in here. You're not a bat living in a cave." She marches directly over to the windows and draws the curtains. Light floods the room and I have to blink a few times so my eyes can properly adjust. "That's better." Amanda spins around and gives me a look over, hands planted on her hips. "You look awful."

"Thanks," I mutter, knowing full well I haven't bothered getting dressed or doing anything to take care of my appearance for the past couple of days.

"Hurry up, go shower and get dressed. After that, we can get the day started." She gently steers me toward the bathroom. "We have things to do and places to be."

I stand rooted in place. "Amanda, I can't go out. I've grounded myself."

"Eddie's filled me in on the four-one-one. If you ask me,

Ali, you've learned your lesson. You won't ditch your security again. I get that it was a traumatic experience, but you shouldn't punish yourself for every mistake you make. We're only human." She sighs. "Did you know I pulled a similar stunt right after Eddie and I became engaged?"

I shake my head.

"We'd planned to have a special date night together and I wanted to have something extra special to wear to it. One of the best places to find vintage clothing is the Notting Hill antique market. I asked the security office about it and my request was shot down. I was told there would be way too many people and the market was too out in the open. Can you see where this is going?"

I nod. Amanda is stubborn, like Eddie. If she wants something bad enough, she'll find a way to get it. "You decided to go anyway on your own?" I guess.

"Yup." She smacks her lips together. "I ditched the protection team, spent the morning at the market, and shopped 'til I dropped. I was lucky that I wasn't recognized, and nothing happened. But Eddie, David, your dad, and the security office made sure I understood afterward *exactly* how badly things could've gone. Like it or not, as Eddie's fiancée, my life as I knew it as a private citizen was over."

I soak in her words, processing how difficult it must have been to transition from being able to go anywhere and do anything to a life in the public eye.

"I knew I'd messed up. Yes, I was mad at myself for making a bad decision. But you know what? Lesson learned, and I moved on. Life is too short to be miserable." From the outer pocket of her handbag, she passes me a slim tablet and a piece of paper. "Now here's what you're going to do. Send an email or text to your man. When you're done, we'll head out for some retail therapy. We have a wedding to plan."

I accept the paper and clutch it to my chest. I'm being

given a lifeline. In the craziness of the situation, I never had a chance to leave my napkin message with Art. "You've set a date, then?"

"Uh-huh. Eddie and I decided we're going to tie the knot with a private ceremony in December. The state wedding will be next June. The news about that one will officially break tomorrow. We're hoping the headlines will squash anything that's still being printed about you."

I charge toward the redhead and wrap my arms around her, hugging her tightly. "Thank you." It's not lost on me that my brother and soon-to-be sister-in-law are doing this for me. They easily could've waited another year, but they didn't.

"Mm-hmm. It was a no-brainer. The wedding makes everybody happy and gets a huge monkey off our backs with the in-laws. The best bit is that my mom and your mum are doing all the work. All I have to do is find a dress for you and me."

"You're not going to be involved in the planning?" My eyes widen.

"I will with the December ceremony. But not the June one. I got a taste of what a royal wedding was like when I helped Clara with hers. I'm totally fine taking a back seat to the parental units this time around."

"I think that's brilliant." For the first time in a week, I'm smiling.

"I'll fill you in on the details later, but the December wedding is our secret for now. Well, my mom knows, but she'll keep her lips sealed. Eddie and I were thinking we'd do our small ceremony at Disneyland Paris. We'll make a long weekend out of it. The castle should be amaaaazing all decorated for Christmas."

"Will you have a photographer or videographer on hand? I want to see it when you guys get back."

"You're going to be there, silly." She elbows me. "Eddie

and I wanted to ask you to be the maid of honor slash best woman. We both agreed you're going to be the only guest we want there. Clara and David were invited too, but they don't want to travel due to her pregnancy. And I can't say I blame them."

"Count me in."

"Awesomesauce." Amanda high-fives me. "Now hurry up. The dress shops of London await us."

"I'll be fast. I promise."

I squirrel the tablet away to the bathroom and flick the lights on. At this point, I *could* send Arthur a text, but I decide on an email. With how the universe has been conspiring against us lately, I think it's better to play it safe. Just in case.

Logging into my account, I quickly pull up a blank template and begin typing a message similar to the one I tried to put together last week.

To: thecatdaddy@email.com

From: a.wales@email.com

Dear Art,

Let me start out by saying how sorry I am for the entire situation you've been placed in. I wanted to let you know what was going on before the news broke, but unfortunately, I failed. I've felt guilty ever since. I didn't want you to be caught by surprise. I'm sure it came as a nasty shock.

I also want you to know how much I miss you! I've been thinking about you nonstop, and I want more than anything to see you. I'm so very sorry that it's taken so long for me to reach out to you. I promise it isn't for lack of trying. Without going into too much detail, let's just say that I understand how prisoners in the Tower of London must've felt.

I wanted you to know that I understand if things might have changed between us, and you feel that you no longer want anything to do with me. Even though I've done a crappy job of it, I just ask that you consider letting me remain your friend.

Best,

Alice

It's not a message written with the grace and elegance of Shakespeare, but rather from a person who's writing whatever comes to mind. There is so much I want to say, but now that I finally have the chance to write to Art, I'm struggling.

I read the message twice to make sure that it's at least coherent, click Send, and watch it disappear from my inbox to the virtual world. I click the power button and the screen goes black. I let out a deep breath. That's one weight that's lifted off my shoulders.

I only hope Art receives it and knows I do care for him. A lot. It's what made writing the last paragraph all the more difficult. If he doesn't want to date me anymore, I understand. I'm probably more trouble than I'm worth. And I care about him enough to let him go so he can be happy. The last thing I'd ever want to do is hold him back.

DRESS SHOPPING WITH AMANDA IS NOT AT ALL what I expect. Instead of going to a familiar shop, like the Clarissa Lee Atelier, we end up popping into a series of vintage and second-hand boutiques along Brick Lane in Shoreditch.

"All right, Ali, let's see if the fourth shop is the charm. Just like the others, pull anything that catches your eye," Amanda instructs.

I nod, still not exactly certain what she's looking for. All she's told me is that she's open to any dress and any color, which basically means use my best judgment. From past experience, I know that Amanda doesn't usually wear large, full skirts. I steer away from the princess-y ballgowns in favor of fishtails and sleeker silhouettes.

"Oh, this one's pretty." She selects a cerulean-blue chiffon dress and holds it up to my body. "What do you think?"

The dress contains a sweetheart neckline with lace cap sleeves and a ruched bodice that continues down the right side of the skirt. The back has an arched opening that shows off just the right amount of skin. As I run my fingers over the material, I love how light and airy the fabric feels. "The color and the cut are amazing, but it needs a little more sparkle."

"Sparkle can always be added. What do you think about it for you? What color are you thinking about wearing for the bridesmaid dress?"

"You want me to pick? Isn't that normally up to the bride?"

"I'm definitely not normal." Amanda chuckles. "I want *you* to be happy and comfortable with the dress you're wearing. I don't care what anyone else thinks."

I stare at the dress for a moment. I do love the color. I've always thought I looked good in blue. It's bold and would definitely make a statement.

"I think with a few modifications it could be perfect. Although, for a winter wedding, I might freeze without a coat."

"Pfft. You'll have a coat. Trust me." She hands me the dress. "Go try it on, and we'll see if you still love it as much when it's off the hanger."

"Okay." I head toward the back of the store as Amanda moves on to the next rack. As I turn the corner, I spot a mannequin dressed in a strapless white tea-length gown that stops me in my tracks. It has a ruched corset top and a lace overlay skirt with scalloped edges. A tingle of excitement shoots up my spine. "Amanda . . ."

"Hmm?"

"I need you. I think I've found something."

She stops what she's doing and joins me in front of the

mannequin. "Winner, winner, chicken dinner," she squeals. "It's like a grown-up, sophisticated *Alice in Wonderland* garden-party dress. I can totally see myself adding a cute white fascinator veil and some strappy heels to go with it. Come to Mama." She wastes no time in running to the front to find the shop's owner.

As I stare at the dress, I'm in love with the fact that it's the polar opposite of what a royal bride would be expected to wear. It's strapless, and the hem will only come down to her shins. I know Mum would expect Amanda in something with a long, flowing train, but that's not her. This is.

When I emerge from the dressing room, I'm surprised to find that Amanda has already changed and is admiring herself in a three-way mirror.

"How did you get dressed so quickly?"

"It's former-flight-attendant ninja skills," she jokes.

I laugh.

"Come stand beside me, I wanna see how we look together."

I carefully lift the skirt and stand off to her right side. We're normally even in height, but in heels, Amanda is about three inches taller than me. The shop owner has clipped the back of her dress, so it fits her frame better. It makes it easier to see the potential it has.

"You were right about the sparkle," Amanda says, looking at me. "You definitely need some bling on the skirt and a necklace and earrings. Aquamarines? Those would look smoking with that blue. Or maybe sapphires? What do you think?"

I study my reflection in the mirror. Instead of envisioning what this dress could look like, all I'm able to picture is Art standing next to me. He'd be wearing a light-gray suit with a matching cerulean-blue tie and a white waistcoat.

His arms would wrap themselves around me and he'd plant a series of long, soft kisses up the nape of my neck. I can practically hear his voice whispering into my ear how much he loves the color on me. I'm filled with a deep sense of sadness. My relationship with Art is over. I can't foresee us finding a way to be together now.

"I think I'd like a flower here." I point to the waist, where the fabric of the skirt drapes downward. "And I agree, either aquamarines or maybe even something like tanzanite. I have a necklace that I inherited from my grandmum that would do well with this."

"Perfecto. And does it feel like something you could wear all day and dance around in? It's not too restricting?"

"No. It's perfect."

"That's one down." Amanda grins widely. "Now give me your brutally honest opinion; what do you think of this bad boy?" She smooths the skirt and slowly pivots in a circle for me.

"I like the style of the dress as a base. It's close to being perfect, but I feel like it's missing something."

She nods. "I agree. I think maybe a little lace jacket and a few accessories would do the trick. And for a hundred pounds, you can't go wrong."

Amanda pulls out her mobile and snaps a couple photos of us in our outfits before we change. I do my best to be positive despite my mood. We decide to purchase them and head to the grounds of Kensington Palace to meet up with Clara.

"My mom is going to die when I tell her we both found dresses. She told me it might take a couple shopping trips, but I knew we'd get lucky. After all, you're my good luck charm, Ali."

"Thank you," I murmur.

The privacy screen in the car is up and I relish the fact that it's just the two of us. "Will she be disappointed she wasn't here to go shopping with you?"

"Nah, Mom understands this dress is for the December

ceremony. She'll be here when we go to the design meeting for the dress I'll wear for the more formal church ceremony." She shakes her head. "Your mother was non-negotiable about that. My dress has to be something custom and have sleeves."

"I hope Mum doesn't find out about the December wedding."

"You and me both. We'll tell your parents afterward. Do you think you can keep from saying anything?"

"You don't have anything to worry about."

"Thank you." Amanda places a hand on my shoulder. "You start school in another week, week and a half?"

"Yeah, I do."

"Are you excited about the move to your flat? Do you need any help finding furniture?" She rubs her hands together, her eyes gleaming in excitement. "You know how much I love interior design."

"I am, but I'm not going to be moving in until mid-February. I'm not ready for furniture yet, but I'd love your help picking out all the designs features for the ground-floor flat."

"Ground-floor flat? You have more than one unit?"

I nod. "Since the construction crew ended up having to tear out more walls than expected, and I don't need all the space, I thought it would be best if we turned the ground floor into its own separate property."

"Smart, but what are you going to do with it? Sell it?"

"Mum and Papa said I could if the right person comes along, and they meet with their approval."

"Uh-huh." Amanda cocks her head to the side. "I know your dad though. What's the catch?"

"The only people allowed would be a family member or friend of the family," I answer sheepishly.

"That's Reggie for you." She chuckles. "Well, don't worry. I'm sure the downstairs unit won't stay vacant forever."

"I hope not. It would be nice to have a friend live next to me."

LATER THAT EVENING, AS I LIE IN BED, I TAP THE email icon on the borrowed tablet from Amanda. It's been a whole half hour since the last time I checked. Maybe something has changed.

As the page reloads, I mutter, "Please, please, please."

The inbox, however, remains empty. Placing the device face down, I groan and slide deeper under the covers, pulling the sheet over my head. "When am I going to hear from you again?"

Twenty-Eight

It's Friday. It's been five days since I sent Art a message and I have yet to hear anything from him. No matter what, I've told myself that if I don't hear from him by tonight, I'll ring him. My patience is running out.

"All right, ma'am, spill the tea. What are you afraid to ask me?" Bruce says. He's temporarily been returned to duty as my protection officer.

I turn my gaze away from the passing scenery of London. We're blessedly alone since it's such a short trip from the flat to the stables. Angela is still hardly speaking to me unless its business related. "Er, what makes you think I have a burning question to ask?"

"Call it my sixth sense."

There is no hiding anything from Bruce. There *is* something that's been on my mind. "How long do internal investigations within your department normally take to complete?"

The car slows and he stops at a red light. A few pedestrians cross, carrying oversized shopping bags with souvenirs from one of the palace's many gift shops.

"It depends. If it's something that's straightforward, three or maybe four weeks. If it involves a person *and* a job performance evaluation, the inquiry may take a few months before a decision is reached."

"That long?" My heart drops.

"I'm afraid so."

"Why isn't he checking his darn email?" I mutter to myself.

The light changes and the car begins moving again. "Did you say something about email?"

"That was off the record." I'm angry with myself for being careless with my tongue. I don't want anyone except Amanda to know I've been trying to get in contact with Art.

"Ma'am, for what it's worth, I'm always on *your* side. What I was going to say is that if Arthur is the person you sent the email to, he's always been hopeless with checking it. If you want to get through to him, a call, text, or in-person visit is best."

"I'd give anything to see him in person, but that's highly unlikely to happen. I'll have to ring him."

"I wouldn't be too sure." Bruce's voice is smug.

That's when I finally notice that we're headed in the opposite direction of the palace stables. We've traveled to the far end of Whitehall behind Horse Guard's Parade. The street narrows considerably. Bruce makes a turn, and we slip into an underground car park.

My pulse quickens. "Um, Bruce, where exactly are we?"

"Great Scotland Yard." He cuts the engine and turns around. "Arthur normally works out of the stables here or at the Bow Street station. I'm taking a gamble, but I think it's more likely he'll be here today."

"You've brought me to see him?" I sputter.

"Yes. I can't stand to see the pair of you so gutted and miserable. It's high time you two hurried it along and reconnected."

"But what if somebody sees us? I can't have you risking your neck for us too. We're already in enough trouble."

"I don't care about me, I'm on my way to being semi-retired anyway." Bruce brushes me off and directs us to a lift fifteen meters away. "I care about you two. It doesn't take a rocket scientist to see that the bond you and Arthur have developed is special. I want to see you both happy."

Many questions are racing through my head about Bruce. About Arthur. About what I'm going to say to the man I've been dreaming about seeing again.

The lift dings and we arrive on the ground floor. As the doors open, I immediately smell hay, mud, and horses. We pass several rubbish bins, oversized bales of hay, and a forklift. Like a duckling following her mother, I trail Bruce as he leads me up a ramp past a stable block containing about twenty stalls. A bay and a dapple horse have stuck their heads out of their stalls, watching us curiously as we walk past.

"How many horses are kept in here?"

"There's room for nineteen Met Police horses and two City of London ones. Greater Scotland Yard happens to be the largest stable in this area. Bow Street has room for about twelve horses."

As we reach the last stall, I see the door is wide open. The lead of a dappled gray is clipped to a post. A man is inside the stall with his back turned to us, mucking it out as the horse munches on some hay. He's in black riding trousers and a black top. My pulse begins to pick up.

"Arthur," Bruce calls.

"Dad? What are you doing here?" He pivots around and drops the broom. It falls to the ground with a clatter.

Dad? Bruce is Arthur's *father?* I blink a few times in shock. My eyes dart between the two men. All the signs have been there. There share a similar height and hair color, but physically, Art seems to have taken more after his mum than Bruce.

"I brought the princess to see you. It's high time you two worked things out. If you need me, I'll just be down here, feeding Yoda a couple treats." He whistles the *Star Wars* theme as he heads to the opposite end of the hall.

For several long moments, we stare at one another, still not believing we're both here. Our chests rise and fall. It's only when the dapple horse stomps his hoof that the spell is broken, and we rush toward one another in a fierce embrace. Our lips meet, and time around us seems to stop. It's as if we've both been wandering aimlessly through the Sahara Desert, and just in the nick of time, we've encountered an oasis.

Art's arms wrap around the small of my back and pull me in so I'm tight against his chest. The fabric of his shirt is coarse against my cheeks. It smells as if he's recently laundered it. It's a fresh, crisp scent.

I've missed these full, silky lips, the laugh lines around his mouth, and being held by his strong arms. I never want to let go. We continue to drink greedily from each other as if we'll never reach our fill.

When we do finally break apart for air, I tilt my head up and manage a quiet, "Hi."

"Hi," he replies, continuing to hold me close, stroking the side of my face lightly with his thumbs.

My throat constricts. "Art, I'm so, so, so sorry."

"Ali, you have nothing to be sorry for."

"Yes, I do," I emphasize. "This mess we're in is all my fault."

"No, it's really not, it's all *my* fault. I should've been the one who realized something was amiss at Locked in London. I failed you when I didn't catch the bloke who was taking our photos." His tone is stoic and his body stiff.

"Art, you couldn't have known. The bloke at the escape room was sneaky."

"That may be true, but the point is, I was distracted. This is exactly why the no-relationship rule is there. To protect you from situations exactly like this. What if—"

I take my hand and place it over his lips. "No. We're not playing the what-if game. There are too many unknown factors at play here. If you really want to take a part of the blame, we'll split it down the middle."

He blinks slowly. "I don't know."

"Art, please. For me."

He studies me for several long moments, then sighs deeply. "As you wish."

"Thank you." I pick up his hand and run my fingers over each and every one of the rough calluses on it. It feels so good to be able to be so near to him again. My body is growing increasingly warm the longer I stand here. "Now enough of the blame game." I bury my head in his chest. "I've missed you so much."

"Me too, Ali. Me too." I listen to him breathe deeply. "Not seeing you has been the hardest two weeks of my life. It's taken everything in me not to take one of these horses and charge the gates of the palace, demanding to see you."

I lift my chin and meet his eyes. The flecks of gold are glowing. "Why didn't you? I've been waiting for so long to hear from you! Why didn't you email me?"

"I *did*." He releases me and glances away. "When I didn't receive any response from you, I figured there had to be a valid reason you'd dropped me, and so I've been waiting."

"I haven't had proper access to my account." I groan. "My old smartphone was stolen, and the security office was worried everything connected to the old phone and number could be compromised. Everybody in my family has had to get new mobile numbers because of me." I take a moment to bring him up to speed on my failed attempt to see him after he was pulled from my detail.

"I can't believe you risked your safety like that! What were you thinking?" He crosses his arms.

"I wasn't. I just needed to see you. At the time, it seemed like a brilliant idea. I know now how foolish it was." I've had ample time to relive everything over and over again in my head. My life isn't a Hallmark or Disney movie. I have an understanding of the realness of the threats that are out there now.

"I want to stay angry with you, but I can't." He sighs. "I'll only admit this to you, but I happen to find this royal rebel streak to be incredibly attractive. I can't imagine another woman who would throw caution to the wind like you did to go after me."

I grin. "For now, I think my days of being a royal rebel are over, unless you're by my side."

"I respect that." Art flexes his muscles. The dapple horse neighs in agreement, causing us to laugh.

"I can't believe you've been reassigned to the mounted police force. I would've come searching for you sooner if I'd have known."

His cheeks color. "It doesn't compare to seeing you on a daily basis, but for the time being, this is the next best thing. I'd forgotten how much I miss working with horses like Quixote." He bends over to retrieve the rake and balances it against the door. "Being here again has gotten me thinking about the future lately."

"Uh-huh." I tense.

"What are your thoughts if I decided not to return to your security team, and instead, asked to stay attached to the mounted unit?"

My mouth opens and closes. I'd miss seeing him, but if that's what he wants after putting up with this media circus, I respect his choice. "Would it make you happy?"

"Yeah, it would. Do you know why?"

I shake my head.

"First, it would mean that the investigation would be called off. Second, and more importantly, if you'll still have me, it would mean that I'd get to be with you. There's nothing in the rules and regulations stopping a mounted officer from dating a princess."

"It's not even a question. Of course I want you." My heart flutters. "You would do that for me?"

"Not just for you. For us." He cups my cheeks. "Ali, you've become such an important person to me. I can't imagine you not being a part of the picture. I don't just like you. I love you. I need you to be in my life."

My heart suddenly swells so much that it feels like it no longer fits inside my chest. Art doesn't merely like me. He loves me! He's said that magic L word that I've been too terrified to say or even think to myself. Until now.

"I can't imagine a future without you either. I'll support whatever you decide you want to do. That's what people do when they're in love. I love you too, Art."

He closes the distance between us and spins me around in a circle. I've never seen him smile so wide. "I never thought I'd hear you say those words."

We kiss. Suddenly, I'm a hummingbird that's discovered one of the world's largest flowers. No, scratch that. A flower that contains a never-ending supply of nectar! I'll never have to travel frantically from flower to flower again to ensure I have enough to eat. Everything I need is right in front of me. I couldn't be any happier.

~

A LITTLE WHILE LATER, AFTER ART'S FINISHED mucking out the stall, fed Quixote, and put everything away, we slowly walk toward the end of the stall block toward Bruce, who's probably reading a detective novel on his mobile.

"I can't believe I missed that Bruce is your father!"

"We've always kept our relationship on the down low. I never wanted anyone to think that I'd gotten a spot on the security team because of who my dad is. I wanted to earn it." Art's fingers are laced through mine. He squeezes my hand. "Dad didn't even know I'd been transferred to you until the day we met."

I think back to our first meeting, recalling his stoic demeanor and one-word answers. "That explains a lot. Is that one of the reasons why you were such a grump?"

"Sort of." He clears his throat. "Ali, I'm not proud of this, but when we met, I was determined *not* to like you. I had it in my head that you were some spoiled, entitled royal."

We stop walking. He drops my hand. I tilt my head to the side and stare at him, eyes wide.

"The more time I spent with you, however, the clearer it became to me that I couldn't have been any more wrong about you. You're one of the smartest, kindest, most genuine people out there. The truth is, I was *jealous* of you." He takes a deep breath. "Growing up, Dad was *always* working. Mum would end up filling in for him, explaining that he wished he could be with us, but he was busy. I understand now how the nature of the job works, but back then, I resented that he spent more time with you than his own family."

I squeeze my eyes shut and let his words wash over me. Art and his brother were those kids with the missed birthday parties, graduations, and other major milestones. I don't blame him two bits for resenting me. I would resent me too.

I inhale sharply. "Art, I'm so sorry."

He runs a hand softly down my arm, causing my pulse to skip a beat. "Ali, there is nothing for you to apologize for. You were just a child. My father is the one who made the decisions of when he'd work and when he'd take time off. If there's anyone who owes my brother and me an apology, it's him."

He shoots a glance in Bruce's direction. "But like I said, having walked in his shoes, I understand how the job works now. Being a bodyguard is both an honor and a privilege. Protection officers don't just do an important job. They put their lives on the line on a daily basis to serve the country."

"I'd add that it's not just protection officers—there are members of the police force, fire service, military, and countless other individuals too." My brother's face pops into my mind.

Art nods. A few moments of comfortable silence envelop us. The anxiety I'd felt earlier has dissipated. Knowing that Art and I remain on solid ground helps quell the doubt and uncertainty of what comes next.

"Your school term begins this coming week?"

"Mm-hmm. It's Fresher's Week. From Wednesday on, I'll be at Imperial most of the day."

"Hmm, maybe I'll see if I can trade for a shift or two out of Hyde Park." His eyes twinkle. "There's nothing stopping us from meeting if we just so happen to run into one another."

"I'd like that." I smile, already thinking about a few of the different places where Art and I can "accidentally" cross paths just outside campus.

As I watch my man's eyes continue to twinkle, I can picture him riding onto the center of Imperial's campus just to have lunch with me. I'm kind of excited about him scaring away all the people who will try to get to know me just because of my title. Art is as close to a real-life knight in shining armor as they come, and I'll be counting down the days until I can officially call him my boyfriend.

Our relationship may not have started off on the best of terms, but the journey we've taken to reach this point was important for us to be able to get to where we are now. I suppose what they say about everything happening for a reason is true.

<h1 style="text-align:center">Epilogue</h1>

THREE AND A HALF MONTHS LATER

Amanda whistles loudly and slightly off-key as I zip up the back of her wedding dress and take a step back. "My brother is going to cry when he sees you," I whisper, awed by how stunning my soon-to-be sister-in-law looks.

The vintage dress we found a few months ago has retained many of its original features, but Amanda has also added a few of her own touches to it. It now contains straps and a giant bow on the back.

My eyes travel up to her face. She's used a champagne-colored eye shadow and a light layer of mascara, and offset it with some hot-pink lipstick. Her cheeks are rosy, and as she moves under the light, I notice a few sparkles. "Is that glitter?"

"Of course. It's my wedding day. Well, my secret wedding day. When else will I get to dress up like a real-life Disney princess? Would you mind helping me sprinkle some in my hair?"

"Sure." She hands me a brush and some white and gold

297

glitter. I dip the end into the container and carefully brush it on the crown and ends of her hair. She's straightened her normally wild red curls and styled her hair so it's half up and half down.

"Do you want me to sprinkle some in your hair too?" she asks.

"Why not? If we're going all-out Disney, I want to be a part of it."

A goofy grin crosses her lips. "That's the spirit." She begins humming "Oh I Just Can't Wait to Be King."

A short while later, after I've slipped into my own blue dress, we grab our coats and walk arm in arm from our suite to the waiting glass carriage.

"Bonjour, madame," a footman greets Amanda as he opens the door, assisting us inside. "You look very beautiful this morning."

"Merci," she exclaims, beaming with pride.

We settle ourselves and the doors close.

"Don't get me wrong, your family's carriages are amazing, but you have to admit, there is something extra special about this baby!" Amanda says.

I nod. "One, it's much comfier. And two, it's the *Cinderella* carriage. Riding inside of it is one of the things my brother was most looking forward to."

Amanda sighs. "I can't wait to take a sunrise ride around the park with him in it."

Taking out my mobile, I take the opportunity to snap a few photos of us, the horses, and a view of Disneyland Paris without any people inside of it. The popcorn lights of the Main Street shops elicit a soft yellow glow. A few maintenance workers are power washing the street, but stop and wave to us as we pass them.

The sun has just begun to rise, and as we get closer to the castle, it transforms from an inky black to a purple and golden orange. With the twinkling Christmas lights of the castle as a backdrop, it's as if we've stepped into a real-life fairy tale.

Suddenly the carriage slows, and my pulse begins to race. Amanda slips on a pair of gloves. I make one final adjustment to her fascinator. "You look perfect. Are you ready to do this?"

She nods.

The door opens, and as we descend, I notice that a white carpet has been sprinkled with red rose petals. At the end of the aisle, standing under an archway of fairy lights twined with red and pink roses, I spy Eddie. He's fidgeting as he speaks to Art. Both men look handsome, but I have to admit, Art in a form-fitting tuxedo is an image that will live in my mind for a long, long time to come.

"Ladies." The deep voice of my cousin David causes us to spin around. He, too, is dressed in a black tuxedo.

"David! What are you doing here?" I squeal.

"You didn't expect Clara and me to miss this, did you?"

Clara is seven-and-half months pregnant. Travel around London has been uncomfortable for her; neither Amanda nor I thought she'd be coming. But now that she's here, I'm extra excited. A moment like this necessitates Amanda having her bestie here. And from way she looks like she's about to burst out of her skin, she shares my thoughts.

"When? How?" she sputters.

"We flew in last night. Clara can fill you in on the details later. She's sitting at the end of the aisle, waiting for us."

I turn my head and see her petite form covered in a few blankets as she watches us. I wave and she waves back.

David extends his arm to Amanda. "First, let's get you married. Then we can spend the rest of the day talking and celebrating."

I accept a bouquet of fragrant roses from a Disney cast member and trail behind Amanda and David. A hidden string quartet plays the traditional wedding march. It's a strange sight to see Clara as the only guest sitting among the ten chairs on either side of the aisle.

Both my parents and Amanda's were invited to the affair at the last minute, although Amanda's mum technically knew about it. After some heated conversations, they both agreed it would be best not to intrude on the event and that the happy couple should be allowed to have the ceremony of their dreams. Especially since their London ceremony, scheduled for next June, has turned into a circus.

I release my breath and begin down the aisle after Amanda and David. The moment my brother spots her, his head snaps up and he stands at attention. His eyes are locked on Amanda. All the tension in his face melts away and he smiles wider than the Grand Canyon. I've never seen him appear so happy. My heart leaps with joy. This moment has been a long time in coming, and I'm beyond thrilled to be able to share it with them.

We reach the end of the aisle. David places Amanda's arm in Eddie's, kisses her on the cheek, and takes a seat on the bride's side next to Clara. She snuggles into his chest. I take up my spot to Amanda's left, directly opposite Art. Our eyes meet and he mouths *You look beautiful* to me. I mouth *Right back at you.*

The ceremony is over in the blink of an eye, and after Amanda and Eddie share a long, passionate kiss, I officially have a new sister.

It's only after the photographer steals the newly married couple away for a few minutes that I finally have the chance to greet Art.

"Good morning." I kiss him on the cheek.

"Good morning to you too, Ali." He chuckles and wraps his arms around me. "You must be freezing—that cape doesn't look like it's doing a very good job of keeping you warm."

I shrug. "Up until now, I really hadn't noticed it. I've been thinking about other things."

Art slips his jacket over my shoulders. "Better?"

"Much, but aren't you going to be cold?"

"I'll manage until we get back to the hotel."

Flashes go off as Amanda and Eddie ham it up for the camera, not wasting a single moment of their precious time. "Are you still all right with exploring the theme park after breakfast?"

"Of course, I'd be concerned if you didn't want to do a full Disney day, seeing as it's your first time here." He glances at David and Clara. "Do you think they'll be joining us?"

"I doubt it. Knowing David, they'll probably fly back after Clara fits another nap in."

"What about your brother and Amanda?"

I lower my voice so Art is the only one who can hear me. "I love them both dearly, but I can't handle the mad pace they'll want to keep to make sure they fit literally *everything* in today. If they try to join us, we'll find a way to ditch them."

His body shakes with laughter. "It can't be that bad."

"Yes, it can. Amanda is notorious for choreographing the day's activities down to the loo breaks."

He arches his eyebrow. "Loo breaks, huh?"

"Uh-huh. Trust me. We'll be better off on our own."

"As you wish."

I picture us taking a slow walk up to the bridge of the castle, where we'll share a romantic kiss.

"Are you picturing us in the castle again?"

My cheeks warm. "Yes," I admit.

"Brilliant, because I'd like that to be our very *first* stop of the day. Angela and Dylan have even agreed to give us a few minutes of privacy."

"What's the catch?" I ask.

Dylan is the protection officer who was hired to replace

Art. A former Royal Marine, physically, he's a lot like Art. Personality wise, however, they're opposites. Dylan is always laughing and manages to keep me entertained. He's nowhere as serious as Art. If you ask me, it's no surprise Angela is smitten with him. Or so I think.

"They want us to purchase them mouse ears, churros, and some popcorn buckets. Apparently collecting them is a thing."

I nod. "Done."

It's a small price to pay for a few moments alone with my boyfriend, but worth it. Art and I deserve to be able to enjoy our own fairy-tale moment.

~

THREE MONTHS LATER

"I'M SO PROUD OF YOU. YOU'RE GOING TO DO brilliantly Ali." Art kisses my cheek. "Just remember to breathe."

"You're not going to tell me to try and imagine the audience in their knickers?" I joke.

"No," he deadpans, crossing his arms. Our eyes meet and we both snicker. It's just the distraction I needed to push the bundle of nerves away. Sometimes it's hard to believe we've officially been together for about just over six months. We've gotten to know one another so well.

"We're ready for you, ma'am," my mum's secretary says as she joins us behind the curtain separating Art and me from the press. A clipboard is tucked under her arm. She's my assistant for the day. "The teleprompter is loaded with all the speaking points you've prepared."

"Thanks, Lynn."

"Be the Alice I know and love." Art squeezes my hand one last time as I stand by the entrance and take a deep breath.

Squaring my shoulders, I plaster a smile on my face and walk out. There are three rows of schoolchildren in uniform seated crossed-legged, watching me with wide eyes. I can hear their whispers as they wonder why they're here. Their teachers stand off to the side, also chatting quietly amongst themselves.

Behind them are about twenty members of the media. Some are taking photo after photo of me, while others are filming. Placing my hands on the side of the lectern, I take a few moments to myself before focusing on the children. They're the reason I'm here.

"Good morning, everyone."

I'm greeting with a chorus of "Good morning, Princess Alice."

"Thank you all for being here." My eyes flicker to the script as it flows across the screen. "Today I'm thrilled to announce the launch of United Voices. It's an initiative I hold close to my heart, aimed at stopping bullying and supporting those who are being bullied." Although my pulse is racing rapidly, I feel a surge of adrenaline racing through my body. "Let me tell you a little story about a girl who was just like you all."

Art has joined the teachers off to the side. He nods as I speak, urging me on. Meeting the eyes of the students, I open myself up and share with them about how school was for me, how I was bullied, and the mental and emotional toll it took on me.

It's the first time I've shared such an intimate piece of my life with the public. But when I practiced in front of Eddie, Amanda, David, and Clara, they all agreed sharing my story was the most effective way to get my points across. My experience is one that many others can relate to. I want them to see themselves in me and know that bullying can happen to anyone. Even a princess.

". . . and so it's my mission to make sure that none of that ever happens to you." My legs are shaking. I squeeze my knees together as I nod to Lynn to pop the first slide of my Power-Point presentation onto the screen behind me. "United Voices will run several different programs at schools and community centers across the country. The first of which is our support network, where victims of bullying will be able to anony-mously share their stories and ask for and receive advice."

I mention how victims can feel powerless and ashamed at what's happening. It's important that they have a safe way to ask for help.

"Our second program will be training for our Kindness Ambassadors. These are specialists who have been trained to identify and support victims of bullying, and promote kind-ness and inclusivity through various activities and campaigns."

By the time I finish taking questions from the students and everyone else in the room, I'm mentally exhausted, but beaming with pride at what I've just accomplished. I've been working hard on United Voices for weeks, stealing time where I can between classes and dates with Art, and now, it's finally live and out in the world. Who would've thought that the girl who considered giving up on becoming a working royal at the beginning of summer would be standing here today? Not me.

I've changed so much in the last six months. I don't even feel like the same person at times. The old Alice was still growing out of her shell. She was a princess who was afraid to make mistakes. She wanted to hide away from the world in her little bubble and craved a life where she could be just like everybody else.

Well, the woman I am today is the more matured version of the old Alice. When I started taking classes at uni last fall, I got a taste of what it was like being just another first-year student. I was expected to show up for my modules, do the reading and assignments, and participate in the discussions. I didn't have any royal duties assigned to me. When I wasn't studying, I spent my free time with Art, or working part-time.

At first, it was blissful. But as the weeks wore on, and I saw pictures of Eddie, Amanda, and my parents working, I felt this gnawing sense of incompleteness. Here was my family using their platform to shine light on so many worthy causes. And what was I doing? Nothing. I realized then and there that I *wanted* to join them. I *needed* to use the voice I was given to help others, and that's when I started working on the United Voices campaign.

When I approached Eddie and told him about my plan, he was excited for me, but also nervous. He reminded me that being a working royal meant being in front of the media. He wanted to make sure I knew what I was getting into. The funny thing is, the media was the last thing on my mind. As I spoke to my brother, my father, Art, and my therapist about it, I found that when I have a cause I'm so passionate about, I don't care about what's printed about me.

I've already been to the lowest point a person can go. It can't get worse than it was when I was a teenager. But if it does happen again, this time, I have the tools to handle the situation. Experience has taught me to use my family and the people I love as my support system. The media will always be looking for their next storyline, be it good or bad, ugly or pretty, true or false. All I can do is shrug it off, because life is too short to worry and be miserable.

"There's my strong, confident princess," Art gushes. I let his strong arms envelop me in a tight hug. "You. Were. Amazing."

My body warms like a piece of chocolate melting inside a fondue pot. Whenever I'm in his arms, I never want him to let me go. I rest my head against his suit jacket and soak in the scent of vanilla and spices.

"I did do pretty well, didn't I." I pull back slightly, grinning.

"I heard some of the reporters in passing talking about how impressed they were with the layout of United Voices. Something about it being one of the most well-thought-out programs they've seen the palace come up with."

The muscles in my cheeks begin to ache as I smile even wider.

Art releases me, lacing his hand through mine. "How should we go celebrate your success?"

"I'd *love* to have a long lunch with you and go out for a nice long ride, but I have class at three."

"Could I persuade you to be a rebel and skip it?" Art asks, a hopeful tone in his voice.

I chew on the inside of my lip. "We only meet once a week, and I can't miss out if I want Dr. Jackson to write me a letter of recommendation for the summer Historic Royal Palaces internship I want to apply for." I've become really interested in structural engineering work that involves repairing listed and historic buildings. It's something I can see myself doing in the future. I offer him my puppy-dog eyes. "A rain check for this weekend?"

"Throw in dinner with me tonight and you have a deal." Art rubs his hands together. "I have some new recipes I'd like to try on you. *If* you don't mind me using your kitchen."

"Of course I don't. What's the saying Amanda likes to use? Mi casa es su casa? My house is your house."

Art helped me move into my flat in early February. Since then, he's spent more time at my place than his. We've even gotten to the point where Cinnamon and Peppermint spend Thursday through Sunday with me since Art tends to work unpredictable hours on the weekends. Lillian seems to think of them as her puppies.

His lease will be up for renewal next month, and I've been waiting for the right moment to ask him if he'll consider moving in with me. Maybe dinner this weekend would be a good time. It's not like we'll ever be completely alone since a security team member is always inside the property with me. That would probably be enough to convince Papa to sign off on it. Even if technically, I don't need his permission, I'd still like to have it.

Speaking of Papa, he was surprisingly okay with us dating. I'll admit that I was terrified of what he might think of me falling for my bodyguard. But when we met with him and explained the situation, he gave me a knowing smile and said "You can't choose who you fall in love with." Art thought later that my being a daddy's girl and his being one of the top graduates in his protection officer course might've helped our cause. Whatever the case may be, I'm just relieved to have his support.

"Any special requests for dessert? I was planning on making either a Victoria sponge or an apple crumble with fresh vanilla ice cream, but I'm flexible."

"Anything you make is okay with me. Your desserts are the best."

We arrive outside the school and slide into a waiting car with Angela up front. She gives me a wink and rolls up the privacy screen. Art and I lock eyes. A pair of cheeky grins appear on our faces.

"Are you thinking what I'm thinking?" Art's voice comes out husky.

"Uh-huh." I lick my lips.

We lean toward one another and kiss.

The day I met Art, I won the lottery. We're living,

breathing proof that no matter what, you should always follow your heart, for it always leads you in the right direction. You just have to be willing to listen to it.

Dear Reader

Thank you for reading *Engineering Love*

If you enjoyed Alice and Art's story, you can access exclusive bonus content here:

https://tomitabb.com/engineering-love-bonus-content/

If you have a moment, please consider leaving a review on Amazon, Goodreads, BookBub, or wherever you discovered this book.

Reviews help other readers find the story and mean so much to authors.

Stay connected with Tomi by subscribing to her newsletter:

https://tomitabb.com/newsletter/

You can also scan the QR code below.

Acknowledgments

"Engineering Love" is not a story I imagined writing when I first penned the *Unexpected Royals* series. Princess Alice was always intended to be a side character—the baby sister of Prince Edmund.

However, as I've grown as a writer, my characters have evolved alongside me. When I finished *Designs on Love*, I knew Alice deserved the next spotlight. Her journey was a joy to craft, and I loved the challenge of writing a character navigating both the pressures of royalty and the transition into adulthood. Reaching the finish line, of course, was a team effort.

First, I'd like to extend my sincere thanks to Joanne Lui, one of the best editors in the business. You always find a way to make my words shine and push my writing to the next level. I truly could not do this without you. Beyond your editorial brilliance, you've become a dear friend, and I'm so grateful to have you just a text away.

To my friend and fellow author, Brooke Gilbert: thank you for your unwavering support. Whenever I hit a roadblock or lose motivation, you always know exactly what to say to keep me moving forward.

To my proofreader, Charity Chimni: thank you for catching those elusive typos and ensuring this story is as polished as possible.

To my Beta Readers and ARC team: your kindness and thoughtful feedback mean the world to me. Thank you for your continued support and for championing my stories from the very beginning.

To my family: you are my rock and my foundation. Without you, none of these stories would exist.

Lastly, to my readers: each and every one of you is a treasure. By becoming a part of Alice and Art's story, you allow me to keep doing what I love. From the bottom of my heart, thank you.

About the Author

Tomi Tabb writes closed-door romantic comedies filled with heart, hope, and happily-ever-afters. From royalty and bodyguards to engineers, athletes, and performers, her stories celebrate kindness, found family, and the joy of falling in love. Inspired by *Pride and Prejudice*, Tomi writes the character-driven  romances she loves to read—equal parts swoony, hopeful, and satisfying.

A California native, Tomi holds an MA in History and is putting the finishing touches on her doctorate in History, blending her love of research with her passion for storytelling. She lives with her family, one very spoiled cat, and an energetic toddler who keeps life wonderfully unpredictable.

When she isn't writing, you'll likely find her figure skating, watching tennis, or hunting down the newest pumpkin-flavored treat—one of the many reasons fall will always be her favorite season.

Website: TomiTabb.com

Also by Tomi Tabb

The Unexpected Royals

Dancing With a Royal

Jiving With a Royal

Designing for a Royal

Friends of the Unexpected Royals

Designs on Love

Engineering Love

Coasting Into Love

Set to Love

The Skaters of Sequoia Valley

The Rules of the Rink

The Sloth Zone

Caught in a Loop

The Royals of Isola Nostrum

The Great Austen Adventure

For the Love of Dinosaurs

Standalones & Companion Stories

More Than a Passing Shot

Pointe Shoes and Sugar Plums

Jingle Blades

Historical Romance

The Mysterious Mr. Marcellus

www.ingramcontent.com/pod-product-compliance
Lightning Source LLC
Chambersburg PA
CBHW071236300726
48975CB00002B/440